TO CATCH A RUNAWAY BRIDE

Helen Dickson

MILLS & BOON

First Published in Great Britain 2021
by Mills & Boon, an imprint of HarperCollins*Publishers* Ltd,
1 London Bridge Street, London, SE1 9GF

www.harpercollins.co.uk

HarperCollins*Publishers*
1st Floor, Watermarque Building,
Ringsend Road, Dublin 4, Ireland

To Catch a Runaway Bride © 2021 Helen Dickson

ISBN: 978-0-263-28443-0

12/21

MIX
Paper from
responsible sources
FSC™ C007454

This book is produced from independently certified FSC™ paper
to ensure responsible forest management.
For more information visit www.harpercollins.co.uk/green.

Printed and Bound in Spain using 100% Renewable Electricity
at CPI Black Print, Barcelona

Chapter One

～～～～～

1887—early spring

The early morning was cool and crisp when Edmund Fitzroy rode his horse in Hyde Park. Few riders were about at that early hour, which suited him perfectly. Later on it would be filled with the cream of London society, on foot, in elegant carriages and curricles, the ladies bobbing parasols, feathered hats and a colourful array of turbans, the gentlemen on high-stepping horses.

As he rode beneath the leafless boughs of the tall trees, he was taken by surprise when two horse riders, a man and a woman—by his plain apparel he assumed the man to be the lady's groom—came thundering past him. The lady was perched atop a raw-boned gelding, a glossy chestnut, its coat gleaming almost red—a huge beast, which would take some handling at the best of times and would challenge even his own.

Utterly transfixed, he watched as the competitive spirit of the lady's horse flared—it seemed determined to keep ahead of its mate. Its mane and tail flying, legs flailing, the horse, setting a cracking pace, was galloping its heart out. It was evident the other horse was beginning to tire and didn't stand a chance.

Pulling his horse to a halt, with unconcealed appreciation he continued to watch them, filled with admiration for the woman's ability and daring.

'Come along,' he heard her shout over her shoulder. 'Keep up if you can.'

The groom laughed and pulled back. 'You go on, miss. I can't keep up. You and Vulcan are too much for me.'

The woman laughed, a joyous sound to Edmund's ears, and he watched as she urged her horse on.

It was clear that she was utterly fearless seated precariously in the side saddle. Hair the colour of auburn had come loose from beneath her hat and was flying behind, a tangled pennant of glossy waves. He could see brown leather riding boots beneath the skirts of her blue riding habit spread out over the horse's rump.

With a watery sun spilling its grey light, the park stretched before them. Giving up the chase, the groom slowed, following his mistress at a sedate pace, but the woman carried on, riding beautifully, her slender and supple body, arresting and vigorous, bent forward to get every inch of speed from her horse, urging him on harder and harder. The hooves pounded, sending divots of turf up behind, her gloved hands almost touching the horse's flicking ears. Leaping a low hedge and landing soundly, she then soared over a wide ditch with an effortless, breezy unconcern and rode on, her body moving with her horse like a lover's, encouraging him every step of the way.

Reaching the edge of the park, she slowed her mount to a canter and proceeded to head back to her groom. Edmund continued to watch her as she rode through the entrance to the park. Without a backward glance she disappeared. Breathing deeply, he reflected on what he had just witnessed. Whoever she was, the young woman had been like some comet flashing by, leaving a kind of afterglow and a hint of consternation in Edmund such as he had thought he could never feel.

Long after he could no longer see her, Edmund continued to stare at the spot where she vanished, half expecting—and hoping—to see her appear once more. He could imagine how she looked—with a flush of exertion in her cheeks, her eyes bright and her expression animated. Never had he seen a woman ride with so much skill. By God, she was magnificent! It was a long time since he had enjoyed seeing anyone ride as much, or as fast and unrestrained, who could handle a horse and the going as well as she. Deeply impressed, he was curious as to who she might be. He hadn't seen her features, but he would recognise her again by the magnificent colour of her hair.

Marietta thought of the day ahead and her forthcoming wedding with little enthusiasm. Today she existed in a state of jarring tension, fighting to appear calm, clinging to her composure as if it were a shroud she could use to make herself disappear as her mother and a succession of maids scurried about the room and dressed her in her finest for her wedding to Gabriel, Viscount Mansel.

When her mother was in the room their chatter was subdued, but when she had gone quips and inuendoes as to what would take place between the newly wed bride and groom made Marietta uneasy. Embarrassed, she wanted to tell them to be quiet, but she held her tongue, wanting to keep her unease of what was to come to herself. She was going to have to build a number of skins on her if she was going to survive.

Gabriel was the son of the Earl of Waverley of the vast Elton Park Estate in Sussex, which was on the brink of ruin, the fortunes of the Mansel family having depreciated over the years from heavy gambling and profitless business ventures, hence the marriage to Miss Marietta Harrington. Her father was Samuel Harrington, a businessman, stronger, wealthier, more powerful than the Mansels, prepared to go to any lengths in his relentless pursuit of profit and an exalted title for his only child.

The announcement of the betrothal in the papers had struck London society with the force of a thunderbolt. It was common knowledge that the Earl of Waverley was about to go under and that Samuel Harrington, who lived in a large, elegant establishment lining Berkeley Square, was a social climber who would stop at nothing to see his daughter married to a title, which was a common enough practice so it should not have come as a surprise.

But Marietta wasn't like any of the young ladies society was familiar with. She was quiet and demure and there were many who never missed the opportunity to criticise or disparage. She was never seen unless it was in the company of her parents. Because her father was so strict, insisting everything be done his way, he expected much of his daughter, and she tried to do and be what was expected of her. Some said she was an unusual young woman—unnatural if they wanted to put it that way.

But if anyone had been inclined to look deeper they would find that behind the unprepossessing young woman there was a veritable treasure trove. Nineteen years of age, and formidably intelligent, Marietta had a distinct and memorable personality and could hold the most fascinating conversations on most subjects. She had a genuinely kind heart, wasn't boastful and rarely offended anybody. As a child she had taken most things for granted. She'd had to, having known nothing else. She rarely showed her feelings and seemed to have the ability to put on whatever kind of face was necessary at the time.

If she was left alone young men would be drawn to her like moths to a flame, but not for her kisses and gropings in dark corners, to be handled and touched and her self-respect squandered for the dubious pleasures of some gentleman seeking a quick thrill, not when her parents had their hearts set on a loftier destiny.

Seated at her dressing table, through the mirror Marietta watched her mother march into the room. Beatrice Harrington was a striking woman, tall and robust with auburn hair streaked with silver. With a domineering husband—a trait she shared—and Marietta's society wedding to arrange, she presided over the preparations with a stern eye. Draped in a royal blue silk gown with a low square neckline that revealed the swell of her ample breasts, she had been in and out of Marietta's bedroom all morning to check on the proceedings. She had instilled in her daughter the discipline to make her an obedient, biddable young woman and was satisfied that Marietta's exquisite manners and skills in everything a young woman of quality should possess would make any man a perfect wife.

She was watching Marietta having her hair brushed when she caught sight of a maid coming out of the dressing room carrying Marietta's wedding gown. Reaching up to hang it on the large wardrobe, she gasped when it slipped off its hanger on to the carpet.

'Heavens!' Beatrice exclaimed crossly. 'Be more careful, girl. With treatment like that it's not going to be fit to be seen. If it's creased, then take it and iron them out. We don't want it to look like it's been slept in. It has to be perfect.'

The maid blushed crimson and gathered the dress up from the floor and hung it back up, checking it carefully for any offending creases.

Beatrice went to her daughter, meeting her eyes in the mirror. 'Everything appears to be on schedule, Marietta. Your father is getting ready. Think yourself fortunate to be marrying into such a distinguished family,' she said, casting her eye around the room for the hundredth time to make sure everything was in order. 'And try not to look so glum.'

Marietta had heard this criticism all her life and, much as she wanted to complain, she held her tongue. No one would listen to her either way. She stared at her image in the dressing table mirror as the maid continued brushing her hair. Her mother's life consisted of daily promenades around Mayfair and the park, shopping and sipping tea with her friends in the pleasure gardens, her evenings one long round of entertainment. None of that appealed to Marietta. She dreaded any social event she attended with her mother and usually spent the entire evening in a corner, playing cards with some of the more sedate elderly ladies. She preferred to be at Lime Hall, their home in Surrey, riding through the meadows and indulging her passion for painting.

She listened to her mother giving orders to the servants, who bustled to do her bidding. She had always been a remote figure to Marietta, for all that they lived in the same house. Theirs was not a loving mother-and-daughter relationship. They were not friends or even companions. She was the one who gave instructions rather than confidences. When she had been small Marietta had tried so hard to please her parents, but her mother was always brusque and impatient to be doing other things—important things, she said—and her father was always so stern, unreachable, and she'd been more than a little afraid of him.

Marietta had been raised in a comfortable world created for her by her parents, with everything a girl could want, but it was also a narrow world, insulating her from real life that existed outside her sphere. She had been tutored at home and spoke French. She was also fluent in Italian, which she had learned when on her visits to her maternal aunt in Siena.

Marietta was so tired of her parents' control. She closed her eyes to hide the sudden tears that flooded her eyes. As far back as she could remember she'd learned what to be alone meant. She remembered peering out from an upstairs window, watching families passing by, children playing and skipping along, and she had longed to be invited to play with them. But it was not to be. Not for her. When she'd visited her Aunt Margaret in Siena with her mother, everyone had always welcomed her with warmth. Her young cousins had drawn her into their games and for a short time she had known what it was to be happy, to be like those children she had watched from her window. And then it would be time to leave and they would return to England. That was when she really learned about being alone. She often likened herself to a bird in a gilded cage.

At that moment Marietta couldn't bear to think about what lay ahead. Her youth was crying out for experience, for life. She wasn't looking for love—how could she when she had no idea what love was? She didn't want to marry Gabriel. Desolation was squeezing her heart tighter and tighter the closer the time came when she would have to leave for the church, knowing there was no way out.

'Just think, Marietta,' her mother said, breaking into her thoughts. 'You will go and live in that fine house in Sussex, and remember that one day, when you become a countess, you will be mistress of it. Despite the family's lack of wealth, Gabriel is a good catch, handsome and of a good disposition—better by far than some young men your father has considered in the past. Many young ladies would be glad to have him.'

Yes, Marietta thought bitterly, she must count herself lucky. After all, what did she know of Gabriel Mansel to object to? An expression of boredom she caught in his eyes on the four occasions they had met, never alone? Perhaps she had just imagined it, as she imagined the reluctance he had shown to the marriage when his father had insisted on it. He had made no attempt at courtship. A settlement had been made. Her father was handing over a substantial amount of money along with his daughter. She was not free to marry where she may. She would have to learn not to shudder when Gabriel touched her.

The time of the wedding had been set for midday. The house had never known such excitement as it prepared for the important day. She was bathed and pampered, her rich auburn tresses brushed until they gleamed. Only when Marietta's mother vacated the room to supervise the dressing of the four giggling bridesmaids and prepare herself for the wedding, and they were no longer under her watchful eye, did the maids relax and chatter excitedly among themselves.

Marietta did not share in their excitement. If they noted her quietness, they put it down to nervousness, which was often the case with a bride before her wedding.

Marietta was dressed and went downstairs for her mother's inspection. Servants were busily putting finishing touches to the banquet and her father's voice could be heard issuing orders in his study. Not usually one to be moved by such things, her mother surprised Marietta by stopping in her tracks when she appeared, her eyes wide with a mixture of admiration and satisfaction that she had produced such a beautiful daughter. She suddenly seemed to be looking at a different person. For once in her life she was speechless.

'Why, Marietta,' she said at last. 'You look… You look quite lovely. You remind me of myself when I was your age.'

Marietta thought her mother regarded her with more kindness in those moments. There was a softening to her eyes and a small smile played on her lips. The memory of herself as a nineteen-year-old girl had perhaps brought its own reaction. Looking at her now, Marietta regretted the years that they had not shared these memories.

'Lord Mansel will not be able to take his eyes off you.'

'But I don't love him, Mother,' Marietta said in one last appeal to have the wedding called off.

'Which is all to the good,' her mother said sharply. 'Then he cannot hurt you.'

Marietta looked at her. Was there hidden meaning in her mother's words? She knew nothing about her father's private life but that things weren't always in accord with her parents, whom she saw on a daily basis, when angry words were exchanged. Had her parents ever been happy together? As she had grown older she had often wondered. They never sat together or laughed together. Did her father keep a woman somewhere in town and, if so, did her mother suffer because of it?

Stepping back, Beatrice surveyed Marietta's ivory satin gown, the skirts full and flowing and embroidered with tiny seed pearls. Its low, square-cut bodice hugged her firm young breasts, then tapered to a miniscule waistline. The sleeves were long and tight fitting, terminating in points to rest on the back of her hands. Her thick mane of gleaming hair was drawn back from her face and secured with a diamond headband and left to flow down her spine in a glorious burst of colour, with wispy tendrils brushing her cheeks.

'I am aware of your reluctance to marry Gabriel Mansel, Marietta, but it is happening so try putting a smile on your face. It will not do to have you frowning and looking mutinous.'

'Very well, Mother. I will try.'

From an early age Marietta had learned not

to argue back, although as she had grown older acquiescing gnawed at her. Words and excuses filled her mouth, clamouring to be spoken. It nearly choked her to hold them back, to tell both her parents how she felt, but she knew how badly they wanted her to marry Gabriel, so she held her tongue. Her gaze was drawn to her father coming out of his study. He looked her way, but his eyes did not linger on her. If only he would look at her and tell her that she looked nice, she thought, concealing the hurt she felt. Seldom courteous, often impatient and occasionally quite cruel, he often didn't notice she was there.

She wanted to believe that on her wedding day he would take her in his arms in some loving way, but he had never done that and never would. Samuel Harrington was a man of medium height and no excess weight. His hair was tawny and going white at the temples. He also had a temper that was easily roused, his anger like an explosion when he was, which was why those who knew him always tried to keep on the right side of him.

'We should leave early,' he said brusquely, addressing his wife. 'I've had word that spectators are gathering, carriages blocking the streets round the church, which we must try to avoid.'

'I'll go on ahead with the bridesmaids— their mothers and nannies have already left.' She looked towards the door when a stranger was admitted. He'd come from the church to inform them that the Viscount had not yet arrived at the church and for them to delay their departure. Word would be sent when he turned up.

'Not turned up?' Samuel barked. 'Blast it! How can a man not turn up on time for his own wedding?'

'I do hope he hasn't changed his mind,' Beatrice said, a worried frown creasing her brow. Her husband threw her an exasperated look, taking his watch out and glancing at it.

'Don't be ridiculous, Beatrice,' he uttered impatiently. 'Of course he won't change his mind. There's too much riding on this wedding for him to do that. He'll turn up all right—probably got caught up in the snarl up, which he should have taken into account and set off for the church sooner. We'll just have to wait it out until he gets himself there.'

Marietta went into the drawing room to wait it out, quietly hoping Gabriel had had a change of heart and decided not to turn up—although should he not then he would feel all the force of her father's wrath. However, the humiliation she would suffer as a result of being jilted would be immeasurable. She vaguely noted the activities in the dining room, where footmen in immaculate uniforms hovered near the huge sideboard while another was inspecting the tables.

It promised to be a wedding which satisfied her mother's need for show and spectacle. She planned to make the maximum effect on the guests, even bringing in extra staff so that everything should function as smoothly as possible. The dining room, where the wedding banquet was to be served to eighty distinguished guests, shone with only the finest crystal and silverware, and above the tables the delicate prisms of the Italian crystal chandeliers twinkled. Each place setting had its own individual napkin embroidered with the initials of the bride and groom. Only the finest foods would be served, so that the banquet would be talked about for long after platters of meat and fish and delicious desserts had been consumed. Huge ice sculptures would form the centrepieces, some in the form of animals and graceful birds. It was extravagant to the highest degree, with an army of servants to dance attendance on the guests.

For the next half-hour her father walked from his study to the hall and back like a caged tiger, hoping for news from the church. The longer he waited the harder it became for him to contain his fury. He was beginning to contemplate the thought that Gabriel Mansel might not turn up after all when news arrived to say that he had and was waiting at the church. There was such a flurry of activity as bridesmaids piled into the carriage and Marietta prepared herself to follow on with her father.

London seethed with noisy activity as Edmund Fitzroy travelled towards St George's in Hanover Square, Mayfair's most fashionable church. Cursing his decision to accept the invitation to the wedding of his cousin, Gabriel Mansel, he looked irritably at the congestion on the approach to the church. The wedding had had the traffic tied up all morning.

At twenty-nine, three inches over six feet tall and with whipcord strength, Edmund was a man diverse and complex and could be utterly ruthless when the need arose. It was acknowledged that he was one of the richest men in Britain, with heavy investments in the railways, oil and industries worldwide. The kind of money he had at his disposal was difficult to conceive of and had won him the envy of men of business both in Britain and abroad. He always listened to his head and he had learned in the hardest way possible as a boy to trust no one but himself. Nothing he did was impulsive or accidental. Everything was carefully thought out.

He was admired and favoured by women, but he did not favour encumbrances that would tie him down. A wife and children were not part of his plan at this present time, although he supposed he would have to give it some thought in the future. When he took a mistress they were always beautiful and unattached. From the beginning he made it clear that marriage was not on offer and never would be. The issue was never raised again. Once this was established he remained faithful to her until the affair had run its course.

Clean shaven, his face was one of arrogant handsomeness. There was a hard firmness to his jaw and his wide, well-shaped mouth was held in a stern line. His intelligent face was lean and dark brows slashed across his forehead. His hair was thick and ebony black. In the midst of so much darkness his eyes were silver-grey, striking and piercing. Hidden deep in them was a cynicism, watchful and mocking, as if he considered the world a dubious place to be. He possessed a haughty reserve, and there was a strength of purpose in his features. From the arrogant lift of his dark head, he was a man with many shades to his nature.

Momentarily diverted from his thoughts when he saw a street urchin holding out his hand to beg a coin from a passer-by, memories of his former miserable life crowded in around him until the coach was filled with them. An odd emotion flickered across his features and his jaw tightened as he tried to hold back a memory that rose unbidden into his mind. An image of another boy doing exactly the same leapt out at him and his heart began to hammer in painful beats, his mind to drift away into a past he tried daily to forget. That boy had been himself, desperate to survive a life he had no choice but to endure, a life of misery, of begging and scrounging whatever he could find to feed himself and a father who could see no further than the bottom of a bottle of liquor, a father who was in a vegetative state in a clinic in Switzerland as the result of a street brawl and with no hope of recovery.

Leaning over the door of the carriage, he called the urchin over, handing him coin from his own pocket, averting his gaze from the grime-streaked face and the gratitude that filled the urchin's eyes.

Eventually his carriage deposited him outside the church. Forcing his way through the crush of people, reluctant to enter the church until the groom had arrived, he held back. There was no sign of Gabriel.

Gabriel was seriously late—the minutes had stretched to half an hour and the guests jamming the entrance were becoming restless and beginning to question the lateness of the groom. Edmund was beginning to give up on him when a carriage halted and Gabriel got out. With sighs of relief, the guests began filing into the church. Seeing Edmund, he stopped to have a word.

'Cutting it fine, aren't you, Gabriel?' Edmund said. 'Your parents have gone inside and your father looked none too pleased.'

'Oh, Lord! Thanks for the warning.'

'Isn't it the bride's prerogative to be late at her wedding, not the groom's?'

His cousin looked at him, brushing a heavy mop of unbrushed brown curls from his forehead and grinning broadly, as if all was well with the world and he had done no wrong.

'Heavy night, Edmund. I spent it with a ravishing young lady I couldn't tear myself away from—and I'm damned if I can remember her name—you know how it is. Fell asleep and by the time I woke it was way past the hour I intended to leave.'

Edmund knew exactly where Gabriel had spent the night. He'd watched him leave the club they both frequented with a fetching harlot on his arm, clinging on to him like a limpet. Edmund was tempted to tell him to slink back to his whore, but common sense won out. There were qualities in Gabriel that he detested. He was lazy and reckless to a fault, and overconfident in his ability to outwit and hoodwink his parents, who could see no wrong in their precious son, the heir to a noble pile in Sussex and an earldom—although the title was the only thing he possessed to recommend him.

'Hardly the behaviour of a man about to wed the lady of his choice.'

Gabriel frowned morosely. 'More my parents' choice, Edmund. Truth is, I know absolutely nothing about her. Funny little thing, she is—pretty and very much under her parents' thumb all her life. Don't think she'll present any trouble—as long as her dowry fills the family coffers my parents will be happy.'

Blithely ignoring Gabriel's ill humour, Edmund gave him a look of disdain. 'I find it odd that you have agreed to wed a girl you know very little about and that you have no intention of being charitable or accommodating towards. Have a care, Gabriel. You are late for your wedding. The lady might take exception and not turn up.'

Gabriel's scowl deepened. 'Damn it, Edmund! I do believe you're enjoying my predicament. You are being quite unfair. I cannot be accused of being either uncharitable or unaccommodating in this instance. I'm sure we'll rub along well together—providing she knows her place. She'll turn up—you can bet on it. Her father's hankering after a title for his daughter. He'll make sure she doesn't back out. Besides, the rumour about you and Lady Francine Russell is hardly anything to write home about.'

Something in the romanticism of Gabriel's words irritated and irked Edmund. He despised being the subject of gossip and speculation.

Francine Russell was a neighbour of his at his home in Kent and the widow of his closest friend, a woman he had befriended in her loss. She meant nothing more to him than that, but she did have a habit of seeking him out. It was unfortunate that their relationship had given rise to gossip.

'I credited you with more sense than to listen to gossip, Gabriel.'

He grinned. 'Can you blame me? When I hear that my illustrious cousin—a man who seems to avoid young ladies of impeccable background as if they have some kind of dreadful disease—is seen visiting a beautiful socialite at her home in Kent? And on more than one occasion, it would appear.'

Edmund's brow quirked in sardonic amusement. 'At twenty-seven, and a widow of four years, Francine Russell can hardly be classed as a *young lady*. We are close neighbours, Gabriel, and Francine often goes to Ashborne House to visit my aunt.'

'Yes, so I have heard—although you are an added attraction you cannot deny.'

'I wouldn't know,' he replied drily, shrugging off Gabriel's remarks. 'Now I think you should go inside, Gabriel. You don't want your bride to find you gossiping on the steps—or her father either, knowing how quick he is to anger—and I imagine your own father will have a few choice words to impart.'

Edmund watched him go inside, reluctant to follow him, and joined the throng of guests. The presence of Gabriel's father inside the church resurrected a time in his life he would prefer not to dwell on—which was exactly what had happened in the carriage. He took a deep breath as the dark recollections of his past sneaked once more into his wandering thoughts, a past he still struggled to overcome. It was as if a hand clutched his heart. It always happened when the unthinkable would lay siege to his subconscious and claim a thought for itself. Clenching his fists, he would try to think of other things whenever this occurred, to make the memories go away, not to intrude on the present—not a perfect present, for his past still haunted and tormented him, but it was a present much better than the past.

Sometimes when consumed by his work, he forgot entirely whom he had once been—a boy trying to survive in the slums of Liverpool where disease and dying, and children abandoned and forgotten, were all part of the rituals of life. Life had been piteous and unpredictable and the prospect of death had been almost enviable. As a boy, Edmund had deep down resigned himself to his fate.

He was still outside the church, tempted to walk away, when the carriage conveying the excited bridesmaids followed by the one bringing the bride and her father pulled up. A groom jumped down to assist her. From the shadows cast by the tall columns at the front of the church, the vision Edmund saw snatched his breath away. Small of stature and attired in a stylish ivory silk wedding gown, placing her hand on her father's arm, she moved towards the entrance. Was it his imagination or did she falter? Her eyes were fixed on the door to the church so she failed to see him standing some yards away. He watched her idly, wondering how it was that that moment of immobility could yet manage to convey an unmistakable impression of reluctance to join the bridegroom.

Her lovely face was young and unguarded. It was a small face, wide at the brow and pointed at the chin, with enormous amber eyes under delicate dark brows that curved upwards like a swallow's wings. The thick waves of her rich, auburn hair hung freely down her back, some wayward tresses resting on her shoulders. Her mouth was soft and full—a mouth to set a man's pulses beating.

Looking at her more closely, he observed there was a faraway look in her eyes and, hearing her sigh as she passed him by, his heart wrenched. There was a sadness about her, but he sensed that with the right words, she could be made to smile. She did not look as a bride should. There was a lifelessness about her and yet there was something that flickered, like a small flame that needed kindling to bring it to life and she would burst out of herself.

That was the moment Edmund realised she was the young woman he had seen in the park galloping hell for leather over the turf.

Numb to the world, Marietta walked down the aisle on her father's arm, which was strange, she remembered thinking afterwards, for it was the first time she could remember touching him. Roses had been arranged in the window recesses and the aisle was illuminated by candles. The church was packed on either side with lavishly dressed guests, family, friends and acquaintances, but never had she felt so alone. This was supposed to be the most important, happiest day of her life, yet she felt no joy. Seeing Gabriel standing waiting for her at the altar, for a moment she was tempted to turn before the vows were spoken and flee from the insanity of what she was doing. But even as she argued with herself, she took her place beside him, to join her life with his. Time stood still as they were swept into the wedding ceremony. Casting a sideways glance at him, she noted the sloppiness of his cravat and his red-rimmed, bloodshot eyes. She smelled liquor from his closeness. She was clearly so unimportant that he couldn't even be bothered to turn up on time for their wedding or attend to the cleanliness of his person.

She shuddered. It was as if a cold wind had stirred in the quiet of the church, had swirled about the congregation and settled on her. It was as if it was telling her to attack the established order of things, to dare, to seize the opportunity to take charge of her own life. It was as if she had been touched by a force she did not fully comprehend and could not now withstand. Something sprang to life within her. A spasm of pure disgust wrenched through her and caught her stomach into a tight knot. She was aware that everyone was watching her, waiting for her to respond. A raw anger replaced her numbness and real hatred unknown to her until today filled her and gave her courage for what she did next.

The vicar was intoning the words of the ceremony. When he came to *Will you take this man...?* she listened and, facing Gabriel, in a clear voice that rang out in the hallowed church, said, 'No, I will not.'

Ignoring the incredulity on Gabriel's face, which quickly turned to an expression of horror that penetrated his impassive features, and the collective gasps of the wedding guests, with her back ramrod straight and her head held high and ignoring her immobilised parents, without more ado she walked back down the aisle with as much dignity as she could muster and left the church.

Outside, breathing deeply, she looked about her, unaware of the chill March air, wondering where she might find refuge before her father came storming after her. 'Now what?' she asked herself, knowing there would be terrible reprisals for what she had done. Noting the crowd gathered outside the church, waiting to see the bride and groom emerge together, she made a move towards it.

'One moment, if you please, young lady.'

The authority in the calm voice brought her up short. She turned slowly, feeling like a child who had been caught misbehaving.

'That was a turn up for the books.'

Raising her eyes, she met those of the gentleman towering over her. They were focused intently on her, the expression she could not fathom. In the surrounding haze, Marietta no longer saw anyone but him. She stared at him fixedly. Had she wanted to look away she could not have done. Never had she seen such a figure of masculine elegance. His movements, his air of power and languid indolence, hung about him like a cloak. The perfect fit of his coat and the tapering trousers accentuated the long lines of his body. It was impossible not to respond to this man as his mere presence dominated the scene.

'I suppose it was. It wasn't what everyone was expecting—or myself, come to think of it. Who are you?' His gaze narrowed a little as his eyes passed over her in a manner which she recognised as appraisal. His attitude was all courtesy, although he gave a slight shrug of his shoulders, as if in wonderment at the foolishness of some people.

'Edmund Fitzroy, Gabriel's cousin, at your service,' he said, inclining his head slightly, his voice deep. 'Am I correct in thinking that you would like to get away from here?'

The planes of his face were sharp, the mouth a straight line, and then he offered her a smile that softened the harsh lines of the arresting face and seemed to melt the gloom in her heart. 'Yes. As you see, sir, I am in dire need of rescuing.' She glanced back at the church, seeing people beginning to appear through the doorway.

'You don't intend going back inside and continuing with the wedding ceremony?'

'No. The matter is settled. The only way I can be tied to Gabriel Mansel is to bind me to him hand and foot. Even then no one could force me to agree to wed him. I must leave. I have no time to explain.'

A slow smile that curved his lips widened and he gave a careless shrug. 'You don't have to. I was there—at the back of the church.'

'Then you will understand my need to be gone from here—and quickly, before my father comes storming out of the church and drags me back inside to marry Gabriel.'

He chuckled softly. 'What a charming escapee you are. I'm so glad I was on hand when you decided to run away. Come with me. My carriage is just round the corner. Where would you like to go?'

If she wanted to escape the full force of her father's wrath, then she had no option but to throw herself on the mercy of this stranger. 'I don't care as long as it's away from here.'

'You do realise that before the day is out, what you have just done will be the talk of the town.'

She looked at him. There was an openness about his handsome face that Marietta trusted and she smiled. 'Will it really?' Her smile broadened. 'Yes, I suppose it will.'

'Don't you care?'

'At this moment—no, I don't, but I will be made to answer for it, you can be sure of that.' Falling in with Gabriel's handsome cousin's long strides, then glancing back, she saw the wedding guests pouring out of the church, her father at the head of them. He appeared to be furious.

Chapter Two

Edmund Fitzroy gave Marietta no time to dwell on what was happening behind them. He had taken her arm and at the same time was beckoning the man who stood by the carriage some way from the church. 'Marsden, we must be away. Miss Harrington will be coming with us.'

The man gaped with astonishment. 'The bride, sir?' But then he stopped and quickly climbed atop the carriage, taking up the reins and waiting for a signal from his employer to drive on.

Marietta allowed herself to be hurried along, her decisions made for her. And why not? She had no wish to linger. Her immediate problem had been solved— she was grateful.

Her saviour assisted her into the elegant, shiny, black open carriage drawn by four matching, prancing bay horses. Immediately they were heading away from the church.

Seated in the carriage with no idea of where he was taking her, Marietta took a moment to give thought to her situation as the driver negotiated his way between the carriages waiting to take the wedding guests to Berkeley Square and the grand reception that would not now take place. Her mother would be furious. Marietta had behaved so out of character. Now she could see that what she had done was shocking and beyond any forgiveness. And to her humiliation and her sense of guilt was added the fear of what her father would do.

She shivered.

'Are you cold?'

Before she could reply, her companion had shrugged out of his jacket and, leaning over, draped it around her shoulders. Marietta was cocooned in a comforting warmth along with a masculine smell of spicy cologne. The gesture was as intimate as it was chivalrous and she was suddenly conscious of how much of a stranger he was to her As she glanced across at him lounging back against the rich upholstery with his long legs crossed in front of him. He was studying her with a watchful curiosity, appearing composed and unfazed by the whole affair, while she was struggling with mortification. Now she had time for calm reflection, she was sorry her recklessness would have hurt so many people, but she did not regret it. What she had done had changed everything, but she would still have to face everyone and deal with the situation later.

'Well, Miss Harrington. Now that we've established that you are not going to marry Gabriel, what will you do?'

'The truth is, sir, that I have no idea. I don't know what I would have done had you not been there.'

'I could not have left you standing there. Whatever the reason that had you fleeing from the church, then the least I could do was save you from some of the consequences of your folly. You were in distress. That alone can provoke the chivalrous nature of a gentleman however unaware the lady might be of her charm. And charming you undoubtedly are. I don't think Gabriel will be at all that happy with being jilted at the altar—and his father will be furious.'

'Perhaps he will. We'll have to see.'

'Would you like me to instruct my driver to take you home?'

Perched stiffly on the cushioned seat across from him, having spent a moment adjusting her skirts in an effort to avoid meeting his gaze, Marietta now raised her eyes and looked at him.

'I will have to at some point, I suppose, but I'm in no hurry. In fact, the longer I avoid coming into contact with my father the better. Where are you taking me?'

'My home is quite close. We will go there for tea and decide what is to be done—although I don't imagine it will be long before your father comes knocking on my door. We were seen leaving the church together. My uncle, the Earl of Waverley, will be sure to give him my address.'

'Oh, dear!' she gasped, suddenly mortified. 'I do so hope I haven't got you into trouble. My father can make the earth tremble when he's angry.'

He nodded, not in the least concerned. 'So can I, Miss Harrington, so can I. I should tell you that I am acquainted with your father. Some of our business interests cross over from time to time.'

'I see. Then you will agree that he is quite formidable and I dread how he will react to what I have done.'

Edmund Fitzroy's town house was situated in the heart of Mayfair. It was imposing without being ostentatious or austere. Huge windows admitted light to the hall, where an elegant curved staircase rose to the upper floor.

He led her into a spacious drawing room with long French windows which overlooked a creeper-draped terrace and an immaculate garden beyond. The room was furnished to suit masculine tastes. They sat at a table close to the windows and waited for Henry, the butler, to bring refreshments.

Edmund Fitzroy smiled at her, a pleasant smile, so that Marietta felt called upon to smile in return. She sighed, gazing at the well-tended garden, thinking it really was a pleasant place to be and would be even better in summer when it was in full bloom.

'That's better. Now, tell me, how did you come to be in this position? What made you do it? It was a brave thing you did in the church.'

Marietta drew in a shuddering breath and shook her head. 'It wasn't brave. I simply knew

I could not marry Gabriel. I would have said so before, but I knew no one would listen to me—and if they did they would take no notice.'

'But why wait until you were in the church and about to say your vows? Do you have an objection to marriage?'

For a moment Marietta debated how to meet this unexpected and sudden frankness, but his expression held no derision. 'No, not at all. In the ordinary course of events I would never have contemplated doing anything so drastic as what I have done today. But I was desperate. I didn't intend leaving Gabriel at the altar—but—he—he made me feel so unimportant. I thought arriving late for his wedding was bad enough, but turning up and looking as if he had slept in his clothes and smelling strongly of drink—well, I—I was so angry I knew I could not marry him—that marriage to Gabriel would not be a pleasurable experience. I am sure he must feel he is lowering himself by marrying me, even though his father would be receiving a substantial amount of money to relieve his situation. How desperate he must be to taint his noble heritage by marrying into trade. I imagine Gabriel will be feeling angry and put out, but I don't think I will have broken his heart—only his pride. The wedding seemed all wrong.'

'Then you are exonerated—at least in my eyes. Better to do it at this late hour than live to regret it.'

'As a result of what I have done I will be talked about and laughed at.'

'While half the young ladies who marry without a say will envy you your courage.'

'And the other half will think I am peculiar.'

'Exceedingly.'

Marietta looked at him, ready to defend herself, but found him regarding her seriously and with some interest. 'You don't laugh.'

'You refused to bend, to accommodate your parents' plans they tried to impose on you. I cannot laugh at that.'

'But I have been like that all my life—never once questioning what they wanted for me. It was only when I saw Gabriel in the church, who didn't do me the courtesy of turning up on time and looking unkempt, that I knew I couldn't go through with it.'

'It's a great shame there aren't more like you. As it is there are far too many sad young ladies in unhappy marriages because they did not have the courage to speak out. Many young women are considered unimportant until they are old enough to marry. Then everything changes and they become bargaining tools for their parents.'

'You are very frank, Lord Fitzroy.'

'Mr—I do not have a title. Do you mind my being frank?'

'No, not in the least. I find it rather refreshing. I wish more people were equally so. I apologise for giving you a title. I—I assumed…'

'Don't worry about it. It's a mistake easily made. Too much importance is put on titles.'

A silence fell between them. Marietta turned her attention to the garden, watching a blackbird as it hopped about on the lawn.

'What are you thinking about?' Mr Fitzroy asked softly.

'Nothing in particular.' She sighed, dragging her eyes away from the bird. 'I'm trying not to think of what I have done—and dreading the reprisals. It's so peaceful here. You have a lovely house. Do you have property elsewhere?'

'I have an estate in Kent.'

'Is it very large?'

'Several hundred acres.'

'I can't believe that you were so quick to rescue me when I ran from the church.' She smiled, her cheeks rosy in the heat of the room.

'Like my knight in shining armour. You must know Gabriel very well—although you don't resemble him in the slightest. I can't recall him mentioning you—although why would he? In fact, I know nothing about you.'

'Then allow me to enlighten you. Gabriel takes after his mother and he is six years my junior. We are cousins, but spend little time together. Gabriel's father and my mother were siblings. My mother died when I was a child.'

'Oh, I'm sorry.' Her sympathy was genuine, although never having lost anyone close to her she could only imagine how it might have affected him.

Marietta sat back in her chair when Henry appeared carrying a tray of tea things. She was surprised—her mother, always one to stand on ceremony and do the correct thing, would frown on such a procedure being carried out by the butler instead of a maid. Favouring her with a smile, Henry began placing the delicate china cups and saucers on the table.

'Thank you, Henry,' Mr Fitzroy said. 'I think we can manage now.'

Henry ignored him and began pouring the tea.

Marietta found the relationship between Mr

Fitzroy and his butler very odd. Tilting her head to one side, she looked across at her congenial host. 'Do you spend much of your time in London?'

'I do. I am a businessman, Miss Harrington, which frequently brings me to the city. From a youth I have lived in Kent with a paternal uncle and aunt. He died two years ago—after spending the latter years of his life trying to talk me into marriage—but he failed. In fact, I think he despaired of seeing me suitably married and fell in with my unequivocal wish to remain a bachelor—for the time being at least.'

'Why? What's wrong with you?'

'Nothing.' He chuckled, glancing at Henry. 'I think Henry can attest to that, can't you, Henry?'

'Oh, absolutely, sir,' he said, handing Marietta her tea with a smile.

'There you are, you see. Henry agrees with me.'

Henry's eyes twinkled. 'You will find, Miss Harrington, that Mr Fitzroy is an exacting man, who insists on the highest standards from all those he employs. However, he can be quite charming, when it suits him, I grant you.'

'Thank you, Henry,' Mr Fitzroy said, scowling at his butler.

'What does Mr Fitzroy really do with his time, Henry?' Marietta asked, already in awe of Edmund Fitzroy, thinking that he had all the markings of a prize catch—with one exception. A title. She was bewildered by the strength of her feelings, whatever they were. She was not all that sure and she was frail in her ignorance, but she found herself defenceless against the strange magnetism, the masculine vitality of his which she could not resist.

'I work,' Edmund informed her. 'Quite hard as it so happens.'

'At what?'

'I have an estate to run. I also handle all my own business and financial affairs—which are considerable.'

'And he has a brilliant mind, Miss Harrington,' Henry informed her, handing her a delicate little iced cake in a napkin, 'and a head for figures that shames me. He also drives himself hard, demanding too much of himself—and others.'

'And you, Henry, let your tongue run away with you.' Mr Fitzroy chuckled, stirring his tea. 'He is also deaf, Miss Harrington—which is why he remains to play the maid—although he is too proud to admit it.'

Henry grinned. 'It's one of my faults—and now I am in my dotage it is one I get away with.'

'Don't count on it. You are also old and infirm and ready to be put out to grass, so you would be wise to have a care,' his master said.

Henry laughed, supremely confident of his place. 'You wouldn't do that. You couldn't do without me. Admit it.' Without more ado, Henry inclined his head towards Marietta, a definite twinkle still in his eye, and left them to their tea.

Marietta was surprised to find laughter bubbling up inside her. 'What a lovely man. You must be very fond of him.'

Mr Fitzroy nodded, placing his tea on the table and leaning back in his chair. 'I am. He's been with the family for many years. In fact, when I was a youth and in London, I don't know what I would have done without his support.'

'How fortunate for you to have such a loyal retainer. My father's butler is so po-faced I think his face would crack if he smiled.' Taking a sip of her tea, she gasped softly when she spilled a little on her dress. 'Oh, dear! Had I done that in front of Mother she would make me feel that I had committed the ultimate sin.' She laughed when he passed her a linen napkin which she took and dabbed at the stain. 'It is nothing and will wash out.'

'And it just happens to be your wedding dress.' A crooked smile curled his lips as he let his leisurely perusal sweep over her. 'It's the perfect dress for a bride. You look quite enchanting.'

His smiling eyes captured hers and held them prisoner until she felt a warmth suffuse her cheeks. 'Thank you. My mother chose it— but I'm not, am I—a bride?'

Resting his elbows on the arms of his chair and steepling his fingers in front of him, he said, 'Tell me, Miss Harrington. Do you enjoy riding?'

Her eyes lit up. 'Oh, yes. Absolutely.'

He grinned. 'A girl after my own heart.'

She darted him a sharp glance. 'Really?'

He nodded. 'You may be surprised when I tell you that I've seen you before.'

'You have? When?'

'It was when I was in Hyde Park early one morning. I like to ride there myself when I'm in London. I saw you with a groom. I had no idea who you were—until today. You were riding a chestnut gelding. I remember it was a huge beast—I thought at the time it was far too big and spirited for such a small woman to ride, but you soon put me right. You are one of the most skilled female riders I'd ever seen mounted. I can see you are no ordinary young woman. I'm impressed by your prowess.'

'I had no idea I was being watched.'

His grin was boyishly disarming. 'How could you? You were flying like the wind at the time.'

They sat in silence as Marietta drank her tea. 'I had no idea I was being watched.' She was surprised and quietly pleased and flattered by his praise.

This house, this beautiful garden, this man, all crowded in on her senses. She felt something stir in the pit of her stomach and at the same time a long sigh of contentment engulfed her. This was so right. A sudden peace came over her—she was sure he felt it, too—an awareness of one another. It was a beautiful moment which came to an end when Henry came in to announce the arrival of her parents.

'We were expecting them. Show them in, Henry.'

Marietta's heart was pounding as she rose

from the table, dreading the moment when she would have to face her mother and father. Henry swept open the pair of carved doors and stepped aside to admit her parents.

'Mr and Mrs Harrington.'

The air was charged as her parents moved into the centre of the room. Polite greetings were exchanged before her father cast a disapproving eye over her.

'I apologise for the intrusion, Mr Fitzroy,' he said sharply, 'but you know why my wife and I are here.'

'Of course. I was expecting you.' Mr Fitzroy turned and looked at Marietta several paces behind him. 'You are here to see your daughter.'

'Yes. I do not know what happened back there, but my daughter must realise the enormity of what she has done and return with us to the church at once.'

'Mr Fitzroy has been most kind,' Marietta said in a small voice, 'and was kind enough to bring me—'

'I'm sure he has been,' her mother said sharply, her wintry eyes fixing on her daughter with anger smouldering in their depths. 'I really don't understand you, Marietta. Most young ladies would give their right arm to be in your position—a fortune and a title.'

Edmund inclined his head. 'Perhaps you should listen to what your daughter has to say, Mrs Harrington.'

'Nothing she says will make up for what she has done. No groom likes to have his bride run out on him at the altar.'

'I am sure she will explain what it was that prompted her into such an action,' Mr Fitzroy persisted. The lines around the sardonic mouth had deepened and the furrows across his forehead were more marked, the finely moulded lips more compressed. His stance gave the impression not of force, as did his features, but of disciplined power and energy.

Mrs Harrington took a step towards Marietta. 'You show no sign of repentance for your appalling lack of propriety and good manners, Marietta. What were you thinking of? Do you have any idea what you have done, you stupid girl? Do you? You have disgraced yourself beyond recall. I'll never forgive you for this. If you don't return with us now, you will be throwing away the chance of a lifetime. You have made us the laughing stock of London.'

'No, Mother,' Marietta whispered. 'All that

you do—everything you do is worthwhile and appreciated. People will not laugh at you.' This brought a look of contempt from her mother.

'Foolish girl. Such is your naivety. A lot you know about people,' she said and Marietta was shocked at the virulent rage emanating from her mother.

Marietta stood mute, which seemed to infuriate her mother further and to enrage her father who tightened his lips into a line so thin his mouth completely disappeared. Her mother's face grew puce with rage at what she saw as her daughter's defiance.

'You have been raised as a decent young woman with a good education and the prospect of a decent marriage. A worthwhile life—'

'Does she not have a say in this, Mrs Harrington?' Mr Fitzroy interrupted.

'Certainly not. My husband and I know what is best for her.'

Glancing at Mr Fitzroy, Marietta suspected he was struggling to make a pretence of politeness to her parents. However, his granite features softened when they settled on her. He seemed to know how humiliated she was feeling and she could not believe her ears when he came to her defence.

'It seems to me, Mrs Harrington, that if you continue treating her like a prisoner she will do her best to escape her prison—which is what you have just witnessed when she ran from the church, leaving her future husband at the altar of matrimony.'

Affronted that he should speak so frankly, Mrs Harrington gasped. 'Prisoner? Marietta is not a prisoner. She does very much as she likes. And you, sir, exacerbated the situation by carrying her off in your carriage. Did it not occur to you that we would wish to speak to her, that she was suffering from some kind of hysteria and that she should have been persuaded to return to the church?'

'Your daughter looked perfectly sane to me, Mrs Harrington, and was not in the least hysterical. She was distressed and would have run away from the church in any direction open to her. It was fortunate I was there to offer my assistance.'

'And you are Gabriel Mansel's cousin, you say?'

'I am.'

'Then did you not consider the humiliation and shame he might be suffering?'

'No, I confess I did not. I very much doubt

Gabriel has suffered anything resembling humiliation and shame in his life.'

'Well, he is most put out, I can tell you, and his father is outraged.' Mr Harrington looked at his daughter. 'You have much to answer for, Marietta. And now enough time has been wasted. The rector has very kindly said he will wait for you to return when he will then continue with the ceremony. Everyone is still there so we had best return.'

Mr Fitzroy looked at him in cold incredulity. 'You do not propose to take her back, to force her into a marriage she has no liking for?'

Marietta looked at her father in horror, backing away as though he was about to strike her. 'No, Father. I will not go back. I cannot marry Gabriel—not now. Not ever. I do not like him. I do not want him. I *will* not marry him.' Her voice was passionate.

'Enough of this, Marietta. You will do as I say. You will return to the church and marry Gabriel,' her father snapped.

'No, Father. Not this time.' Did he not know how this hurt her? Did he care? Had either of her parents ever cared?

Her father looked at her as if she had taken leave of her senses. From the stupefied look on his face it was obvious that he couldn't take it in. He did not like to be argued with and he spoke in an irritated, angry tone. 'Wretched girl,' he expostulated. 'To cause a scene like that in the church was a disgrace. Your only goal in life is to cause me as much aggravation as possible. Have you any idea of the expense this day has cost me? No, of course you haven't. Clearly it does not concern you. You have brought disgrace on the whole family. I will not have it, Marietta. You cannot ruin your life like this.'

This outburst caused Mr Fitzroy's face to tighten with anger and, noting how his hands clenched into fists, Marietta could almost feel his urge to toss her parents out into the street and close the door on them.

'What do you think will happen to you now?' her mother retorted. 'No decent man will have you. For pity's sake, Marietta, pull yourself together. Now come along. You have prevailed upon Mr Fitzroy's generous hospitality long enough.'

It was not often that Marietta could withstand her domineering parents. It was not often that she even tried, but she seemed to have about her now a grim air of coldness, of fixed, unbending resolution. She shook her head, backing away further. 'No, Mother. I will not. I am sorry for all the trouble I have caused, but I will not marry Gabriel. Not now. Not ever.'

'Allow me to make a suggestion,' Mr Fitzroy said, having made a quick assessment of the situation. 'Since your daughter is unwilling to continue with the wedding, nothing will be gained by forcing her to return to the church. However, you will have to return to speak to the rector and inform the guests that the wedding will no longer take place. I will put my carriage at Mrs Harrington's disposal to take your daughter home where you can discuss what is to be done in private.'

Samuel Harrington glared at his daughter as he considered Mr Fitzroy's suggestion. 'I would be grateful,' he reluctantly conceded. 'Thank you.'

The four of them filed out of the house. After having a quick word with his wife and thanking Mr Fitzroy for his assistance in this unfortunate matter, Marietta's father climbed into his carriage to return to the church.

About to place her foot on the step of Mr Fitzroy's carriage, Marietta stumbled. Mr Fitzroy's hand automatically shot out. He took her hand to steady her. As he did so there was a strange transmission between them, something purely physical that had not been there earlier, or at least only on the edge of their consciousness. Marietta wasn't at all sure of what was happening, what she was saying when she thanked him, but whatever it was she knew she wanted something from him and she didn't want to leave him, but she could not put a name to what it was. She held his hand trustingly, his strength enfolding her as she climbed into the coach, and whatever it was that had happened to her she held it close to her heart like a newly found treasure.

Once inside the coach and seated across from her mother, she looked directly into Mr Fitzroy's eyes as he stood back and waited for the coach to move off. There were no barriers between them, just the two of them and an invisible force that touched and communicated and needed to be resolved. It lasted for just a moment in time, but it was enough.

And so she returned to Berkeley Square, to the house she had left as a reluctant bride earlier, back to the silken luxuries and cold cruelties of parents who tolerated her for the kudos that would come their way from their daughter's advantageous marriage. But the wedding was indeed over, Marietta had seen to that, leaving behind consternation and scandal. If ever there was a time in one's life when one wished the ground to open and swallow one up, this was the moment for Marietta. But she had to live the next minutes and days and a lifetime with it. Perhaps it would be worse for her parents, but she doubted it. They had learned long ago not to languish in defeat.

It was a thoughtful Edmund Fitzroy who watched the carriage carrying Marietta Harrington disappear down the street. He could only wonder what had just happened, the like of which had never happened before. Miss Harrington had certainly impressed him. She had a femininity he could have put to his lips and drunk and she had been so close he could feel her breathing, feel the warmth of her and smell her natural scent. Never had he seen such shimmering perfection in his life before as he had when he had met her, when he had gazed at her deep auburn hair curling in soft, feathery wisps, framing a finely proportioned and flawless visage.

He found himself dwelling on the perverse

quirk of fate that had brought them together. When he had offered her the use of his carriage, he had wondered what he was letting himself in for by offering to take her to his home. When he had witnessed her impressive horsemanship in the park several days ago and again seen her at the church when she had arrived, he had been completely captivated by her, equally so now he knew her a little better. Then her manner had marked her as strong of character whereas when she had been driven away in his carriage with her domineering mother, he had seen a fragility about her, a softness, an elusive gentleness that declared her to be as fragile and vulnerable as the roses that had decorated the church.

She was young and he suspected this was her first revolt at life. Clearly she was a person of ever-changing moods and subtle contradictions. While her physical beauty first arrested the attention, it was this spectrum, this bewildering, indefinable quality that had held him captive. A strange, sweet, melting feeling softened his innermost core without warning, the place in him that he usually kept as hard as steel.

Later, looking back, this was Edmund's first transgression in getting to know Marietta Harrington—setting a precedent for what followed.

He should have stopped there. But even then it was too late to stop. In many ways his fate was already decided. With her shining auburn hair and soft amber eyes, she was beautiful, exquisite.

As he turned and went back into the house, there was a lightness in his heart that he hadn't felt before. It took him by surprise and for a long time his thoughts were taken up with that bright-eyed girl. He let himself recall how he had felt when he had been close to her, visualising the sensations of how it would feel to hold her in his arms, to place his lips on hers and feel her sweet response. His body tightened at the thought.

Yet what he felt for her was somehow more than lust, more than desire. However unwittingly, Marietta Harrington had proved a focus for his dark thoughts, an escape from his ghosts.

Chapter Three

Now Marietta had decided that nothing in the world would persuade her to marry Gabriel Mansel, the wedding was called off, the marriage settlement cancelled and the guests went home. It had never occurred to Marietta's parents that their quiet, biddable daughter, totally dependent on them, would do something as outrageous as to leave her future husband at the altar.

The following morning had a normality about it for Marietta. It was as if the previous day with all its upset had never happened. But it had and it was the day she had met Mr Fitzroy. She sighed, deeply troubled by the recollections of their meeting. She could not understand this strange fascination that claimed her whenever she thought of him. She was ignorant of how to deal with it, that was the trouble. She had not been prepared on meeting him for the blow which had struck her, right in the spot in her chest where she supposed her heart to be.

Faith, her maid, woke her, pulling back the curtains and bringing her hot water.

'I thought I would let you sleep in a bit this morning because you would be tired after yesterday,' Faith said as she prepared the clothes Marietta would wear that day.

Dearest Faith, Marietta thought. What would she do without her cheerful patter? She was always happy, competent, thoughtful and never one to judge.

Having no wish to come face to face with either of her parents, Marietta had her breakfast brought to her room. All that morning and into the afternoon she was aware of the activity in the house, as her mother went about the business of removing all evidence of the wedding that had never happened.

The scandal, when it became known, rocked London society. The newspapers reported every humiliating detail. Mrs Harrington wanted to retire to their country house until the scandal had passed over, but her husband was of a different mind and steadfastly insisted on staying in London and braving it out. Every day Mrs Harrington, unrelenting, glared at her daughter with displeasure whenever she came into contact with her and she would abruptly dismiss her from her presence.

Her mother's anger and sniping and stony silences snapped the slender thread of control Marietta managed to keep on her emotions. As the days passed a strong sense of depression and loneliness was settling on her. The only relief open to her was the passion she had for painting. Art was something she had become familiar with as a small child and she had insisted on having a room where she could draw and paint to her heart's content. Her studio had become a place of refuge where she could be herself, where she could express herself in her painting. Her parents couldn't see the point of it, but allowed her to indulge her passion.

When Marietta mixed her colours and picked up her paintbrush, to hold these things and to apply the brush to canvas and create images of the people she had seen on occasion, images burned into her memory—their expressions, the way they dressed and moved, a solitary child in the park, perhaps rolling a hoop or throwing a ball—there was comfort and release in doing this and order was restored.

It was cool in the early light of the morning, two weeks after she had walked away from her wedding, when she rode Vulcan into the park accompanied by a groom. She liked to come early to avoid the influx of riders that came later. The dawn light was a clear, opalescent hue which shivered in a challenging point of brightness where the sun was just beginning to appear on the horizon. There was a faint swathe of mist floating on the grass and among the trees, the birds waking and warbling.

With the groom following in her wake, she had been riding hard for several minutes when she saw a rider emerge from a fringe of trees. At first the rider was indistinguishable in the dull light. She recognised him as he came closer. Her heart surged and instead of slowing her mount she urged it on, laughing delightedly when he rose to the challenge and fell in beside her. They rode at full gallop. With a challenging shout, Edmund Fitzroy went ahead. The exhilaration of speed and the rush of the morning air had brought a glow of colour to Marietta's cheeks and she was laughing as she reined in beside him beneath a clump of tall trees, where he had pulled up to wait for her.

His face looked relaxed and unguarded in the pale light of the morning and he looked terribly handsome in his brown well-cut riding coat and fawn-coloured breeches atop his highly polished brown riding boots.

'Good morning, Mr Fitzroy. I didn't expect to find anyone riding this early. I usually have the park to myself at this time.'

'I ride most mornings, but later. However, hoping to see you, I decided to leave the comfort of my bed and come to the park before my usual time.' His eyes warmed as they swept over her. 'I am happy my efforts are rewarded for here you are and looking quite splendid and as pretty as a picture.'

Marietta smiled. She had often been paid compliments and called pretty, even though in her opinion she was just passably so. 'I'm flattered that I generated so much interest. Our meeting two weeks ago is hardly one I care to think about.'

'And how are you now?'

'Well, it's behind me, thank goodness. I pray it will be some considerable time before my parents find someone else for me to marry—although my mother is still very angry with me.'

'So they have no plans for you.'

'No—at least none that I am aware of—although I am sure my father is already seeking a needy title for me to marry. He's not known for letting the grass grow under his feet. At this present time my whole future is a question mark.'

'It needn't be. There is a whole future ahead of you. It will be what you make it.'

'Perhaps, though I do not see it myself. I've never been one for the glitter of society and the company my parents keep. I take little pleasure in them—I feel like an outsider looking in.' She sighed, shaking her head. 'As for what the future holds for me—I shall have to wait and see what happens.'

'When I think of what you did that day, I think you are impatient to give fate a prod. Am I right?'

'In truth, I've never thought about it. Up to now the only prodding of fate I have done is to refuse to wed Gabriel—the results I suspect hit his parents much harder than they did their son when Father cancelled the marriage settlement.'

'I'm afraid you are right—although my uncle

will have to curtail his pleasures until Gabriel finds another wealthy young lady to wed. Where Gabriel is concerned, he will carry on doing what he does best—playing the scene.'

'And he was going to be my husband. I shudder when I think of it and consider myself well rid of him.'

Mr Fitzroy chuckled softly. 'Perhaps—although he has his agreeable points. I think he could be described as a likeable rogue.' Marietta laughed and he said, 'You should laugh more often. How different you look when you do. You look less severe than you do when in repose.'

'Do I? I didn't know. No one has ever said.'

'Perhaps it is only when you are in my company and that you disapprove of me,' he said with an amused gleam in his eyes.

'I can't think why you should feel that. The disapproval is in your imagination. I don't know you well enough to disapprove of you.'

'Perhaps my reputation has gone before me.'

She frowned, putting out a hand to soothe her horse which was growing restive. 'I don't know anything about that.'

'There! Now you are wearing your severe expression again. I think if we meet more often to ride in the park I will have you smiling all the time.'

Again she laughed. 'I shudder to think what my father's reaction would be to that. I feel I must thank you for what you did for me that day—rescuing me when I most needed rescuing. Had you not taken me in hand I would probably have ended up being married to Gabriel.' She glanced at the groom who was waiting for her close to the entrance to the park. 'I'm afraid I must go. I must get back to the house.'

'I'll ride with you to the gate. I hope we meet again.'

She turned her head to look at him as they rode on. 'I can't imagine why you would want to.'

There was no laughter in his eyes, no amusement lurking on his lips when his intense gaze settled on her face. 'Can't you? I'll tell you some time. In the meantime here you are back with your groom.'

'Yes, he always accompanies me when I ride.' She looked at him. 'I'm glad we met. I did so want to thank you for what you did for me that day.'

'And you have—several times, in fact. Good day, Miss Harrington.'

Marietta rode out of the gate where she turned and looked back at him. For a moment his gaze held hers with penetrating intensity and unexpectedly Marietta felt an answering frisson of excitement. The slight smile that curved his lips warned her he was aware of that brief response. His eyes moved over her face as if he were memorising it and then, with a slight satisfied nod of his handsome head, he rode on.

And then Marietta knew. The comfort she sought in her art was here also, with this man she barely knew, but already he had made inroads into her heart. What she felt was almost holy in its intensity, so strong that she was certain he must be aware of it. It tore through her senses and she knew it would never diminish. In that moment he had scattered her thoughts like fairy dust, stirring into life a longing she did not recognise. It disturbed her, for how could it be that she could feel this way after such a short time? The feeling was exquisite, something quite joyous and unique which had been spun between them.

Edmund headed back home, his thoughts very much on Miss Harrington. When he had watched her ride to the entrance of Hyde Park with her groom, she had turned and smiled, a smile that had transformed her whole face. There was a kind of power in that smile and the way she used her eyes, as if she were bestowing some kind of favour. Young as she was and completely ignorant to the ways of the world and the opposite sex, that power could stir and arouse.

She had intrigued his male sensibilities from the start, stirred his senses, her sharp mind stimulating his own, and had captured his imagination. She was coolly confident and showed a capacity to think for herself and to assess what went on around her. He admired her spirit and her sweetness—especially her honesty. Seeing her again had increased his interest and he intended seeing her again.

Never had he been touched by another human being as he was by Marietta Harrington, but his thoughts were aggressive when he considered what her life must have been like as an only child growing up in an establishment where there was no one she could be herself with, no one she could be a child with when she had been a child herself, with stern unloving parents foisting on her the manners of their kind, the stiff and proper adult kind.

After stabling his horse he strode into the house, marshalling his thoughts with the precision taught him by doing business with shrewd players. His head was clear and an elated gleam, a pinpoint of clarity, shone in his silver-grey eyes and a smile, lurking at the edge of his mouth, quivered as though longing to burst into laughter. He didn't know why she had such a volatile effect on him, but he understood that he wanted her. He wanted her warm and willing in his arms—in his bed—and he told himself that it would be by some holy miracle if he managed to keep his hands off her.

He had a choice to make. Either he could arrange another meeting between them before he had to leave for Kent in two weeks' time—his aunt was to entertain a few guests over a weekend and he had promised he would be there—or he could wait until his return in a month's time, in which case her father could well have found another suitor for her to wed. He would take it upon himself to extend the invitation to Mr Harrington. A weekend with his daughter within reach was extremely appealing to him.

With his mind made up, he considered only the advantages of haste and ignored any disadvantages. Whatever steps he took he knew he must handle things carefully. There was too much room for misunderstanding and misinterpretation.

It was late morning when Edmund Fitzroy was admitted to the Harrington house. Unbeknown to him, from an upstairs window Marietta had watched him approach. Mr Fitzroy had a strange and strong effect on her—he invaded her consciousness and took over her mind. She found it hard to explain because it was something she had never experienced before. The way he had of looking at her was a new, very powerful and profound thing. That something was happening to her she knew, but she didn't know the exact nature of it or how to deal with it.

Always one to be in control of her emotions, she fought her feelings, telling herself she didn't want to see him, even going as far as to change the time she rode in the park, but there was some strange and mysterious pull drawing her back. She watched him enter the house, knowing she would have to see him because her parents were not at home.

* * *

Striding with a natural exuberance into the spacious hall, with elegant, sumptuously carpeted and furnished rooms leading off, when Edmund enquired of the butler if Mr Harrington was at home, he was told in stentorian tones that Mr and Mrs Harrington were visiting friends and were not expected back for another hour.

'And Miss Marietta Harrington? Is she at home by any chance?'

'I will see, sir. If you will wait in the drawing room.'

Edmund waited several minutes before the door opened and Miss Harrington entered. He was totally unprepared for how she looked and he couldn't suppress the smile that stretched his lips. He could not take his eyes of this radiant sprite of a girl. Rich auburn hair spilled about her shoulders without discipline, her full soft lips ready to smile and warmth in her golden amber eyes in her perfect little heart-shaped face. But what amazed him more than anything was that she was shrouded in a garment that was neither an apron nor a dress and it covered what she wore beneath. One of her cheeks had smudges of what he could only surmise was red paint. She was wiping her paint-stained hands on a cloth.

'I'm sorry my parents aren't at home just now. I'm afraid you've had a wasted journey.'

'Not at all. It means I get to spend time with you.'

'As you see I'm not dressed to receive visitors—in fact, I'm a bit of a mess really. I paint, you see, and I tend to get more paint on myself than I do on the canvas.'

'So, you are an artist. I'm impressed. And what do you paint? Do you have a favourite subject?'

'I paint all manner of things—landscapes and whatever else takes my fancy, but painting people is what I like doing best.'

'And are you good at what you do?'

'I think the people who view my paintings are the ones to ask—not that many people do, only the occasional acquaintance of my parents. But I think so—and I wouldn't spend all my time doing it if I didn't. I get a lot of pleasure from painting.'

'Perhaps I could see some of your work—if you would like to show me,' he said, his expression one of genuine interest.

'Yes—of course.'

'I would like to see your studio or wherever it is you paint, while I wait for your parents to return—if that is acceptable to you, of course,' he said when he saw her hesitate. He smiled knowingly. 'You can always leave the door open and have a maid hovering outside if you are concerned about the impropriety of being alone with me.'

She laughed softly. 'Of course not—although my mother might be of a different opinion. I will be delighted to show you my work—and as you say,' she said, laughing softly, 'I can always leave the door open.'

She led him back out into the hall and up the stairs to a fair-sized high-ceilinged room at the back of the house, which she told him was ideal because the light from several windows gave her near-perfect light for her painting.

Edmund stepped inside. The smell of turpentine and paint immediately assailed his nostrils.

'Welcome to my studio,' she said, opening her arms with a flourish to embrace her work. 'Look around if you like. I don't mind.'

Edmund wandered about, looking at everything. Windows along one wall overlooked a well-kept garden and the April sunlight streamed in through them along with a skylight in a sloping ceiling. Dirty rags, sketch-pads, pots of pigment and jars of brushes and dilutants littered tabletops. It was filled with pictures of every size and description, from ladies in sparkling jewels and fabulous gowns to the ordinary person on the streets of London—water colours and oils, landscapes and some of an equestrian theme.

Edmund, who took great pleasure in the arts and had an impressive collection of his own at his house in Kent, was lost in wonder and astonishment—so many beautiful and accomplished pictures he could hardly believe his eyes. His experienced eye could tell that they had been painted with a degree of confidence and sureness and love that stamped them with the mark of a proficient artist. The subtleties of Miss Harrington's palette and the masterful quality of her brushstrokes struck him immediately.

Tentatively he reached out and touched the face of a child dressed in vivid blue with a white collar. He was holding a golden puppy close to his chest and his cheeks were plump and rosy, a blond curl dipping over his forehead. The colours were exquisite and he felt the silken smoothness of the oils. He valued the portrait's taste and for what it revealed about the exquisite sensibility of the subject and the artist.

'It must give you great satisfaction to be able to record the beauty of life so well, so vividly.'

'Thank you for the compliment,' she said softly, her cheeks flushed with pleasure. 'And thank you for wanting to see them. I'm glad you have. It's not often I get the chance to show them. Mother thinks I'm wasting my time, that I should be occupying myself in more feminine pursuits. But there is satisfaction in the accomplishment when I finish a painting. When I'm painting I get so involved with my subject that I lose all track of time.'

'I imagine you do. And what are these?' he said, crossing the room to take a closer look at some canvases stacked against the wall, lifting several and taking a closer look. They were watercolours of the Tuscan landscape, with gently rolling hills, cypress trees, sun-kissed olive groves and sheep being herded across the Tuscan meadows. 'I recognise the Tuscan hills—and this—the Ponte Vecchio over the Arno in Florence.' He turned to look at her. 'You are familiar with Tuscany?'

'Yes. I have an aunt—my mother's sister—

who lives in Siena. I've been to stay in her home several times over the years.'

'And you like Siena—but that's a stupid question. It's obvious you do when I look at the paintings and the love that has gone into the painting of them.'

'Yes. I love going there. Italy is a mixture of tradition and enlightenment and has always fascinated me. I've always wanted to see Venice, but I've never got that far. As I painted those scenes of Siena I would let my mind wander back to those times I spent there—how I would have liked to remain there for ever. Aunt Margaret's house was always full of laughter—I have three cousins and loved their company. They always make us so welcome.' She sighed, a faraway look in her eyes as she remembered those times. 'I often wondered what it would be like to have brothers and sisters. How I envied my cousins their life in Tuscany.'

Edmund heard the yearning for those days in her voice. 'I can understand what you're saying. Like me you are an only child. There were times when I would have liked siblings. Sadly my mother died when I was a young child— my parents had been married two years when

I was born. I imagine there would have been more children had she lived.'

A remembrance of how it had been for him living in the squalor without a mother to guide him, of a backstreet in Liverpool, flashed into his mind, but in that moment he could not bear to revisit the awful memories of his childhood, of how his father had gambled away what money they had and was eventually set upon by thugs, the brutal beating he received leaving him in a vegetative state, unable to speak or recognise him, his son.

He drew his attention back to the paintings, having no wish to divulge anything of his past. 'I know something about art—I know what I like, but even to my inexperienced eye it is plain that you are a true master—a genius.'

She laughed. 'You are too generous, Mr Fitzroy. I call myself a dabbler—although not without some talent—but as far as being a genius goes, that is something I see in others, not in me.'

'Nevertheless it is a gift as well as an art.'

'To paint my subjects takes what talent I possess. That is not greatness.'

Edmund faced her in surprise, seeing a different Marietta Harrington. She was no carefree young woman with no ambition or direction. She was absorbed, an artist who cared deeply about colour and light. He was drawn to her intensity, and he wanted to know more. 'How do you define greatness?'

'I can't. I can smell it, touch it and feel it, but what I know is that I do not possess it.'

Glancing at the picture of the small boy once more, Edmund could not agree with her. 'How can you pass judgement on yourself like that—so harshly? Where did you learn to paint like this?' he asked, looking at her. 'Who taught you?'

'I didn't go anywhere and no one taught me. I enjoy going to the Royal Academy and looking at paintings of the masters—of Reynolds and Gainsborough—and I knew that was what I wanted to do. I taught myself—starting at a young age. My parents didn't approve, but when they saw I wasn't to be deterred, that I was serious about it, they relented and let me have this room—not that they come in here. My mother can't stand the smell of turpentine. She says it gives her a headache and she would have a fit if she got paint on her lovely gowns.'

'Did your governess encourage you? I assume you did have a governess.'

'Yes, I did. Mother wanted to send me to an academy for young ladies, but Father wanted me to be taught at home. I had three governesses in total and, no, they did not encourage me to paint.'

'And no doubt you were well tutored in all subjects.'

'I believe so.'

'And what are your pleasures?' he enquired softly, waiting for her reaction and her reply with enigmatic eyes, knowing perfectly well that her idea of pleasures would not conform to his own—which were the kind she would not approve of and certainly not admire. He was ten years her senior, wiser and centuries older than she in experience. There was an innocent vulnerability in the purity of her features and, when she replied and he noted the enthusiasm that crept into her voice and the glow that lit her wide amber eyes, he suddenly felt ancient and worn out beside her youthful idealism.

'You have an intelligent mind, Miss Harrington—one most women would envy.'

'I do and there are many things that give me pleasure. I certainly don't have the time to be bored. I take pleasure from music and reading, riding—and painting, of course—and visiting the theatre with my parents. I also enjoy discussions on current affairs—but I do have opinions of my own which do not always agree with those of my associates and that often leads to arguments,' she told him, her light laughter bursting from her like sunshine.

Edmund's reaction was sharp, his voice holding a trace of irony. 'Whatever happened to such things as needlework and housewifery and etiquette? I was under the impression that the curriculum for young ladies was heavily weighted in favour of those accomplishments so as to make an appealing wife.'

'And so it is, but unfortunately—and much to my mother's dismay—I am not much good at any of those things—although she would hate to hear me say that,' she confessed without embarrassment. 'She insisted I had to be informed with charming manners. But most of all she desired that I be instilled with high principles with more than a cursory knowledge of mathematics and language.'

'But isn't that what all parents want for their offspring?'

'I expect it is, but I don't think other parents would be looking over their offspring's shoulders to make sure everything was done right.'

Edmund smiled crookedly. 'I expect you sing, too.'

'I play the pianoforte, but unfortunately I do not excel at singing. My voice is less than tuneful so I always avoid inflicting it on sensitive ears,' she answered, undaunted by his tone and with laughter still shimmering in her eyes.

'I expect you enjoy attending balls and the like.'

'No—not really. I like London well enough, but I prefer the quietness of our home in Surrey. What about you? Do you attend society events?'

'Not if I can help it, but I do escort my aunt to this and that—she insists.'

'You don't seem the kind of person to endorse the dictates of polite society.'

'No, I'm not.' He looked again at the painting of the child. 'When you paint, do you have people to model for you?'

'Usually the servants—when I can get them to sit for long enough and my mother isn't demanding of their time. The child in the painting dressed in blue is the son of one of the kitchen maids. He proved to be an adorable and well-behaved model. I intend to give the painting to his mother.'

'Do you ever show your work?'

'Oh, no. Besides, my parents would be horrified if I should suggest such a thing. Painting in private is one thing, but my parents would never allow that—to make an exhibition of myself as well as my paintings.'

'But it's ridiculous not to sell any of them. It's a terrible shame that so much talent has to remain hidden away in a studio.'

'I don't want to be famous. Besides, I am a woman. Can you name any women artists?'

'I see what you mean. I hadn't thought of that.'

Her face actually creased in a genuine smile and was incredibly altered by it. Edmund decided from that moment that he would do all he could to draw it often from her.

'Because I'm a woman, to most of your sex—and some of my own—I may sound stupid about things most men have knowledge of.'

'Don't you believe it. You are not stupid or you would not be talking to me like this. Yes, you are a woman, but women can be shrewd and wise, because they hide their cleverness so well—which, I suspect, is what you do, Miss Harrington. You have certainly taken me unawares. Where women are concerned, men are not very deep.'

'That is not very complimentary about the character of your sex.'

He laughed softly. 'Men have no character when it comes to women.'

'But they must do—when it comes to love.'

'Love turns us into complete idiots or dishonourable rogues—or both.'

'Even you?'

He dropped his gaze to her lips, his brows drawing together in a fierce scowl. 'Even me,' he said quietly, 'when I am least expecting it.'

'I'm sorry,' Miss Harrington murmured. 'I should not have mentioned it—only, when two people marry, there should be love—not that I know anything about that emotion,' she said softly, her face flushed with embarrassment. 'Which is why I'm glad I didn't marry Gabriel. I could never have loved him.'

'You might have grown to love him—or at least become close enough to have a happy marriage.'

'I don't think so. When two people marry there must be respect—and perhaps love. How else is it to succeed? Men are so much more fortunate in life than women. My marriage to Gabriel would have been advantageous to him—and to my father for the title that would come my way. Sons are bred to continue the line. Daughters are bartered and married young, while still malleable, passed like possessions from father to husband. Like many young women I am owned and possessed, the property of someone else and when I marry I will be passed on to a new owner—and so it goes. We are expected to obey and be happy with this change in guardianship. But it saddens me that my father sees me more as a commodity than a daughter.' She gazed at Mr Fitzroy, her head tilted to one side. 'Have you ever been in love?' she enquired quietly.

'I've discovered, with age and experience, very few of your sex are actually capable of feelings or behaviour that even approximates that tender emotion—though women talk as if it were as natural to their sex as breathing.'

'Dear me, Mr Fitzroy, you are a cynic.'

'Maybe I am. I will not utter false protestations of undying affection that I don't feel to any woman. But,' he said, reaching out and slowly wrapping a lock of her hair round his finger, his knuckle brushing her cheek, 'I am sure I could be persuaded—should the right woman come along. On the whole, in my world, marriages are arranged for profit and gain—which was the case when your father arranged your marriage to Gabriel. Those who believe they are in love find their pleasures elsewhere. They throw caution to the wind.'

'Do you mean—even when they are married to someone else?'

'Yes.'

'But—that would not be agreeable to me. I would not stand for it.'

'No,' he said quietly. 'No, you wouldn't and I wouldn't blame you. Tell me, are you happy with your life?'

Since it was such an intrusive question she did not reply at once. After a moment she said, 'Happy? I've never considered it in such terms. What consists of happiness? I've always been well provided for, with everything I could possibly want. I suppose I've been content with my lot—but happy? I don't know. My life could be worse, I suppose. I live a placid, quiet life. Nothing exciting ever happens—always predictable, demanding, no emotional responses. My whole life has been one of acceptance.'

'And love? I suppose you have never been in love, Miss Harrington.' She looked at him sharply—it was a look that told Edmund that she would not be pitied or made to feel uneasy by his question, which could be considered impertinent.

She answered quickly. 'I have never experienced the kind of love you speak of—that overblown passion that was long ago sung by troubadours—and if my father has his way then I never will.'

Edmund inclined his head in acceptance. 'It was not my intention to make you feel uncomfortable. If I have offended you, I ask your pardon.'

'You have not,' she replied on a softer note. 'I find it a relief to speak openly about such things. It's just that, at times, things can be difficult.' She sighed and looked at him thoughtfully. 'Mr Fitzroy, why have you come to see my father? For what reason?'

'It is a business matter.'

'I see. Then you are fortunate. All my father ever does is discuss and attend to his business. But I suppose that is why he is so rich.'

'Miss Harrington, you do realise that you will have to wed one day. Your parents will see to that.'

She looked him straight in the eye. 'Maybe so. But when I do he shall be *my* choice. The man *I* want. None other. I will not be possessed by a future that is dictated for me. I will take nothing I do not want myself. There has to be willingness and love.'

There was a tap on the door. The servant had come to inform them that her parents had returned.

Marietta watched him leave. She felt uplifted by their conversation—it was a rare thing for her to be so forthright and speak so openly about her feelings and opinions with another person. She was curious about him and had been tempted to ask about his life, about his family and his background, but she held her tongue. She was in no position to ask him about his past. He would find her intrusive at best, unjustified at worst. So she had let it be.

The bluff, expansive look of the successful businessman her father always wore was by no means diminished, but on receiving correspondence from Derbyshire, there was a slight change in both her parents and Marietta began to feel they might have forgiven her.

'I want to speak to you about Mr Fitzroy,' her father said when the two of them were alone at breakfast, her mother in her sitting room instructing the housekeeper on domestic matters. 'What do you know of him, Marietta?'

'Very little. Have you known him long, Father?'

'Our paths have crossed in business from time to time and occasionally socially.'

'I believe his parents died when he was a child and that he lived with his paternal uncle at Ashborne House in Kent until his death.'

'Where he continues to live with his aunt, apparently. I have to say that he has brilliant abilities in business that have served him well. Like me he is self-made and is probably one of the wealthiest men in Britain. Ever since he was a youth he has controlled his own world and never left himself vulnerable. Wherever he goes people court his favour. Success has brought him notoriety. He cannot be manipulated. In business he is ruthless and if crossed he can be a dangerous man. Few people want to test that.'

'Why are you telling me this, Father?'

'Because he has kindly invited us to his house party in two weeks' time. Unfortunately I have too much on at this present time so I won't be able to accompany you. But it should give your mother adequate time to prepare for it.'

'His house? Here in London?'

'No. Ashborne House in Kent.'

'And you have accepted the invitation?'

'Yes. An invitation to spend a weekend at Ashborne House is not to be turned down, Marietta.'

Marietta could not believe her good fortune. Her meetings with Mr Fitzroy had invigorated her. When he had left her after viewing her work she had wondered if she would see him again, then reproached herself for that vain wish that lay behind the thought. But that did not stop her thinking that someone very nice and surprising and exhilarating had come into her life. She wondered why she was so drawn to him and why their meetings remained so intensely with her. So when her father told her they had been invited to Ashborne House, she grasped and held the thought and the excitement this brought her like a child holding its favourite toy.

When her father told her that her mother was delighted by the prospect, he could not have said a truer word. The invitation to visit the house of the illustrious Mr Fitzroy drew her mother out of the sour mood she had been in since the debacle of Marietta's failed wedding to Gabriel Mansel.

'I shall look forward to seeing Ashborne

House, Marietta,' she said as she walked slowly beside her daughter in the garden, enjoying the late afternoon sunshine despite the chill of the wind. 'We are honoured to have been invited—although it's a shame your father will be unable to accompany us. He has already made plans to travel to Derbyshire—on business, I believe. Still, it will be an enjoyable weekend and it will be nice to become reacquainted with the Dowager Lady Fitzroy.'

'The Dowager Lady Fitzroy?'

'Mr Fitzroy's aunt. She lives at Ashborne House and doesn't come to town as frequently as she did when her husband was alive. She is a woman highly thought of and respected.' She cast Marietta a shrewd glance. 'What is your opinion of Mr Fitzroy, Marietta? Do you like him?'

'He—has always been courteous towards me, but I do not know him well enough to have formed an opinion.'

'You are bemused by him—I can understand that—which is natural with a man of his character. There will be some illustrious people at Ashborne House so we must look our best. I think a visit to the shops is in order—something cheerful to bring the colour out in you.'

'But I have gowns aplenty we purchased for my trousseau when I was to marry Gabriel. Besides, I am sure Mr Fitzroy won't notice what I'm wearing.'

'Then we must see that he does. A man who is respected, important, rich and powerful, with a large estate in Kent, is a highly desirable prospect for any parent seeking a husband for their daughter in every sense.'

Marietta stopped abruptly and stared at her mother in shocked amazement. 'Mother! You don't mean to parade me as a prospective wife for Mr Fitzroy? If so, then I will not have it. Please do not go to Kent with that in mind otherwise I will not go.'

'I simply think it will be good for you to get out of London for a while. And worry not. Marriage to Mr Fitzroy is not on the agenda. Your father wants a title and a title he will have—which is probably why he has arranged to travel to Derbyshire. But we will not think of that now, so stop frowning. It spoils your face. You must look forward to your visit to Kent and your meeting with the illustrious guests who will be there.'

Marietta didn't know what to think—and she didn't want to speculate on what her father was up to. Business or another prospective bride-groom for her—no doubt she would find out soon enough. Since the debacle of her failed wedding to Gabriel she had kept to the house, not wishing to be seen and recognised and gossiped over. On the other hand she could not remain hidden away indefinitely, so the sooner she faced public scrutiny the sooner it would die a death. She wanted to see Edmund Fitzroy again. She enjoyed his company and he had made a favourable impression on her, but anything else was quite out of the question.

Their shopping done, they were about to return to the house when Marietta's attention was caught by a woman who emerged from a shop further along the street. She was a striking woman attired in an oyster-coloured fitted gown and matching hat, worn at an attractive slant on her dark hair, the net attached to her hat shading her face. While Marietta waited for her mother, she sat watching the lady in fascination, wondering who she could be. Suddenly a man appeared behind her. The woman turned and threw back her head and looked up at him, and Marietta could almost picture the beatific, dreaming smile on her face. She said something to the gentleman and then laughed, her laughter as light as a balloon sailing up into the sky. The man was poised, debonair. The two were easy with each other—familiar. They walked towards a waiting carriage, sleek, black and shiny and drawn by four bay horses.

Suddenly Marietta started, for the gentleman was none other than Edmund Fitzroy. She watched him bend his head towards the woman's upturned face to listen to what she was saying. He assisted her into the carriage before climbing in himself, sitting across from her. Whoever the woman was, Marietta wondered if they would meet when at Ashborne House. When Faith came out of the shop carrying their packages, seeing where Marietta's attention was directed, she placed the packages on the seat and glanced at her mistress curiously.

'Do you know that gentleman, Miss Marietta?'

'Yes, yes, I do. It is Mr Fitzroy—the gentleman I told you about. He was very kind and courteous to me at the church.'

Faith studied the couple for a moment and started to shake her head in the negative, then stopped abruptly and looked at the gentleman with renewed interest. 'Yes, I do remember. I've never seen him before, but I've seen the lady he's with.'

'You have?' Marietta shouldn't have been surprised by this. Faith was a mine of information, picking up gossip from the kitchen staff and other kitchens in other houses where she was friendly with the servants. Nothing seemed sacred in the lives of those who depended on their servants for their comforts and needs. 'Who is she?'

'Her name's Lady Francine Russell—I'm certain of it. Lovely, isn't she? She's a popular figure on the social scene—I'm surprised you haven't seen her before.'

Faith went back into the shop to fetch more packages and to assist Marietta's mother. Marietta watched Mr Fitzroy's carriage move away down the street. The pair seemed relaxed together, close, even. With a familiarity that seemed to be born of long acquaintance, the woman leaned across and touched his arm—it was an intimately possessive gesture. Then the carriage became swallowed up in the traffic and she lost sight of them.

Looking forward to her visit to Ashborne House more than ever, and determined she was going to enjoy herself, Marietta fixed her eyes on the shop to see her mother emerge followed by an arm-laden Faith.

Chapter Four

Edmund stood by the window looking out over the gardens, watching as the guests who had arrived sauntered and sat and met old friends and acquaintances. It was a blessing the weather was fine if somewhat cool. He would have preferred to have invited Marietta Harrington and her parents to Ashborne without all this fuss, but it was important to him that he didn't overwhelm Marietta with what he had in mind. Better that she came to Ashborne to enjoy an informal weekend.

A longing to see her again gripped him and he thought of her with the feverish longing of a man who had just found what he had been unconsciously searching for his entire life. Marietta Harrington was a woman who could love him for himself. From the moment he had set eyes on her he had not tried to deny the feelings that were coursing through him. Yet he was no fool to believe that men and women fell in love with each other at first glance. He had not believed in love at all until he had seen her. But things had changed for he believed it now. He wanted the beautiful, idealistic young woman to love him and no one else. For the first time in his life he had found something rare and unspoiled, and he was determined that she would be his wife.

'You are looking for Miss Harrington to arrive if I am not mistaken, Edmund,' his aunt said, coming to stand beside him. A tall, slender woman with a strong personality, she was well liked and respected in the area.

'Yes. I sent the carriage to meet her and her mother off the train. They should be here any time.'

'Really, Edmund, the haste and enthusiasm with which you have invited Miss Harrington to Ashborne has come as a surprise, for you have shown no such interest in a young lady before, despite your amours in London and the eligible daughters of marriageable age of friends and acquaintances I have brought to the house and paraded before you in the hope that one of them would catch your eye. And now, just when I thought you had found the right woman in Francine, you have shattered any expectations that the two of you will eventually marry.'

'Marriage to Francine was never on the cards, Aunt. She is a friend—the widow of a man who was my closest friend, nothing more than that.'

'Your refusal to accept invitations to social events makes it virtually impossible to introduce you to suitable young ladies. You cannot blame me for beginning to hope for a match between you and Francine. It is obvious she is strongly attracted by you—although it has not gone unnoticed by me that you do not appear to be enthusiastic about forming a close relationship with her. I had thought that now you have returned to Ashborne, something might develop between you and give both families reason to hope that a marriage might be hovering blissfully on the horizon.'

'Then I'm sorry to disappoint you, Aunt Dorothy. Miss Harrington is unlike any other young woman I have met. It will all be explained when you meet her—and is why I've invited her this weekend. She will be among people and will not feel uncomfortable with people around her. I am already impatient to have everything completed, but because of what happened with Gabriel I intend to proceed with caution.'

'I can understand that. Have you spoken to her father?'

'Not yet. But I will—as soon as he is back from the north where he's gone on some business venture. By her actions his daughter has brought his name into disrepute. I can remedy the situation by making her my wife.'

'And what makes you think he will accept your suit? From what I know of him Mr Harrington will be satisfied with nothing less than a title for his daughter—which is something you do not have at present.'

'Not yet—but I will—in time—when my father…' He faltered, his jaw tightening, unable to go on. His aunt placed a comforting hand on his arm.

'I know, Edmund. While ever your father is alive—I do understand why you will not take the title. But you know as well as I that he will never recover.'

'I know, but it is his by right—be it a minor one. I will not take it away from him. I know what he was, Aunt Dorothy—a drunk and a gambler—but he did not deserve what happened to him when he was beaten to within an inch of his life and left for dead. It would have been a blessing if he had not survived that. Mr Harrington is desperate to marry his daughter to a title, but after what she did to Gabriel, no other family will consider her suitable for their sons.'

'But you will.' He nodded. 'And you are fixed on it, I can see. If Miss Harrington is as rebellious to walk away from marriage to Gabriel at the altar, do you realise she may reject you?'

His shoulders lifted in the slightest of shrugs. 'I sincerely hope not. Following the scandal that ensued when she publicly jilted Gabriel at the last minute, her situation is not an enviable one.' Not for one moment did he doubt his ability to entice Marietta into his arms, but her father might prove to be a different matter.

'And your uncle—the Earl—and Gabriel? How do you think they will receive the news that you are to wed Miss Harrington after that debacle she created?'

Edmund's eyes hardened. 'I long ago ceased to consider my uncle's feelings—as well you know, Aunt Dorothy. The Earl of Waverley had precious little time for my father when he was in dire need—which could have prevented the tragedy that ultimately put him in a clinic in Switzerland. It is the Earl's misfortune that he gambled away his wealth and is forced to look outside his own class for a wealthy wife for his son.'

'Who will have to look for someone else to marry. I look forward to meeting Miss Harrington—but you cannot have forgotten that Francine will be here. It could be awkward.'

'I fail to see why that should make a difference to my inviting Marietta Harrington.' He sighed in exasperation, perfectly aware what was passing through his aunt's mind. 'Francine is privileged, beautiful, spoiled by an adoring father and used to getting what she wants. But if it's marriage to me she has in her sights then she is going to be disappointed. Besides, do not forget Thomas Sheridan in all this. He's been in love with her ever since Andrew died.'

'Unfortunately Thomas isn't as wealthy as you are, Edmund—although his background is impressive. But Francine doesn't see him when you are within her sights.'

'She might have to when I marry someone else.'

His aunt sighed, shaking her head somewhat sadly. 'How often have I told you that it is about time you settled down and filled the house with your offspring. It is far too big for one man to rattle around in—for as you know I shall eventually retire to the dower house. Is it so unreasonable of me to want to see you settled with a wife—the right wife?'

'No.' He turned and looked at her, smiling and taking her in his arms. 'You worry too much about me. It is not unreasonable of you to want to see me settled—and you will. You will like Marietta Harrington, Aunt Dorothy. I promise you.'

His aunt took a deep breath and nodded. 'Very well,' she conceded. 'You must want her very badly, Edmund.' She smiled at him, making no attempt to hide the deep affection between them. 'What girl in her right mind would not want to marry the handsome, charming— and often infuriating Edmund Fitzroy. I look forward to meeting her.'

When his aunt had left him to welcome more guests, Edmund turned back to the window to continue his wait for the young woman who had occupied his thoughts since meeting her. Inwardly, he smiled at the bizarre turn his life had taken. He had given up trying to understand the reasons for wanting Marietta Harrington in his life. He wanted her and that was that.

Never in his wildest imaginings had he visualised anything like this—for in all his adult life, after many affairs with some of the most beautiful women in the land, he had fallen for an enchanting creature in the form of the delectable, adorable Marietta Harrington. She was a veritable treasure of contrasts, with an unspoiled charm, the smile of an angel and the promise of tantalising things to come in her warm amber eyes.

He did not doubt his ability to woo her, to persuade her into marriage, but remembering the words she had spoken when she had shown him her work in her studio, *she* had to want *him*.

People crowded the platform of the railway station at Charing Cross. Between them, Faith and her mother's maid took charge of the luggage and they managed to find a compartment to themselves. It was a relief when the train moved off and they had left London and travelled through the sunlit countryside of narrow lanes and pretty villages strung together in a seemingly endless chain. On arriving at their destination, they found Mr Fitzroy had sent his carriage to the station to meet them. It wasn't Marietta's first visit to Kent. The last time had been two years ago when she had accompanied her parents to visit friends in Canterbury. It was a county she had always liked.

Ashborne House nestled in a fold between the gentle hills which protected it from wind and weather. There was something stately about the tall beeches that lined either side of the long and winding drive leading to the house, their branches meeting overhead and virtually shutting out the sunlight. Marietta's first glimpse of the stately house, built of brick which had mellowed over the years did not disappoint her in the least. It was a fine, square, three-storeyed house with a columned porch and stables at the rear. The lawns had been mown to resemble smooth velvet and the terraces all around had pots of flowering shrubs.

The carriage came to a halt at the bottom of a short flight of steps. Immediately, as if he had been waiting behind the door, Mr Fitzroy came out of the house to meet them, his thick black hair glossy and brushed back from his forehead. Stepping towards the carriage, he opened the door himself and reached inside, taking Marietta's hand to help her alight after one of the servants had pulled down the steps. That was the moment Marietta was glad she had taken her mother's advice to look her best and had taken time with her appearance.

Mr Fitzroy drew in a deep breath, his eyes glittering as they flicked over her with undisguised approval, from the tips of her shoes to her auburn hair coiled expertly about her head that she hoped made her appear older and more seductively alluring.

After greeting Mrs Harrington politely, then sensing Marietta's nervousness, he took hold of her hand, feeling her fingers tremble slightly.

'You look lovely,' he murmured in a gentle tone, his gaze searching her face. 'I trust you've had a pleasant journey.'

'Yes—thank you. It's always a pleasant experience to travel on the railways.'

'Come and meet my aunt. You can be assured of a welcome. She's looking forward to meeting you—although you, Mrs Harrington, are already acquainted with her. Some of the other guests have arrived—some you may be acquainted with. Try not to be nervous.'

Marietta quivered beneath his touch, thinking he looked breathtakingly handsome. She felt the force, the vital, physical power within him, and the warm grasp of his hand reassured her and she was strengthened by it. He conducted her and her mother into a large square hall with tall doorways and marble pillars. An elegant blue-carpeted staircase rose up from the centre to form a gallery. Marietta's first impression of the house was one of elegance and good taste, but so intent was she on her meeting with the Dowager Lady Fitzroy that she paid little attention to her surroundings just then.

The Dowager Lady Fitzroy was happily conversing with her other guests, but became distracted when she saw her nephew. She glanced at Marietta standing by his side and immediately excused herself and made her way towards them to welcome her and Mrs Harrington.

'Aunt Dorothy, allow me to present Miss Marietta Harrington. I believe you are already acquainted with her mother, Mrs Harrington.'

After Lady Fitzroy had welcomed her mother, and when her mother was claimed by an acquaintance she had not seen in a while, she turned her attention to Marietta. 'How do you do, Lady Fitzroy,' she said politely. Dressed in a wonderful shade of jade green with diamonds at her throat, she looked younger than Marietta had expected, a slim, elegant lady radiating calm and confidence who was completely at ease. There were no reservations in her welcome.

'I am well, thank you, and happy to welcome you and your mother to Ashborne House. I have heard so much about you from Edmund that I am glad to meet you at last. I am sorry your father wasn't able to come, but that's what often happens in business, I'm afraid—Edmund will vouch for that,' she said, smiling fondly at her nephew. 'Now you are here you must relax and enjoy yourself, but first I will have someone take you to your rooms. I expect you would like to freshen up after your journey, then you must meet our other guests, although some of them your mother will already be acquainted with. I'm sure at some point Edmund will show you the house.'

As Edmund and Lady Fitzroy watched them being escorted to their rooms by a servant, he said, 'Well, Aunt Dorothy, what is your assessment?'

'Miss Harrington is a lovely young woman, Edmund—not at all what I expected. I feel better for having met her and I can see why you have spoken so highly of her. Any doubts I felt prior to meeting her have been quashed—and when I saw the way you looked at her—your eyes held an open admiration and something else, something I have never seen in your eyes before—it gladdens my heart. There is an open honesty about her that I find refreshing and I find myself curious to know her better. But she looked nervous—we must make sure we put her at ease. I informed some of the guests of her expected arrival earlier and already it has caused some arched eyebrows and given rise to speculation.'

When Marietta and her mother reappeared, with a certain amount of indolence Edmund stood back while Marietta was taken in hand by his aunt. His silver-grey eyes smiled as he observed, but his expression gave away nothing of his thoughts.

'You don't mind, do you, Edmund, if I take Miss Harrington away and show her the house?'

'Of course not,' he replied. 'Although I was hoping to do that myself.'

'Thank you. I would like that,' said Marietta. 'But I should hate to take either of you away from your guests.'

'Don't worry about that.' Lady Fitzroy smiled.

'The weekend is very informal. There are still several guests to arrive, but Edmund will receive them.'

Edmund raised his eyebrows, but before he could reply his aunt said, 'Rest assured that I shall not neglect our other guests for long. You can stay and entertain them, Edmund, while I get to know Miss Harrington a little better. We can gossip as we go along. No doubt the gentlemen will converse about what is going on in Parliament and the financial situation, but I will not tolerate any discourse on those subjects at the dinner table later. By that time I hope those topics will have been well and truly exhausted and we can concentrate on more pleasant discussions.'

'Very well, Aunt,' Edmund said, knowing there was no irresistible argument he could raise that would have any effect on her and allow him to show Miss Harrington the house instead.

'Don't worry, Edmund. I will not deprive you of her company for too long.'

As Lady Fitzroy gave her a quick tour of the house Marietta took an interest in everything she saw, listening to her hostess as she chatted animatedly, clearly proud of the house one of her late husband's ancestors had built. The house was as elaborate inside as it was out—ornamentation, decorative scrollwork, heavy furniture, gas and lamplight on polished panelling. There was a feeling of antiquity and history that was absent in the Harringtons' Surrey house, but there was taste and elegance in the spacious rooms and furnishings. There was also a quietness about the house, a calm distancing from the world at large, and the noise of London seemed far away.

Marietta admired the fine paintings that adorned the walls of every room, along with some family portraits. She would have liked more time to browse these works of art and promised herself that before she left she would take a closer look. Lady Fitzroy paused in front of one particular painting.

'That particular gentleman was my husband, David. He was a military man—until his time in the Crimea put paid to that. He was wounded out of the army and had to settle down to running the estate. He was a man of excellent character, respected by all who knew him, and he worked hard all his life to achieve success, devoting all his time to his work and the affairs of the neighbourhood. He brought me here as a bride. I loved him dearly and fell in love with the house as soon as I saw it.'

'Are there any portraits of your nephew's father?'

Immediately a shutter came down over Lady Fitzroy's face. 'No—unfortunately not. Edmund had a difficult childhood, Miss Harrington— it affected him in ways you would not imagine. He—he doesn't speak of it. As you will know through your knowledge of Gabriel's family, Edmund's mother was the Earl of Waverley's sister—she died when Edmund was quite small. He was deprived of his father when he was a youth. It was left to my husband to guide him. I love Edmund as I would a child of my own—which we were never blessed with. He is marked with the same pride and indomitable will as most of the Fitzroy men. He is like a whirlwind, my dear. He is an exacting master who demands that his house and estate, like his many business ventures, are run as smoothly as a well-oiled machine. Anyone meeting him for the first time cannot help but be swept along with him.'

Lady Fitzroy's comments raised Marietta's curiosity about Edmund Fitzroy. What had happened to him in the past? Whatever he wanted to leave behind him was surely his affair, but perhaps it would do him good to talk about it—but then, what good would it do except to ease her own curiosity.

Observing Marietta's puzzlement, Lady Fitzroy smiled. 'Come along. I'll return you to the others. I imagine you are nervous among all these strangers. That is understandable. You will soon relax. The ease of the garden will work its usual charm, I am sure. It never fails to help break down the formal barriers that exists when one comes here. I'm just thankful the weather is favourable.'

'Thank you for showing me the house. It's quite splendid.'

'It is, isn't it—and steeped in antiquity.'

'It's no worse for that.''

'You are quite right. A house as old as Ashborne has some fascinating stories to tell—they do enrich a house, I always think, and make it more interesting for the inhabitants.'

They arrived back in the hall and, as if he had been waiting for her to return, Mr Fitzroy strode to meet her. Lady Fitzroy drifted away to greet the newly arrived guests.

'How do you like the house?'

'Very much. How could I not? I see you have some interesting paintings. I would like to take a closer look at them later.'

'It will be my pleasure to show them to you. And now I would appreciate it if you would let me show you the gardens—if you are not too fatigued after your grand tour of the house.'

'Yes, I would like that, but shouldn't you be with your guests?'

He arched one dark brow. 'I am. You are my guest, Miss Harrington, and I intend showing you as much of Ashborne House—inside and out—before you return to London.'

'Then what can I say except that I would love to see the gardens,' she said, unable to quell the stirring of pleasure his offer caused. 'I don't suppose my mother will miss me.'

'If she does and seeks to chastise you for disappearing without her knowledge, then I shall make a point of becoming better acquainted with her later to soften her attitude towards me. I don't think she quite forgave me for whisking you away after you fled the church.'

Marietta searched his bold visage, unsurprised by his nerve. 'Your intention to placate my mother amazes me. I really shouldn't be going off alone with you.'

He chuckled. 'Why not? I am your host and we will both enjoy the walk through the gardens—and I shall endeavour to be on my best behaviour and as charming as my nature will allow.'

Marietta laughed. 'Then it should prove to be an interesting outing.'

'It will be what we make it. Now, come along before my aunt tries to draw me away should some guests need entertaining.'

As Marietta accompanied him out of the house to the terrace, she felt a strange exhilaration. She felt wonderfully, gloriously alive for the first time in as long as she could remember. There was something undeniably engaging about her handsome escort. He made her feel alert and curiously stimulated. He introduced her to guests as they went. There were so many it was impossible to be introduced to all of them or remember their names. Swarms of titled, wealthy and influential people invaded the house, lawns and terraces, their colourful gowns, jackets and painted parasols echoing the bright colours of the flowerbeds and the graceful sculptures.

Liking everything she saw at Ashborne House, she breathed deeply of the sweet-scented air and let her eyes wander, looking with appreciation at the gardens spread out before her, gardens that would be filled with flowers as spring turned into summer. A line of dark yews marched down to the lake beyond. This particular area of the garden was laid out in formal flower beds forming a circle, the centrepiece being a fountain where water spouted from a cornucopia held by three exquisitely carved cherubs, the fine mist of its spray drifting on the slight breeze.

Mr Fitzroy pointed out the greenhouses where carnations, orchids and exotic house plants were grown. The greenhouses were on the edge of the kitchen gardens that provided all the vegetables for the house as well as delicious peaches and nectarines and grapes in the vineries. Camellia trees grew against the huge brick wall that surrounded the kitchen gardens. He told her that when they were in bloom, the various coloured flowers were so profuse there was scarcely a gap between them.

'How ever I may look to the outside world, I am of a solitary turn of mind, Marietta—you don't mind if I call you Marietta?' He took her silence for assent. 'Please address me as Edmund—I would like that. I like coming down to Ashborne. For me the great attraction of it is that it's far enough away from London, so apart from Aunt Dorothy's friends—who call to see her, not me—I do not have many visitors, only those I invite.'

'You have plenty of visitors here now,' she remarked, seeing that there was a new gravity in his features, a tightening of the muscles of his jaw. Here was a man with troubles of his own, she thought. There were thoughts in his mind that were not open to her and she did not know him well enough to ask.

'This weekend is an exception and my aunt enjoys entertaining occasionally. Apart from that, since my uncle died I have my work. The family owns a fair slice of Kent and it takes time and energy to keep it going.'

'But don't you have stewards to do that?'

He nodded, stopping when they reached a bench inside a secluded arbour covered with a profusion of creepers. 'I do, but I like to keep my finger on the pulse.' He indicated a bench. 'Let's sit a while.' Seating himself on the bench, he turned sideways better to study her profile, resting his arm along the back. The air settled quietly around them.

'Are you cold?' he asked.

'Not at all. It's so warm today. It feels more like early summer than spring.'

'How lovely you look. I was half afraid that you would not come to Ashborne, that your mother would find a reason to keep you in London.'

He spoke the words almost beneath his breath. Now his face seemed transfigured and he was looking at her as if he could not gaze too long.

'Well, I am here—I am real enough,' she answered, hardly aware what she said, conscious only of his proximity.

'And were you as pleased to see me as I was to see you?'

'I was,' she murmured, unable to quench the sweet pang of pleasure this caused her. Those glowing eyes burned into hers, suffusing her with a growing aura of warmth. How could she claim uninterest in this man when his very nearness and the words from his mouth could so effectively stir her senses? Suddenly overwhelmed by warm rush of tenderness, she was so conscious of her deep attraction for him that she had to make an effort not to throw her arms about his neck.

'You are a strange young woman, Marietta

Harrington,' he murmured, focusing his eyes on a wisp of hair against her cheek.

Without thinking, he reached out and tucked it behind her ear, feeling the velvety softness of her skin against his fingers. Marietta sat still as he ran the tip of his finger down the column of her throat, liking the feel of his touch and making a stern effort to hide her treacherous heart's reaction to the deep timbre of his voice. They looked at each other in silence. His eyes were calm, serious, and they were weighted with something she'd never seen in anyone's eyes before when they looked at her—warmth and compassion.

'Suddenly I find myself wanting to know everything there is to know about you—what you are thinking, what you are feeling. From our short acquaintance I have learned that you are not the prim-and-proper miss I imagined you as being when I heard you were to wed my cousin. I also know you to be an excellent horsewoman and a proficient artist. I am looking forward to knowing more.'

Marietta laughed softly. 'I am not sure there is more—certainly nothing you would find interesting. In my world, there was prosperity and peace—providing I did what I was told.'

'I imagine you were a biddable child.'

'Yes, I was. I didn't know how to be anything else. In my quiet moments I use to invent places that I could dream about—happy places, where everything was perfect and I could accomplish anything I wished and be anyone I wanted to be.'

'Isn't that the dream of every child?'

She looked at him, holding his gaze with her own. 'Is that how it was with you—when you were a child?' She wondered at the depth of his thoughts and where his mind wandered when he came home to Ashborne. And then she laughed, a sound so soft it drifted on the air. 'Forgive me. Of course you wouldn't do that. Boys don't dream of those things.' Her laughter was infectious, causing Edmund to smile broadly, his white teeth strong and gleaming from between his parted lips. Suddenly she stopped smiling and met his gaze. 'Why did you invite us to Ashborne?'

'You know the answer, Marietta.'

Never had her name sounded so like a caress. 'I don't. I would like you to tell me.'

Taking her hand, he laced his fingers through hers and examined it closely. His touch was gentle yet strong. With his head bent and his eyes intent on her fingers, he raised them to his mouth, holding them there for a moment, caressing the cool flesh with his lips. Marissa watched in rapt amazement. A pulsating heat began to throb in her hands, spreading upwards, and she felt shooting, tingling sensations travelling in the tips of her fingers.

With her hands still enfolded in his, Edmund's gaze swept upwards and regarded her in silence, and for a moment his eyes held hers with penetrating intensity. The mysterious depths were as enigmatic as they were silently challenging and unexpectedly Marietta felt an answering response that gave her reason to hope that he might care as much for her as she did for him.

'It was to see you,' he said in answer to her question, 'even though the house is full of guests and we cannot be entirely alone. It is an opportunity for me to get to know you, for you to get to know me, where neither of us needs be circumspect.'

The words shivered over Marietta, through her. She experienced a quickening of her heartbeat—a warmth spreading beneath her bodice as if a flame had been ignited. 'Why—I—I don't know what to say…'

'You don't have to say anything. I remember that moment we met. It was a moment of brilliant awareness—when you scattered my thoughts asunder—nudging into life a longing I did not recognise.'

Marietta stared at him. She, too, had come to know that emotion that had surprised her by its power. 'I—I did that?'

He nodded. 'Absolutely. Do you know, Marietta Harrington, that you are the first woman I have invited to Ashborne? My aunt is quite bemused by it—and pleased.'

'Then what can I say? I am indeed honoured—flattered.'

'You are a very tempting young lady.'

For one shocking moment Marietta thought he would kiss her—she was hoping that he would. Her eyes were trapped in his gaze and she could not look away. At that moment others came into the garden, disturbing their idyll. Still holding her hand, Edmund got up and pulled her to her feet.

'Come,' he said, casting a look of displeasure in the direction of the intruders. 'I'll return you to your mother before she seeks us out and chastises me for stealing you away.'

Releasing her hand, he walked side by side

with her in silence. Not until they were within sight of the terrace did Edmund speak.

'Do you often get down to your home in Surrey?'

'Yes, when we can. I love the solitude of the country. I'm nineteen, soon to be twenty, and already I think I've seen and done everything there is to see and do in London. I see new faces all the time, although their names are a blur and I don't remember them. Mother says I go out of my way to be unsociable, but she is wrong. I don't. I'm just bored with it all—more so since I didn't marry Gabriel.'

'Surely you don't regret it?'

'Goodness, no—but I cannot say the same for my father. Already he's looking for someone else—and I think he might have found someone. No sooner did I extricate myself from one undesirable marriage than he has entered into a transaction with another. I think that's why he's gone to Derbyshire. He said it was business, but I don't believe that. I don't know what to expect when he returns and I dread the battle that will ensue. I cannot go on fighting him for ever over this.'

Edmund looked at her in silence and his face hardened. 'I'm sorry, Marietta. I didn't know.

Life's full of hard luck—that's one thing I had to learn early—that most of the time life's unfair. Who is it your father has in mind for your next husband—a duke? An earl—or perhaps a marquis? Or don't you know?'

She shook her head, wondering at the bitterness underlying his words. 'I'm afraid I don't. I shall have to wait and hope and pray that whoever it is will have heard how I treated Gabriel and consider me a risk not worth taking.'

'Put it from your mind until you return to London.' Having reached the terrace and seeing Mrs Harrington beckoning to her daughter, he looked down at Marietta. 'It's important that you enjoy yourself while you are here.'

Marietta smiled and proceeded to climb the steps to the terrace. Turning, she looked back. Edmund was still watching her and she settled her gaze on him, held by an enchanted thread that bound her whole destiny to this man, unable to explain the feelings that touched her heart.

Marietta's mother sought her out and murmured behind the feathers of her fan, 'You were gone a long while with Mr Fitzroy, Marietta. I'm so glad we came. You look lovely in that dress. I'm so glad you chose to wear the blue—it doesn't clash with your hair like the pink would have done.'

Sitting on the terrace where tea tables had been laid, she sat drinking tea out of china cups and eating dainty cakes with her mother. The afternoon was pleasantly warm. With the sun shafting through the trees and flooding the terrace, the noises from the tennis court as background, people laughing, people talking, birds singing, it was a perfect setting.

Marietta did not speak to Edmund again, but she was always conscious of his silent, attentive presence. The guests commanded his attention and she watched him pass among them. She tried to think of him dispassionately, not to let her emotions become involved, because if she did she was afraid she was in danger of becoming overwhelmed by him. He had made a deep impression on her. This she could not deny. She had never met a man who was so alive, so full of confidence, a man who both stimulated and excited her, and he had a sensuous way of regarding her that set her pulse racing.

Tall and slender and dressed in a coral silk gown and a matching wide-brimmed hat, the woman who stood with her hand on the balustrade overlooking the garden was so beautiful that Marietta could not take her eyes off her—as if held by a powerful magnetic force. Her gaze went at once to Marietta and her eyes, brilliant, blue, exotically set and shadowed with brows and lashes as black as her hair, seemed to scour her with their examination. She had a nose designed for looking down, a nose that gave one the impression that she had a bad smell under it all the time.

So, Marietta thought, this was Lady Francine Russell. She had unassailable dignity and confidence. She exuded a sultry sensuality that men would find impossible to resist. Lady Russell continued to assess her with a cool and exacting stare, then she smiled, a tight, carefully controlled smile. Thinking it would be rude to turn and walk away, Marietta stepped forward. As she moved closer there was a cloying sense of musk about her. She could see that Lady Russell was older than she had seemed. There were fine lines in the skin around her eyes and mouth, but they did not detract from her beauty.

'I do hope I'm not intruding. I've been sitting with my mother for so long I thought I'd stretch my legs.'

'You are not intruding. You are a stranger here, Miss Harrington—I don't recall seeing you at any of Lady Fitzroy's gatherings.'

Her voice was low and cool. Marietta straightened her spine and raised her chin, meeting the other's eyes directly—silently envying her and wishing she had Lady Russell's height. She sensed instant antagonism when she looked into Lady Russell's eyes. When she recalled the covetous way the other woman had clung to Edmund's side when she had seen her in London, she thought that perhaps she would resent Marietta's own relationship with him—even though it went no further than friendship.

'No, this is my first time. But you have the advantage of me since you know my name. And you are?' Marietta asked, knowing perfectly well who she was, but she would not give her that satisfaction of letting her know that.

'Lady Francine Russell. If you are surprised that I know who you are—I am not the only one. Your failed wedding to Gabriel Mansel is still talked about. I have to say I rather admired what you did. Jilting a man before the wedding is bad enough, but to do so at the altar is practically unheard of.'

'It was difficult—and knowing I would have

to face my father's wrath afterwards made it doubly so.'

Lady Russell smiled thinly. 'It caused quite a stir at the time.'

Marietta stood with unflinching poise under the penetrating inspection.

'Then it's a shame people have nothing more interesting to gossip about.'

'Nevertheless, your presence at Ashborne House this weekend has given rise to a good deal of speculation and curiosity.'

'It has? I am surprised. Do they approve?'

Lady Russell nodded condescendingly, smiling tightly. 'To be frank, you are not what I expected. You're quite different. You are really quite beautiful.'

'Thank you.' Marietta was surprised by the unexpected flattery. 'Might I return the compliment.'

Lady Russell merely nodded coolly. 'Do you live in London?'

'Yes—we also have a house in Surrey—I like to get down there when I can. Do you live in Kent, Lady Russell?'

She nodded. 'I am also a widow. My husband, who was a close friend of Edmund, died when he took a tumble from his horse during a hunt.'

'I am sorry to hear that.'

She shrugged. 'It was five years ago. I've had time to get used to it.'

'You are a friend of the family?' Marietta asked with what she hoped was mild interest, determined to remain calm and deliberate. Having seen the familiarity between them in London, she wondered just how close she was to Edmund, but good manners prevented her from revealing this.

'Yes—not only are we neighbours, but close friends also. Edmund and Lady Fitzroy were very kind to me when my husband was killed. I am curious as to why he has invited you down for the weekend. I imagine you must have become well acquainted with him.'

'No, not really. He is acquainted with my father—they are both businessmen, which often brings them together.'

'But your father isn't here.'

'No. Due to pressing matters of business in the north, he was unable to accept the invitation for himself, but Mr Fitzroy insisted that my mother and I should come.' The remark, spoken calmly and in all innocence, clearly made Lady

Russell bristle inside. Her mouth tightened, and her face hardened.

'That's typical of Edmund—always the gentleman. He is fortunate that his aunt is always the perfect hostess. I expect you have been introduced to Lady Fitzroy?'

'Yes, I have. She is a charming lady and gave my mother and I a warm welcome.

'The time will come when Edmund takes a wife and Lady Fitzroy will have to step back.'

'I am sure you are right—and I imagine Lady Fitzroy will know that. For her sake—and his own, of course—I hope that he chooses the right woman.' Marietta met Lady Russell's eyes as she said this, which had darkened to a stormy blue. Marietta was determined not to let her get under her skin and arouse her to an expression of her personal feelings.

'I am quite sure he will.'

Marietta stepped back, half turning. 'Please excuse me. I must return to my mother.'

'Wait.'

Marietta turned and looked at her, waiting for her to speak.

'Do you have an arrangement with Edmund?'

'Be assured,' Marietta returned with cool dignity, 'that I do not. What we have is purely an acquaintance. Mr Fitzroy very kindly offered us an invitation to attend this weekend's house party—nothing more than that.'

Somewhat reconciled and relaxing her features, Lady Russell permitted herself a faint, satisfied smile. 'I see. I know Edmund very well, Miss Harrington—indeed, we have known each other for many years. We are friends— *close friends*,' she informed her, placing strong emphasis on the last two words. 'You are an attractive woman and I can imagine Edmund might be tempted by you. When he sees something he wants, he takes it with the same dispassionate logic with which he approaches his business transactions. So if he does succumb to temptation, do not imagine for one minute it is you he wants.'

Unease slithered beneath Marietta's skin at such a show of unconcealed resentment. She managed to smile in the face of it. 'I think you are running ahead of yourself, Lady Russell— and you insult both me and Mr Fitzroy.'

'Think what you like, but take care. You are an outsider, not of Edmund's class. You will never make yourself acceptable no matter how hard you try.'

Lady Russell's words washed over Marietta,

scouring and abrasive. 'I am not a threat to you. You are seeing things that do not exist.'

Lady Russell inclined her head. 'I hope that is so.'

Marietta merely raised her chin and turned away, refusing to allow this woman to provoke her further. 'Please excuse me.'

With her head held high, Marietta made her way back along the terrace, feeling her defences begin to crumble. She was more disturbed and disconcerted by her conversation with Lady Russell than she cared to admit. Never in her life had anyone shown her such open hostility. She had been demoted abruptly from being Mr Fitzroy's friend to being someone who had no business to be with him, no part of his world. Clearly Lady Russell didn't like the attention Edmund had given her and she was eager to tell her so, to warn her off, but Marietta wasn't ready to be shown the door just yet.

If there was some kind of understanding between Edmund and Lady Russell, then why had he invited her, Marietta, to Ashborne for the weekend? Thinking of how she had gazed into his compelling silver-grey eyes when they had been together earlier, it dawned on her that what she had said to Lady Russell, that she was no more than an acquaintance, was not true. The things Edmund had said to her and the way he had caressed her cheek and held her hand had been lover-like and the realisation pierced her with unexpected poignancy. After the few times she had been in his company, it was pleasant and flattering to see admiration and that warmly intimate look in his eyes when he looked at her—and then there was his smile that melted her bones. How could she deny something that was slowly becoming a part of her?

Chapter Five

Returning to her mother, she sat sipping tea and listening to the talk going on around her with little interest. Glancing towards the house, she caught a glimpse of Edmund among a group of gentlemen, all looking relaxed—all, she though, but Edmund. Even in the midst of his guests he was somewhat apart and he seemed willing to let his aunt take centre stage. Marietta sensed he would have preferred to be elsewhere than among all these people.

A woman suddenly appeared by his side, tall and beautiful with a smile on her lips. Marietta's heart sank when she recognised Lady Russell. She watched the interaction between them, hearing their laughter from where she sat. Another gentleman joined them, a man Marietta hadn't been introduced to or seen before now.

Tall and fair, he had a sunny disposition and she noted how he moved to stand beside Lady Russell.

Feeling a sudden reluctance to make small talk with the company her mother was keeping, she excused herself and wandered into the house, thinking she would take a closer look at some of the paintings she had seen earlier. The interior of the house was quiet, everyone preferring to be outside on such a fine day. Finding herself in the library, which doubled up as a music room, closing the door softly behind and seeing a grand piano in the corner, she moved towards it and raised the lid, idly letting her fingers trail over the ivory keys.

Unable to resist the urge to play and realising she had no audience, she sat on the piano stool and began to play a Chopin's nocturne, closing her eyes and becoming immersed in the music, the notes coming to her like crystal-clear drops of water. Immediately she began to relax, the music releasing the tension inside her that had been present since her encounter with Lady Russell.

She played with a degree of feeling which seemed to carry her away. She did not hear Edmund enter the room through the long French windows opening on to the terrace. She was only aware of his presence when he stood behind her. Sensing she was about to stop playing, he moved to stand beside the piano, resting his arms on its top and looking at her closely.

'No, don't stop. I would like to listen to you play.'

Marietta continued playing, meeting his eyes. The expression in them was unforgettable. He was looking at her with such intensity which, combined with the music, began to awaken all her senses, making her conscious of only this moment which was suspended in time. It was as if it had become identified with the music, for everything that had gone before and everything that was to come were irrelevant as they became as one in an enchanted circle of sunlight. Edmund was looking at her as no man had looked at her before, and she had never felt drawn to another person as she was to him.

When the last notes of the nocturne faded and died away, she let her hands fall into her lap, feeling it had sapped her will. There was complete silence within the room. Both were reluctant to break the magic of the moment, which had held them in thrall. For those few moments, the intensity of Edmund's gaze held Marietta spellbound, weaving an invisible thread about her from which there was no escape—from which she had no desire to escape—until at last he smiled softly.

'That was beautiful. You play well. Another of your many accomplishments. You really are a talented young woman.'

'Thank you.'

'I looked for you. I thought you would be outside drinking tea with your mother.'

'No. My mother is happily taking tea and gossiping with some ladies she is already acquainted with. I thought I'd come inside and take a look at some of your paintings—until I came in here and saw the piano. I hope you don't mind.'

'Not at all. It doesn't get played enough. I told you I would show you the paintings.'

'Yes, you did, but you were otherwise engaged.'

'Ah—with Francine.'

'Yes. I had no wish to disturb you.'

'You wouldn't have been. I believe you have made the acquaintance of Francine? Did she endear herself to you?'

'I don't think she approves of me. I am not truly acquainted with her—apart from a few choice words—and she did not endear herself to me in the slightest. Her manners leave much to be desired.'

A slow smile curved his firm lips. 'I'm sorry. She does tend to be outspoken.'

Marietta shot him a hard look. 'Outspoken? I am not simple. She does not like me and I know rudeness when I hear it.'

He frowned. 'I hope she didn't upset you.'

Marietta smiled. 'It would take more than Lady Russell to upset me.'

'What do you think of her?'

In Marietta's uneasy mind the memory of those cold eyes resting on her was far too vivid. 'I think she considers me less than civilised. She certainly needs a lesson in manners—they are by no means equal to those of your aunt,' she replied, implying that she had found offence in Lady Russell's behaviour towards her, 'but she is extremely attractive,' she conceded.

'Francine is known to speak her mind. She is also adept at manipulating and controlling people—in fact, there is no one better, no one more subtle. People become like putty in her fingers.'

Marietta smiled, having already decided to

avoid Lady Russell's company. 'And you, Edmund? Are you putty in her fingers?'

His expression became serious. 'No, Marietta, I am not. If I possessed any romantic feelings for Francine, then I would have done something about it, but I don't. I never have and I never will.'

'Then it's as you said—she speaks her mind, but I think I came out of our encounter very well.'

He smiled. 'I'm glad to hear it. Take no nonsense from her. She is of no account. You are a guest at Ashborne as much as she is and I won't have her upsetting you.'

'She won't.' Marietta smiled. 'I won't let her.'

'That's the spirit. Now, shall we look at the paintings before my aunt comes to remind me of my duties to our other guests?'

As they walked through rooms and along the gallery that stretched from end to end of Ashborne House, Edmund told her about the everything they passed, about what paintings he considered good in the varied collection staring down at them from the walls, but with a merciless eye for the errors of the century's modernisation, the artists such as Millais who favoured realism and romanticism which his aunt favoured. Marietta made her own pointed remarks about pictures painted by provincial artists which hung beside the Old Masters and they discussed everything in knowledgeable detail.

Marietta paused beside a collection of hunting scenes, fascinated by one in particular because the artist had painted Ashborne House in the background. When she commented on this to Edmund he nodded.

'I was at an auction in London to buy another painting I had my eye on and when I saw these I couldn't resist buying them. You are quite right. That is Ashborne House in the background— the hunting a familiar scene even now. Every year we host the hunt here at Ashborne—it's quite a turn out.'

Marietta's eye shifted to the painting of a man and horse beside the collection. The man she had seen in one of the paintings earlier of Lady Fitzroy's husband. He made a gallant figure in uniform under a smoky blue sky. The horse was a wonderful rich dark brown getting darker towards the extremities. A startling white blaze ran down his head and he had four white socks. 'He's beautiful. He has a wonderful set of limbs and a good head.'

'And the indefinable stamp of class and breeding,' Edmund said with a note of pride. He belonged to my uncle—Samson, the horse's name was. The memory of him lives on at Ashborne. My uncle fought in the Crimean War. Early in fifty-five he sailed with Samson for Constantinople. My aunt has his medals from the battles at Alma, Balaclava, Inkerman and Sebastopol. They both came back—Samson is buried in the park overlooking the lake where he took part in many a hunt.' Distracted by the perfect picture she made in the light shining through the tall mullioned windows, which cast an aura over her, he settled his gaze on her. 'Does your father hunt when you are in Surrey—or you, for that matter? Riding as well as you do, you would be an asset on the hunting field.'

Meeting his eyes, Marietta felt her cheeks flush at the compliment. Her mind was attuned to his and she was suddenly conscious that they were alone in the warm, intimate silence of the long gallery, where the only sounds to be heard were the voices outside as guests conversed and laughed together. 'We don't hunt, but we do like to ride out. Sometimes Father will tag on to a hunt when he's in the mood, but he's more often than not in London. Do you take part in the hunt?'

'Yes. Like most of the males of my family, I was born and bred in the hunting field—but I didn't really take to the saddle until I was a youth.'

'I have to say that I feel reluctant to ride to hounds. Blood sports do not appeal to me. It is not my idea of a pleasurable pastime.'

'It's hardly a pastime, but a way of life—as it has been for generations past.'

'That doesn't mean to say it is right.'

'But everyone enjoys it—you only have to ask them—riders and hounds alike.'

Marietta had to admit that she enjoyed riding hell for leather in the open countryside as much as anyone else, but she couldn't help saying, with a delicate lift to her eyebrows, 'Then it's a pity no one thought to ask the fox.'

He laughed. 'I understand why you feel that way, but the truth is, there is nothing to compare with riding a high-spirited, courageous horse in the hunt. Hunting is one of man's oldest activities—a way of life, where they would hunt not for sport but for food. I think it brings out all the primitive instincts in the hunter. It's the thrill of it, the exhilaration of the chase ending in the final capture and subjugation of its prey.'

Marietta stared at him, blushing crimson, having a distinct feeling he was not speaking of the fox but of herself, and she was aware and hopelessly appalled that she was unable to work up any indignation. His voice was low and he looked deeply into her eyes, knowing she had interpreted his words in the way they had been intended—he smiled without contrition.

They stood motionless for what seemed a long time, but it was, in fact, little more than a few seconds of highly charged emotion. He was standing very close, looking down at her penetratingly. The silence stretched between them, lengthening and becoming dangerous, but Marietta could not move, and, feeling herself to be in the grip of some powerful emotion, she did not want to move—even though it was an emotion that threatened to destroy her sensibilities and overwhelm her.

The moment was one which saw a heightening of both their senses and involuntarily Edmund took a step that closed the distance between them, his eyes darkening and letting his gaze drop to her lips, moist and slightly parted. His closeness made Marietta feel too vulnerable, but she was unable to move away. She caught her breath, able to feel the heat emanating from his body, to feel the power within him. Edmund's silence was more eloquent, more powerful, more successful in impinging on Marietta's emotions than anything she would have imagined. They were aware of nothing else but each other and the dangerous current of attraction flowing between them.

Aware of guests entering the gallery, who smiled at them but did not look long enough to observe the hasty steps they took away from each other, and the look that passed between them, Marietta turned from Edmund's intense gaze in confusion and thanked him for showing her the pictures and portraits. He followed her down the gallery. She turned and faced him once more.

'Thank you for showing me the paintings. Perhaps I can have a closer look before I leave.'

'Of course. Please feel free to wander about at will.'

His eyes glowed warmly down at her, feeling none of the embarrassment which so clearly gripped her. She walked on ahead to join the other guests. The rest of the time when she went to her room to dress for dinner passed in some kind of blur. Edmund did not address her again directly, but his eyes trailed over her continuously. She was aware of his presence, of his regard, which had an unsettling effect on her heart. She could not think coherently, and from the way every pulse in her body throbbed intolerably, how every time their eyes met she felt all the power of his gaze. There were forces at work in her mind she found almost impossible to understand.

Watching Marietta walk away from him after their tour of the gallery, Edmund though of her with fascinated interest, amazed by the ease with which she had insinuated herself into his heart. What was it about her that he found so appealing? Her innocence? Her smile that set his heart pounding like that of an inexperienced youth in the first throes of love? He liked to hear her musical laughter, see her glowing eyes and jaunty, heartrending smile.

She had succeeded in breaking down all his defences and he could not bear the thought of losing her. Her smile warmed his heart, her touch heated his blood. She had the power to enchant him as no other woman had been able to do. Now, more than ever, he wanted to have her by his side, here, at Ashborne House, to feast his eyes on her and hold her, and to know the exquisite sensation of her slender, voluptuous body curved against his. She stirred his heart which he had believed to be dead and she stirred his blood to a passion that given a chance would be everlasting.

Later, Marietta dressed carefully for the evening's entertainments and chose to wear a sapphire taffeta gown her mother had purchased for the occasion. Faith arranged her hair back from her face with two fat ringlets draped over her shoulder. As Marietta accompanied her mother down to the dining room, her mother told her she was suffering a headache, which she was prone to, and that she would not be late retiring to her bed. Hopefully she would feel better in the morning.

The dining room was elegantly furnished, lit by a huge crystal chandelier suspended above the exquisitely arrayed table that glittered and sparkled, the room becoming a kaleidoscope of colours when everyone was assembled. A variety of dishes of different flavour and delicacies was served, all equally delicious.

Edmund presided at the end of the long table,

Lady Russell on his right. Marietta was a couple of seats down the table on the opposite side to Lady Russell. At one point Marietta listened to the conversation between them. Lady Russell manipulated the conversation with such effortless skill, leaving Marietta with no option but to listen and not participate. She realised that getting angry accomplished nothing and that was exactly what Lady Russell had set out to do—and succeeded, she thought, reproaching herself. In the end she turned her head away to converse with the lady she was seated next to.

As the meal progressed, and more wine was consumed, everyone was in high spirits. Cheeks became florid, talk raucous. After the meal everyone returned to the large drawing room and to the terrace for talk and music, the silks and flash of jewels brilliant. Servants passed among them pouring coffee and more champagne, brandy and fortified wines. Marietta sat in the drawing room with her mother among a group of ladies, all feeling the chill in the air. The sun was beginning to go down in glowing lines of crimson, like ribbons flung across a sky the colour of indigo, radiant in its clarity.

Marietta was engulfed in a dull kind of lethargy, breathing in the aroma of coffee.

As the evening wore on and she became engrossed in a game of whist, partnered by her mother, from the corner of her eye she saw Edmund, his figure conspicuous as he moved among his guests with ease. When the game of cards was over she ventured on to the terrace where wilting ladies hid their yawns behind fans. Empty glasses were refilled and gentlemen sat and smoked their cigars, the smoke spiralling lazily upwards to cloud the air.

Close to midnight guests began to drift away, some to their own homes close by and others, who had too far to travel, to their rooms. Marietta's mother, having listened patiently as a lady regaled her of the beauty of the county, decided to retire. Marietta said she would go with her, but was waylaid when Edmund accosted her at the bottom of the stairs and asked her to accompany him around the garden before turning in.

'Oh, but I couldn't,' she was quick to say.

'Yes, you can. I refuse to take no for an answer.'

'But you showed me the gardens earlier.'

'Ah, but that was in daylight. They look altogether different at night. There are enough lanterns in the trees to light our way. Now come along,' he said. 'I am your host after all. It would be impolite of you to refuse—and you can scarcely desert me, can you?'

He was smiling. How could she refuse? She didn't want to refuse. The usual loungers were on the terrace. Marietta cast them a dubious glance as she walked down the steps on to the perfectly mown lawn. 'Tomorrow the story will be bandied about that we have spent some time alone in the garden together. Does that not concern you?'

'Not in the slightest. It will do them good to have something to talk about.'

And so it was that Marietta found herself walking beside him along paths lit by lanterns dangling in the trees. Everything around them was peaceful. The birds were now silent and there was not even a breeze to stir the trees. The night was surprisingly warm for the time of year and a myriad of stars dotted the sky. She sighed, looking up at the glow of the moon, feeling a peace and contentment wash over her—like a whisper, an excited expectancy, of things to come.

She found herself smiling for no reason,

wondering if this sudden feeling of elation and happiness warming her heart had been brought about by the knowledge that she was here alone in the garden with Edmund Fitzroy. She could not help the feelings she had for him. They were not something that could be stopped once they had begun—not even if she was sensible and prudent, as she had always told herself she must be.

They walked in silence for a while. Marietta was not by nature shy, but he made her feel awkwardly aware of herself. He was a disquieting man. She was again touched by the magnetism of his presence, which was the case whenever she was with him. She examined the profile of his face and thought how handsome he was, wondering how he had managed to run the gauntlet of matrimony for so long.

Suddenly he laughed. She thought it hadn't been meant for her to hear, but it had escaped him. 'What are you laughing at?'

Turning his head, he smiled down at her. 'Not much. I was just thinking. I was thinking that this is possibly the first time that you have left a party to walk in a darkened garden with a man without asking your mother's permission.'

She laughed lightly. 'Oh, it's better than that.

Not only is this the first time I've walked in a garden at night with a gentleman without permission, it's the first house party I've attended at all.'

'Really? You surprise me. I imagined that with your father's business and social connections, you would make a habit of it.'

'Not at all. Oh, we visit other people's houses and my mother entertains when we are in Surrey on occasion, but nothing like this. Ashborne is a beautiful house. You must be very rich.' He smiled down at her and she caught a flash of white teeth between his parted lips.

'You are the only person I know who would say something like that.'

'Am I? Well—why not? It's not a bad thing to be rich. Ask my father. Making money is all he ever thinks about—however devious the means.'

'He's done well for himself and, as you say, there's nothing wrong with being rich. Like your father, I am what I've made myself.' He sighed suddenly, looking into the darkness of the night. 'However, I am no saint either and like all men I have many flaws. I do not deny that I've done my share of wrongdoing and attracted much criticism—from myself, mostly, but considering the savage nature of the times when I was a lad, I saw to it that when I began to accumulate my wealth it was made in a decent and proper manner.'

'Did you not think of giving some of your wealth to your uncle—the Earl of Waverley? If you did that, then Gabriel would be able to marry a woman of his choosing and not think about marrying someone with a dowry substantial enough to shore up the family estate.'

Edmund's expression became grim and his lips tightened. 'My uncle and I do not see eye to eye. He is undeserving of anything I might give him. He is deeply in debt of his own making and I refuse to hand over hard-earned money to see it wasted at the gambling tables.' He looked at her gravely. 'You ask an awful lot of questions.'

It was said not unkindly, but with great finality. He was not angry, Marietta thought. It was just that he obviously didn't want to talk about his past. He had said enough. The conversation on that issue was over. She cast him a curious glance, wondering about what had occurred in his past that had affected him very deeply, but it was not for her to pry.

Turning the conversation on another course,

she asked him about Ashborne House. It was plain to her how much he loved the place. When he talked about it a change came over him, a softening to his face. What did it mean? She began to sense an awful loneliness and isolation must inhabit him at times—something she had experienced at first hand so she could empathise with him. Perhaps he was only able to put his thoughts into perspective, to talk about them, at times like this when he was at Ashborne.

The further they walked from the house, there was comparative quiet in the garden. 'It's been a lovely day,' Marietta remarked. 'We often get down to Surrey—I do so love being out of London, but I rarely get the opportunity to visit such lovely houses as Ashborne. I don't know how to thank you for inviting us.'

She turned her face up to his and his heavy-lidded gaze fixed meaningfully on her lips. 'I can think of a way,' he murmured softly. Raising his hand, he traced her cheek with the backs of his fingers. She shivered. 'Are you cold?'

'No, not cold.' In truth, the warmth of the wine she had consumed at dinner, which had spread through her blood, relaxing the knots inside her and releasing the tensions in her mind and body, made her thoughts anything but clear. She looked up at him and he became still, the smile disappearing to leave his face serious and aware.

Marietta drew in her breath. He was close, so close. The way his eyes had settled on her lips made her uneasy and excited at the same time. She had never been so close to a man in her life and it was a whole new experience. She thought he would kiss her—indeed, she was hoping that he would. Her eyes became trapped in his gaze and she could not look away. She was held by some kind of enchantment that bound her to this man whose touch lingered on her face.

'Tell me what you are thinking?' he asked softly.

'Only that I am so very glad you invited us here.'

He sighed, capturing her eyes, his face serious. 'Why do you think I invited you?'

'Tell me,' she murmured.

'I invited *you*, Marietta. I couldn't ask you to come without inviting your parents. I told you earlier that I have never invited a woman here—Ashborne has always been off limits. I have my life in London and wherever my business takes me and my life at Ashborne. I keep the two separate. Do you understand that?'

'I'm not sure.'

'Of course you're sure. A woman always knows when she has drawn a man's interest— when he is attracted to her. I don't think you are the kind of woman who teases.'

'How do you know what kind of woman I am?' she asked playfully, tilting her head to one side and gazing up at him from beneath the sweep of her eyelashes.

'Oh,' he murmured, his gaze settling hungrily on her mouth, 'I believe I have a good idea.'

'I am thinking that you would like to kiss me?' If he was surprised by her reply, he didn't show it.

'I wouldn't be human if I didn't. Tell me, Marietta, have you ever been kissed?' he asked, his gaze still fixed on her lips.

Unnerved and thoroughly confused at the way things were going, Marietta shook her head. 'No, never,' she whispered.

He smiled. 'And I was of the mind that the times you've been kissed may be too numerous to count.'

She laughed softly. 'Now you jest. I've never met anyone that I wanted to kiss me.'

'Not even Gabriel?'

'Certainly not Gabriel.' At that moment she knew she wanted him to kiss her—and she also knew she should repulse him if he tried. She looked at him, entranced, hardly breathing. Strands of hair drifted across her face, and she thought his face bent over her was more beautiful than she had ever known. She saw the deepening light in his eyes and the thick, defined brows and desperately wanted to touch him.

They stood facing one another, intensely aware of each other—how could they not be? The air was sultry and warm, the atmosphere charged with tension and something else each of them clearly recognised. At that moment, all that existed in Marietta's world was this man's eyes upon her and his low voice. His eyes were so tender and she could not bear it if he did not kiss her.

His brow arched, his mesmerising lips quirking at the corners. His eyes intent and oddly challenging held hers. His finger touched her chin, tipping her face up to his. He smiled crookedly. 'I think it's time you were kissed. It seems the natural place to start to undermine your defences. My dear Marietta, I am twenty-nine years old and I know exactly what I want.' He smiled, his eyes twinkling bright. 'I believe I'm quite good at it—and afterwards you can judge for yourself.'

'How can I do that when I have nothing to compare it with?' she asked, breathing faster as he came closer.

'Then you'll just have to take my word for it. I don't give my kisses lightly—and—like my opinions, once uttered, they cannot be retracted. Would you mind if I did kiss you?'

'No—I don't think so.'

'Well then, shall we?'

Placing his hands on her shoulders, he drew her close. His voice was seductive and persuasive as he looked down at her, his eyes gleaming with a sensual luminosity as they focused on her quivering, parted lips. She could feel the hard thrust of her breasts against his chest. She quivered under his light touch, her breath catching in her throat. Without taking his eyes off her face, he caressed her, gliding his hands up her arms, past her low neckline, until he came to the creamy expanse of her neck. She was aware of the hectic beating of her pulse as he touched her, gently stroking her neck with his fingertips.

He bent his head to press his lips to the soft skin at her temple, her cheekbones, along her jaw, her throat, the lovely tender line of it, dwelling at the place where her pulse beat like a fluttering butterfly below her skin. Her long lashes drifted closed and her rosy lips parted in anticipation of the kiss. She did not have long to wait. Moving with care so as not to alarm her, he settled his lips on hers, lightly, gently caressing their softness, claiming her mouth with a kiss.

Nothing in all her nineteen years could have prepared Marietta for what she was experiencing beneath Edmund's touch, the heat of his mouth on hers. Pleasure unfolded inside her like a butterfly opening its wings to fly. Never in her imagination had she experienced anything so piercing and sweet as this. The movement of his mouth on hers, the warm taste of it, the strong touch of his fingers at the nape of her neck and along her spine—all these things were strangely confusing. The confusion spread through her whole body and she could not stop it, she did not want to. Her heart raced with guilty pleasure. Her body came keenly alive, all her senses heightened and focused on him and herself and the touch of his mouth until nothing else mattered.

Suddenly it was over when he raised his head, breaking the kiss. Her eyes slowly opened, then she blinked and stared straight at him. He couldn't stop his rakish grin.

'Well,' he murmured, his eyes glowing and warm. 'Earlier I imagined you to be a prim-and-proper miss. I can now say that you are nothing like my imaginings and that, despite your protestations, you must enjoy kissing gentlemen, that the times you have been kissed are too numerous to count.'

'I told you I have no experience of kissing. But I must thank you,' she whispered, 'for making the kiss one of the most enjoyable moments of my life.'

He gazed down at her seriously. 'High praise indeed, but I think I should let you go while I still can.'

Weak from the turbulence of her emotions, Marietta rested her head on his chest and felt his heart beating as fast as her own, which meant that he, too, must have been affected by their kiss. There was something different about him, something indefinably more tender about him.

'Forgive me,' he said, taking her arms and holding her away from him. 'I presume too much.' His voice was soft.

'No, you don't,' she countered. 'I practically invited you to kiss me.' Now the moment was over, she was shocked that she had actually enjoyed kissing him and annoyed with herself for making it so blatantly obvious to him. 'But we mustn't do it again.'

'No? Are you saying that you didn't enjoy kissing me?' He reached out and cupped her chin in the palm of his hand and kissed her again, gently once more, his lips merely brushing hers.

'No—yes… Oh, please behave yourself,' she said, flustered and confused by what was happening to her. 'This afternoon you promised me you would.'

Edmund was by no means done with her and he grinned. 'That was this afternoon. This is now. Were you speaking the truth when you told me you haven't done anything like that with anyone else?'

Marietta's cheeks flamed with indignation. 'It is not something I would lie about. Now will you please stop tormenting me about my—slip of propriety.'

His grin widened at her embarrassment, and then he laughed. 'I like reminding you. I like seeing you get all flushed and flustered and hot under the collar.'

She glowered at him. 'Now you're making fun of me.'

'I know. I can be quite incorrigible at times.'

Unable to stay cross with him—knowing he was teasing anyway—Marietta laughed and began to walk on.

Falling into step beside her, Edmund took her hand in his and raised it to his lips. 'You should laugh more often. You have a beautiful laugh.'

Hearing the sensuous huskiness that deepened his voice, Marietta shivered inwardly. 'Thank you—but you are only saying that to placate me.'

'Do you need placating, Marietta?'

She sighed, liking the feel of his lips against her fingers. 'No. I'm having too nice a time to be cross.'

'Good.'

They walked on, content to let the night wrap itself around them and to have the lanterns and moon to light their way. Marietta let her face wander over the smooth, thick lock of hair that dipped over his brow and the authority and confidence in every line of his darkly handsome face. She let her gaze travel down the full length of the superbly fit, muscled body walking beside her. He exuded a raw, potent virility that held her in thrall.

As if he could feel her eyes studying him, without turning his head, he quirked the mobile line of his mouth in a half-smile. 'I hope you like what you see.' He sighed and turning his head he stopped and looked at her. 'You can kiss me again if you like, Marietta.'

Marietta's eyes opened wide in astonishment and then she laughed. 'Why, your sheer arrogance confounds me. I most certainly will not,' she objected, beginning to walk on.

Like lightning, his hands caught her arm, slowly turning her to face to him. 'If you won't kiss me, do you mind if I kiss you?' His voice was low pitched and sensual. 'Are you not curious to find out if it will be as good as when I kissed you a few minutes ago?' A slight smile touched his mouth, but his heavy-lidded gaze dropped to the inviting fullness of her lips, lingering there.

Hypnotised by the velvet voice and those mesmerising silver eyes, Marietta gazed up at him, with a combination of fear and excitement.

She tried to relax, but in the charged silence between them it was impossible. 'Shouldn't we be getting back to the house?'

Edmund chuckled softly as he fell into step beside her. 'If there's anything I can't abide, it's an obstinate woman.'

Marietta laughed. 'I suspect you haven't met many. I'm sure you have most women falling over themselves to do your bidding.'

'As a matter of fact, some of them do. My fatal charm doesn't seem to work with you. I've no idea why.'

'I'm immune,' she said, without looking at him.

His eyes narrowed. 'No, you're not—and before we're done I'll prove it. Would you like to ride out in the morning?'

'Yes, I would like that.'

'I will enjoy showing you more of the estate. It will be early.'

'It's the best time.'

'I couldn't agree more. I shall be at the stables at six thirty.' Raising a superior brow, he met her gaze. 'Will that suit you?'

Despite knowing there would be whispers and raised brows aplenty if she were seen riding alone with him at such an early hour, she nodded, her gaze open and direct. 'Yes, that would be perfect.'

He grinned. 'I'll look forward to it.'

They walked on in silence. Marietta loved being at Ashborne House. She savoured every moment to the full. She was discovering new sides to his nature, but she could not escape the feeling that there was an underlying sadness in him, something in his past he kept locked away. Coming to the foot of the terrace where a few guests still sat about drinking, the gentlemen smoking their cigars, Marietta looked at him. She saw the purposeful gleam in those heavy-lidded eyes and drew a swift breath.

'I think your other guests are expecting you to spend time with them.'

Lady Russell suddenly appeared from the shadows. Marietta watched her come close. There was style and grace and an arrogant sureness in every line of her. She looked more beautiful than she had looked earlier. Was it just the dress or was it the company of the two gentlemen she had just walked away from, neither of whom could possibly ignore her, which added an essential sparkle to her beauty, her expression one of cool control?

'Francine,' Edmund uttered. Marietta noted

a flash of irritation cross his face and she was sure he uttered a curse beneath his breath, which made her smile. 'I thought you would have left by now.' He turned to Marietta. 'Francine is a close neighbour—lives just up the road, so to speak.'

'I was about to leave. I was chatting to your aunt and Mrs Harrington earlier.' She looked at Marietta directly. 'Such a charming, down-to-earth lady, your mother.'

'Yes, although she can be a little too direct at times.'

'And you think that is a failing, do you, Miss Harrington? For myself I prefer people to be that way.'

'I quite agree,' Marietta said, moving away. 'Please excuse me. My mother will be wondering what's happened to me.' She looked at Edmund. 'Thank you, Edmund. I've enjoyed our walk.'

Chapter Six

Edmund paid little attention to Francine hovering by his side, his gaze following Marietta into the house through the French doors. He was well satisfied with the way things had turned out. He had watched her throughout the day absorb the atmosphere of the house, confident that she could not fail to be impressed by Ashborne—and by his aunt who was, as always, charm and graciousness personified.

He could only marvel at how much Marietta had lowered her defences and allowed a moment of intimacy between them. It was a small honour, for he knew how reticent she had been towards forming any kind of relationship after the catastrophe that had been Gabriel. Yet she had opened to him. Even now, he could feel her vulnerability and it made him tremble inside to see how much she trusted him when he wasn't even sure if he could trust himself.

She had walked beside him through the garden, small and slender and utterly lovely. Marietta was different to anything that had gone before, like a new world—a place of endless mysteries and unexpected delights. She could paint and play the piano with deep feeling, becoming lost in her love of both and her emotions, and then she could blush all over when he looked at her in a certain way. When he had kissed her he had sensed her inexperience, but also her interest.

After their kiss her reaction to it had been so naive that Edmund thought she was joking until he remembered how inexperienced she was. He was glad that he had managed to win her confidence and felt her respond to his kiss in a way that had startled him. He was completely absorbed in her. He told himself she was the best thing that had ever happened to him.

He found that there was something lovely about being with her. He felt contented and peaceful in her presence. He was not angry and impatient to be about what it was he was doing—not sad or desperate, the way he felt whenever he thought of his past and his father rotting away in a clinic in Switzerland.

He was falling in love with Marietta, which was an emotion he had always thought had passed him by, assuming it was for others, not for him. And yet Marietta affected him deeply, suppressing the troubled times with all manner of desperate and brutal humanity, times when he had lived from day to day in a silent, hardly controlled rage. Circumstances and the injustices he had experienced swept through his mind in bitter recall, sparking his resentment until he longed to shout his rancour to the sky. Experience had been a harsh taskmaster, brutally convincing him that cool-headed compliance was the only way he could ever hope to survive.

An image of Marietta appeared in his mind. In his imagination he felt the warmth of her breath when he had kissed her and he remembered the moments they had spent together in the garden, of the fierce pleasure and ecstasy he had felt holding her in his arms, the sweetness of their kisses and the temptation to step into the dream which had begun to seduce him when he had first laid eyes on her.

* * *

Marietta walked away from them, carrying a warm feeling inside her. She was strangely affected by what had transpired between her and Edmund. When he had taken her in his arms and placed his lips on hers she had been helpless to prevent the response that surged through her. It had been like having the breath sucked out of her and she could no more have forced her lips closed against his than she could have physically wrenched herself from his arms. He had taken her close to him as if he meant to make her a part of him, taking her to a place of passion she had never known existed. The arousing of her desire still trembled in her body and would not let it be at rest. That he could do this to her with a touch of his lips amazed her—that with a mere kiss he had seemed to take possession of her.

There was nothing in her whole life that had prepared her for the swiftness and brilliance of this new awakening. It was the answer to the longing she had felt for him on all the times they had met. She realised it was not only an awareness of him that he had awakened in her, but of herself. She was not prepared to call it love because she had no experience of it. And yet it bore the resemblance of nothing that had gone before.

'Well, here you are.'

Her mother's shrill voice seemed to come to her from far away. Marietta watched her hurry towards her.

'I've been looking for you everywhere. Where have you been? What a splendid place this is, Marietta,' she enthused, giving her daughter no time to reply.

Marietta looked at her mother. Her face was flushed, her eyes overbright—which was always the case when she had indulged in too much wine.

'How is your headache, Mother?'

Her expression suddenly became pained and she placed the back of her hand dramatically on her forehead. 'No better, I'm afraid, and having to converse with that dreadful Lady Russell has done it no good, no good at all. Now, I would like to go to bed. I've been waiting for you to accompany me.'

'Come along then,' Marietta said, taking her arm. 'I'll accompany you to your room and then I will go to bed myself.'

Marietta saw her mother into bed, not leaving until she had taken a powder to alleviate her headache and her eyes were closed. She then sought her own bed, confident that her mother would feel refreshed in the morning.

Unfortunately Marietta couldn't sleep. The day's events played on her mind and she couldn't stop thinking about Edmund. He commanded her attention, filled her thoughts to the exclusion of all else.

Just before dawn her mother's maid came to her room to inform her that her mother was asking for her. She'd spent a sleepless night and her headache was no better. Marietta was disappointed that she would have to cancel her early ride with Edmund, but there was nothing she could do. Dispatching her mother's maid to take a message to the stables to inform him, she sat with her mother until she fell to sleep.

Feeling restless and that it was safe to leave her mother in her maid's hands, she traversed the many passageways of the house and managed to find her way outside. Setting off in the direction of the gardens, she breathed deeply, watching the sun on the horizon rise higher in the sky, bathing the surrounding countryside with a soft glow. She loved the feel of the light breeze on her cheeks and felt the weight of her spirits lighten. The previous day she had spied the dark waters of a lake beyond the perimeters of the gardens and she decided to walk in its direction. She wore a gown of blue the colour of speedwell beneath a warm jacket, her bonnet perched on the back of her head, allowing the arrangement of curls to be seen.

On reaching the lake, she stopped and gazed at the still, large expanse of water. A serene group of water fowl swam placidly and flapped their wings as they preened themselves. She stood and watched the tiny waves lap the shore and smiled at the scene, one of serenity and peace, that opened up before her. She walked slowly along the water's edge. Seeing a bridge spanning the narrow end of the lake, she headed towards it, completely unaware that she was being watched by a woman on horseback.

Reaching the bridge and seeing the water rushing into the head of the lake out of a wood of dense trees, she decided to walk by the side of the river rather than across the bridge. The ground was uneven and boggy in places but, interested in seeing beyond the bend ahead of her, she walked on, seeing no danger as the water rushed by. The trees were dense, the air damp and humid. When the horse and rider suddenly appeared, taken by surprise Marietta inadvertently stepped into the water, feeling its force against her low boots. Looking up at the woman mounted on a splendid grey mare, her heart sank when she recognised Lady Russell.

'What are you doing here?' Lady Russell demanded, her voice sharp.

'Have the goodness to move your horse out of my way.' Marietta looked at her. Her habit was a simple creation, devastating in its effect— a stylish scarlet riding skirt and jacket, and a matching hat set at a jaunty angle on her dark hair secured in a snood. Marietta thought the woman looked as graceful as any she had seen sit a horse and even here, at this early hour, she thought with a stab of envy, Lady Russell belonged. 'In answer to your question, Lady Russell, I am out for a walk. Do you see something wrong with that?'

Lady Russell shrugged and drew her horse back. 'Not if you know the countryside around Ashborne and in particular the lake. I saw you walking towards this direction and I had to come and warn you that it is not as placid as it looks. The water here is deceptive. As you can surely see the river enters the lake with force and it is deep beneath the bridge. There are many dangerous undercurrents that would drag you down.'

At once Marietta was filled with resentment and a sense of shame that she had to be taught how to take a walk by Lady Russell. Suddenly she felt like an interloper here at Ashborne. 'Thank you for the warning, Lady Russell, but I do not intend taking a swim and I do not need to be told how to take a walk.'

'I'm sure you don't.' She made to turn away. 'I thought I should warn you. You wouldn't want to be swept away. The ground close to the bank is uneven and should you stumble you could easily find yourself in the water. The damp undergrowth is also full of adders—I don't know if you are nervous about snakes.'

'I'm not.'

'I don't suppose you informed anyone at the house you were to walk in this direction.'

'I did not, simply because I did not know myself until I left the house. Now if you will excuse me, Lady Russell, I will continue with my walk.'

'Very well. I will leave you—but perhaps you would like me to wait until you are back on the bridge.'

'Why would you do that? I assure you I will

be careful. I am quite capable of reaching the bridge on my own.'

Again Lady Russell shrugged, and the movement was casual, as if she didn't care very much whether she fell into the river or not. 'If that is the way you want it, then there's no more to be said.'

'Thank you, it is.'

Lady Russell hesitated a moment, then she said, 'I must be on my way. I've ridden over from Stanford House, my home which is nearby. I always ride out at this time—as does Edmund when he's at Ashborne. We usually meet up.'

Marietta stood by and watched Lady Russell turn her horse about and move away. She raised her hand in a gesture to call her back, to thank her for her concern—if that was what it was—and remembering their encounter the previous day and Lady Russell's harsh words, she very much doubted it, but the gesture was never completed and her hand fell to her side.

She continued to watch Lady Russell, her skirts billowing over her horse's rump in the swiftness of her leaving, as if she couldn't leave fast enough. Marietta made her way back to the bridge, making no further movement to detain her—nor would she ever.

Retracing her steps, she paused by the bridge and continued to watch Lady Russell ride into the distance. She saw her pause and wait, then a rider emerged from the trees. It was Edmund. After speaking for a moment they rode off together.

The breakfast room was empty when Edmund arrived to snatch a bite to eat, but it didn't remain that way. He was just heaping his plate from the hot dishes on the sideboard when Thomas Sheridan walked in followed shortly afterwards by Marietta, looking positively ravishing in a dress of saffron and gold. His heart wrenched when he looked at her lovely face—so poised, so beautiful that he ached to hold her. He had been disappointed when she'd cancelled their ride together. One of the servants had come to inform him that her mother was still feeling unwell so she felt she must stay with her. Francine had been a poor substitute. Irritated by her unwelcome presence and her constant chatter, he had cut the ride short and returned to the house in ill humour.

'Good morning,' Thomas said cheerily, clearly eager to be introduced as he gave Marietta the once over before helping himself to a generous breakfast and coffee. 'You must be Miss Harrington. May I say I am truly delighted to meet you at last—we never got round to it yesterday—although that said I wasn't here for long. Edmund's told me all about you.'

'Has he? All good, I hope.' Marietta responded to his warm friendliness with a smile, helping herself to toast and tea and carrying it to the table.

'Of course,' he said without removing his eyes from her face. 'I am enchanted to meet you. I'm Thomas Sheridan by the way—a neighbour. I thought I'd come early—in time for breakfast.'

'You're always hungry, Thomas,' Edmund grumbled, taking his place at the table as Francine swept in. 'Don't they feed you at home?'

'Not like this, Edmund. Besides,' he said, his eyes, much to Edmund's irritation, roaming appreciatively over Marietta's face, 'the company isn't nearly as charming as it is here.'

Edmund glanced at Marietta, wishing she wouldn't smile quite so warmly at his neighbour in his ebullient mood. Thomas, tall and strongly built with friendly brown eyes—too friendly he thought when they looked at Marietta— was a reasonably attractive man with an infectious charm that women couldn't resist. It was unfortunate for them that his whole existence was dedicated to capturing Francine—who was proving difficult for him to ensnare—but in the meantime he was not averse to bestowing his flattery elsewhere.

'You are very kind, Mr Sheridan.'

'Please feel free to call me Thomas,' he said, his dancing eyes passing over her face with an impudence that widened her smile and increased Edmund's vexation.

'And you must feel free to call me Marietta.'

'Don't allow this reprobate too much freedom, Marietta,' Edmund retorted. 'Give him an inch and he'll take the proverbial mile.'

Tucking in to his ham and eggs and stabbing a mushroom with his fork, Edmund nodded politely to Francine as with quiet composure she placed scrambled eggs and bacon on her plate and carried it to the table, seating herself to the right of Thomas and close to Edmund at the head of the table.

'I trust you had a pleasant ride, Lady Russell,' Marietta said, spreading strawberry preserve on her toast.

'Very much,' she replied tightly. 'Good morning, Thomas. I didn't expect you to be here for breakfast. Had you come earlier you could have joined Edmund and I on our ride.'

'Too early for me,' Thomas replied. 'Heavy night—and all that. Got completely foxed and woke with a headache that compelled me to remain in bed a while longer.'

'I think we get the message,' Edmund remarked with a disgruntled glance at his friend. 'Thomas lives close by, Marietta- not far from Francine at Stanford House. He is a long-time friend of the family.'

'So I understand.'

Thomas smiled broadly across at her. His teeth shone white and even, his fair hair flopping over his brow. 'Should Marietta like to see more of the place it will be my pleasure to show her around—should you have your work cut out keeping your guests happy, you understand, Edmund. I shall make myself available.'

'I don't think that will be necessary, Thomas,' Edmund replied tersely, scowling his disapproval at Thomas's constant appraisal of Marietta, knowing perfectly well that he was laying it on thick in the hope that his open interest in Marietta might succeed in stirring Francine's jealousy. 'Besides, I would have thought you had enough to do at your own house.'

'Nothing that can't be put aside for a beautiful young lady,' Thomas replied, his spirits undaunted, his eyes gleaming devilishly. 'And if you grow weary of my friend's ogre-like disposition, Marietta, be aware that my house is a close haven. Indeed, I would be sorely tempted to lure you away from this moody friend of mine.'

Marietta bestowed on Thomas her sweetest smile while Francine looked fit to strangle Thomas. Edmund looked on with amusement. Perhaps Thomas's tactics were working after all.

'Thank you, Thomas,' Marietta replied. 'Despite what Edmund says, I do appreciate the offer.'

Edmund's look at his friend hinted of a certain distrust. 'And be certain that when a gentleman makes such a scandalous suggestion in public, one doesn't mean a word of it.'

'It's when he begins seeking you out in private that you must be more wary of his motives,' Francine murmured mockingly.

'Quite right,' Edmund drawled. 'Francine is right to tell you to be wary, Marietta. My good friend's intentions are to dishonour every female who is foolish enough to fall for his silken tongue.'

Thomas accepted this light riposte with a long, heartfelt sigh, his expression one of longing when his gaze settled on Francine's downcast face. 'Ah, well, you can't blame a man for trying.'

'Did you enjoy your ride, Edmund?' Marietta asked, taking a small bite of toast.

'I would have enjoyed it more if you had turned up.'

'I'm sorry. It couldn't be helped. My mother isn't very well—but you were not without company. I managed a walk to the lake later and encountered Lady Russell.' She gave him a thinly veiled smile. 'I believe she thought I would fall in.'

'And so you might have,' Lady Russell quipped. 'You are not familiar with the area and there are parts of the lake that are best avoided.'

'It does have its dangers—particularly where the river runs into it after a heavy rainfall,' Edmund said. 'The sensible thing is not to venture there unless one is familiar with it. Had I known you were to go for a walk I would have waited for you.'

'You had already left—besides, I didn't want to leave my mother for too long.'

He frowned. 'I can't think why Francine didn't mention she'd seen you,' he said, glancing at Francine who purposefully kept her eyes lowered over her breakfast. 'She rides most mornings—it was quite by chance that I met her this morning. This afternoon some of the guests are to ride out.'

'You, too?'

He nodded. 'And Thomas—if his head gets better,' he said, his tone heavily lace with sarcasm. 'I hope you will join us, Marietta.'

'Yes, I would like that. I would love to see more of the surrounding countryside before we have to return to London.'

'And so you shall. You say your mother is still feeling ill. Would you like me to send for the doctor to come and take a look at her?'

'That is very kind of you but it is not necessary. She does suffer severe headaches on a regular basis. The only thing that seems to relieve them is to go to bed in a darkened room.'

'Oh, dear,' Francine purred. 'I hope for your sake she doesn't have to leave for home sooner than intended.'

'On the contrary. She so looked forward to

this visit that she won't let a headache keep her down for long.'

'If that does turn out to be the case,' Edmund said, 'then another invitation will be issued for her to return at a later date.'

'That is indeed thoughtful of you, Edmund. Thank you.'

Francine looked at Edmund. 'Your aunt's hospitality knows no bounds, Edmund. She is indeed generous.'

'Lady Fitzroy is very kind. I am sure my mother would appreciate the gesture.'

'I'm sure she would,' Edmund said. 'Let's hope it doesn't come to that and she will soon return to the company.'

Mid-afternoon, after partaking of a substantial lunch and a rest afterwards, a small complement of guests was out for the ride. After changing into her riding habit, Marietta made her way to the stables. The stable yard was a hive of activity, the air charged with excitement as horses were led out and saddled up. Marietta's breath caught in her throat when she saw Edmund across the yard from her. He was just finishing tightening the girths on his huge dark brown stallion. His cream breeches fitted him to perfection, and his green and brown tweed jacket emphasised his lean, muscular body. His stock was smooth and snowy white, highlighting his bronzed good looks. She looked at him admiringly, thinking how attractive he was with the breeze lightly ruffling his shiny black hair.

As he looked in her direction Marietta saw his face brighten and felt her heart give a sudden leap. Walking his horse over to her, he gestured for a stable boy to bring another forward—a bay mare which looked lively enough. She wouldn't have been happy with anything else.

When the boy brought the horse to a halt, Edmund turned to look at Marietta and the heat of his gaze travelled the full length of her in a slow, appreciative perusal, before making a leisurely inspection of her face upturned to his.

'You look wonderful. I've been thinking of you,' he said for her ears alone, his eyes watching the movement of her lips, far more eloquent than speech.

'Thank you,' she replied, feeling the blood rush to her face, remembering the previous night's walk in the garden and finding it difficult to appear calm and unconcerned at the memory of his embrace—and how she suddenly found herself wishing they were alone now so he could repeat the action.

'I imagine you are looking forward to the ride, Marietta.'

'Very much.'

'How is your mother?'

'Resting.' She ran her hand down the mare's neck. 'Is she for me?' It rubbed its head against her, soft dark eyes alive with intelligence.

'She is—here, allow me to assist you.'

Placing his hands on her waist, Edmund lifted her effortlessly into the saddle, watching as she hooked one leg around the pommel and placed her foot in the stirrup before settling her skirts.

'She's a spirited horse. You'll soon get used to her.'

'So here you both are,' said a clear voice.

Turning, Marietta found herself looking into Lady Russell's dark eyes. She was an attractive sight in her scarlet habit, sitting her horse with a straight-backed easy grace, riding side-saddle like all the other ladies taking part in the ride.

'Do you enjoy riding, Miss Harrington?'

'Yes. I happen to love horses and ride all the time—be it in London or at my home in Surrey.'

'I expect your father keeps a good stable.'

'Yes, he does, although he is so busy most of the time that he finds little time to indulge in such pleasures as riding out—but he does have some fine horses.'

'Racehorses?'

'No, not racehorses—why do you ask?'

Lady Russell shrugged, giving the impression that it was of little interest to her. 'Oh—no reason. Just curious. Only it costs money to keep and train horses—we know that, don't we, Edmund? To do so one must be extremely wealthy.'

Marietta stared at her at the unexpectedness of this conversation, thinking that Lady Russell was being very rude to refer to her father's wealth. 'I am sure that if my father's interest ran to horseracing, then he would do so.'

Fortunately Edmund came to Marietta's rescue. 'That's enough, Francine. The financial affairs of Marietta's father need hardly concern you or anyone else for that matter. Now come along. The horses are impatient to be off.'

Feeling her horse becoming restless, Marietta dragged her eyes from Lady Russell's coolly speculative gaze and looked around her, seeing other riders moving out of the stable yard. She began to follow them, heading off over a well-grassed area. The air was fresh and exhilarating and Marietta breathed in the feel of the horse moving beneath her. Nothing could compare with the thrill of riding out. The sun shone and the trees cast long blue shadows over the land. Fields of newly sown corn and meadows stretched out on either side, and the gentle curl of smoke rose from cottage chimneys.

Breaking away from the more sedate riders, she was lost in her own pleasure of the exercise. The terrain was challenging and alien to her and some of the hedges and ditches were a severe test to horse and rider. Deep, broad ditches, lying in thick thorn hedges, made a formidable jump which could be tackled safely by really bold horses, but the horse that hesitated lost impetus and all too easily crashed into the ditch.

Marietta spotted Edmund ahead of her, riding well in a class of his own, at one with his horse, leaping with absolute confidence over hedges and ditches. She considered going to join him when she sensed someone riding right on the heels of her horse. She wanted to pull up, but dared not for fear of colliding. As the rider behind persisted in following close Marietta became angry, for over-riding was one of the easiest methods of maiming or even killing the rider in front.

She could see a big open ditch which yawned ahead of her like a chasm. She would like to have ridden after Edmund but, but because of the persistence of the rider behind she had to swerve off course, approaching the ditch at its widest point. Her experience told her that falls which occurred in ditches were seldom serious—unless taken at speed and that was exactly what she was about to do.

Unable to check her stride, she had no choice but to gallop straight at it, making an unsound take off. As the horse landed on the other side of the ditch it stumbled badly on the soft edge. Frantically it fought to regain its footing, but Marietta, one of her feet having lost its stirrup, was unseated and, crying out ,was somersaulted through the air and into the ditch, falling heavily and hitting her head on some loose rocks. The horse righted itself and made off. The last thing Marietta saw before darkness engulfed her was Lady Russell sitting on her horse, looking down at her from what seemed to be a great height, her lips curved in a satisfied smile.

* * *

Immediately being made aware of the accident, deeply concerned, Edmund rode back, approaching Marietta's crumpled figure on the ground. Flinging himself off his horse, he fell to his knees beside her, looking at her tranquil face. Her head had fallen back and her eyes were closed. Her face held a deathly pallor. He was stricken. His world turned to ashes.

Dear merciful God, he prayed with quiet desperation, remembering Francine's husband and how he had fallen from his horse and it had proved fatal. *Let her be all right. Please God.*

'How is she?' he asked of one of the male riders who had been first on the scene, unaware that Francine had drawn back.

'It's difficult to assess the damage.'

Edmund ran gentle hands over the prone limbs to determine any obvious injuries. There seemed to be none. There was blood on her forehead and her eyes were still closed. Clearly she had hit her head when she had been thrown. He grimaced. If the wound had been caused by the horse's hoof, then matters might indeed be serious. But however life-threatening her injuries, they could do nothing for Marietta here.

'We'll get her to the house.' He looked at

Thomas who had galloped over. 'Get Dr Jenkinson, Thomas, and for God's sake tell him to hurry.'

It was a subdued group that arrived back at Ashborne. Doctor Jenkinson came immediately and examined Marietta thoroughly. She was suffering from mild concussion and had sustained a nasty gash on her head which, although bleeding profusely, did not require suturing. There were no broken bones. Doctor Jenkinson was encouraged that she had now returned to consciousness and was confident she would recover fully in no time at all.

Ignoring the impropriety of entering her room, Edmund pushed his way inside. The painful, unfamiliar constriction in his chest made his hand tremble slightly as he reached out for hers and looked down into her beloved face. His heart wrenched. Her eyes were closed but the pallor had left her face. She was so beautiful it tore at his heart.

'Dear God, Marietta,' he whispered, driven by desperation and a deep and abiding love, 'don't you dare scare me again like that. If anything happened to you, I swear I would follow you. You belong to me. I cannot live without you.'

* * *

The voice was loud in Marietta's head. Suddenly the voice broke through and the darkness became light. Her eyes flickered open to see the source of that voice.

A pair of silver-grey eyes looked down at her. 'Hello, sweetheart.'

Marietta stared at him. For a moment she couldn't think where she was. Her head ached. Closing her eyes, she tried to remember what had happened to her, and then it all came flooding back. 'I took a tumble, didn't I?'

He smiled, but his anxiety for her was deeply etched into his handsome face. 'I'm afraid so. You had me worried for a while, but the doctor said you are going to be all right.'

'Well, that's a relief. I'm beginning to feel better by the second.'

'Do you remember what I said to you while your eyes were closed?'

She smiled softly, half teasing. 'Vaguely, so you had better tell me again.'

Framing her face with his hands, he gazed at her. When he spoke it was for her ears alone as Faith hovered anxiously across the room. 'I told you that I cannot live without you, that if you left me I would soon follow you. You are my life, Marietta. I love you more than life.'

'Oh,' she whispered, her tone wondrous, her heart soaring with happiness. 'Well then, I shall have to be more careful in future. But how can you love me when you have known me for such a short time?'

'If I could boast to know the wisdom of love, I would be a rich man. But love you I do. But what of you, Marietta? How do you feel?'

'I love you, too, Edmund—at least I think I do. What I know is that you inspire me with feelings that I have never felt before, feelings I could never imagine existed. If that is love then, yes, I do love you—very much.'

His eyes grew languid, sending her senses reeling, and there was a soft union of lips as their mouths clung with leisurely sweetness that held like every moment in time.

Releasing her lips, he gazed down at her. 'I do believe your fever has gone. Your kiss speaks more of passion than of pain.' Hearing a commotion outside the room, he released her. 'I think your mother has come to check on you. I'll leave you for now. We will speak later.'

The doctor had advised Marietta to remain in bed for twenty-four hours, but she was now fully conscious and feeling a good deal better, apart from a tenderness to her forehead accompanied by a headache. She was impatient to be out of bed.

Her mother had been notified of her fall and had risen from her own sickbed to pay her daughter a visit to make sure she was suffering no further ill effects from her tumble—which she was prone to doing all the time when Marietta had been a child. Once her mother was reassured and feeling somewhat recovered herself, she went to take tea with Lady Fitzroy.

As soon as her mother had disappeared Marietta threw back the covers and got out of bed, refusing to take on the figure of an invalid. This was to be their last night at Ashborne and she fully intended to go down to dinner. As her headache began to recede she began to remember the events of the afternoon, of her fall into a ditch and how she was certain it had been Lady Russell who had over-ridden her, intending to cause just such an incident. If this was indeed so, then her resentment went much deeper than she had realised.

Gingerly she touched the dressing the doctor had applied to her forehead to cover the wound. She winced at the sudden pain which shot through it, remembering he had told her it was not as bad as it looked and would soon heal. Carefully removing the dressing, she was relieved to see it was no longer bleeding. She was sure Faith would be able to arrange her hair to conceal it.

When she was ready to go downstairs, Marietta stood before the looking glass, letting her fingers smooth down the fabric of her skirts. Faith had worked wonders with her hair, arranging it off her face, yet managing to hide the wound with carefully arranged curls. Her eyes met those of her maid.

'How do I look, Faith? Will I do, do you think—or do I look terrible?'

'That you don't, Miss Marietta. You look so much better than you did when they brought you in here—and that dress becomes you perfectly.'

'Thank you, Faith. You always know how to make me feel better. Now, I think it is time for me to go down.'

Guests were gathered on the terrace and in the drawing room for an aperitif when Marietta appeared on the stairs. She paused with her hand on the banister, looking down into the hall. Edmund was crossing to the drawing room when he looked up and saw her. It was as if he had been rendered speechless as his eyes fastened on her. Slowly she made her way down the stairs, still feeling stunned after his declaration of love. When he had left her she had wondered if she had imagined it, that she was suffering some kind of delusion brought on by her tumble, but looking at him now, at the quiet adoration that warmed his eyes, she knew it was no delusion.

When she reached the bottom step Edmund took her hand. There was a twinkle in his eyes and a slow appreciative smile worked its way across his face as his eyes leisurely roamed over her body. The unspoken compliment made her blood run warm.

'You look entrancing,' he said in a quiet voice. 'I'm delighted you were able to join us—but I think you should have remained in bed a while longer.'

'I feel fine, Edmund.'

'Then come and have a drink before dinner is announced.'

Marietta was greeted with some amazement—no one had expected her to be recovered enough to make it down to dinner. Lady

Fitzroy's face brightened and she hurried towards her.

'My dear,' she said, stretching out her hand in greeting. 'I am so pleased that you feel well enough to join us for dinner. That was a terrible tumble you took. How are you feeling?'

'Better, thank you, Lady Fitzroy—just a slight headache.'

Her mother came to her, her face solemn and pensive as she took in her daughter's appearance. 'Are you sure you are up to this, Marietta? You really should have followed the doctor's orders and stayed in bed.'

'I feel perfectly all right, Mother. Please don't fuss.'

'I was of the impression that you were an experienced horsewoman, Miss Harrington,' Lady Russell said, sauntering up to them. Marietta's stomach plummeted on seeing her. Her deep-saffron-coloured taffeta skirts rustled like a gentle breeze as she swept towards her. 'Perhaps you would have been more fortunate had the terrain been more familiar to you.' The sour note in Lady Russell's voice was unmistakable. A superior smile played on her lips and her eyes settled on her with deadly coldness.

There was a silence in the room for a long

moment. And then Marietta, determined to stand up for herself against Lady Russell's unkind sniping, replied in a quiet voice, 'Yes, both the horse and the terrain were new to me, but I make no excuses. I should not have been riding so fast—although with a rider hard on my heels it was difficult to pull my horse to a halt without unseating whoever it was at that particular ditch.' She fixed Lady Russell with a direct, knowing gaze and she was rewarded by seeing her step back awkwardly, her eyes flickering over those around her.

'How very considerate of you.'

'Yes,' Marietta replied. 'Wasn't it?'

Having seen Marietta enter the room and being accosted by Francine, Edmund immediately made a beeline for her, full of concern. He had an uneasy feeling about Marietta's tumble and he had the dreadful suspicion that Francine might have had something to do with it.

Of late he had developed an aversion to Francine and he only put up with her for his aunt's sake and his close friendship to her dead husband, Andrew. There was a time when he had enjoyed her company, her low, throaty laugh and her enjoyment of life. But she lacked the things he had come to appreciate. Her eyes weren't that warm, wonderful shade of amber and her hair was not the rich colour of auburn and she did not stir in him the emotions only one woman could stir in him now. She was certainly pleasing to the eye, but she was also greedy and ambitious, and he was under no illusion that he was included in her ambition.

Approaching Marietta, he noted with some satisfaction how the flash of tension in her face vanished almost immediately when she saw him. He looked at her, his eyes intent. Her face was pale, the fragile skin below her eyes bruised with violet shadows. He still thought she should have remained in bed.

'How are you feeling now, Marietta? If you find dinner an ordeal, you must retire.'

She smiled softly. 'I'm fine, Edmund—truly. Please don't fuss.'

Holding her gaze, he scrutinised her intently, his eyes drawn to her mouth. He smiled, wondering not for the first time what went on behind her tranquil exterior and those liquid, bright amber eyes. She was truly lovely, like a delicate flower. He felt a rare peace when he looked into her eyes. A slow, lazy smile swept across his handsome face as his eyes passed over her shapely figure. He caught a glimpse of the wound where the curls parted on her forehead and felt a surge of admiration for her. She was not one to be kept down for long. The lowering sun slanting on to the terrace had turned her hair a darker shade of auburn, touching her lips to a deeper red.

'Considering what happened to you earlier, you look wonderful.'

'Everyone has been very kind and considerate, but I will not stay in bed. I took a tumble from my horse—just one of many in my life and I am sure it won't be the last.' Her voice was clear and steady, but toneless as if her mind was engaged elsewhere.

'You were riding towards the back with Francine, Marietta?' he said, watching her closely. 'Did she have anything to do with your fall by any chance?'

Marietta stared at him, considering his question carefully before answering. 'In truth, Edmund, I don't know for certain what happened. If she did, then I will not take her to task over it—and neither will you. Not here. Not now. This is your aunt's weekend. We will not spoil it.'

'As you wish, but it will not be forgotten—not by me.'

'Thank you. It is what I want.'

'You are a strange young woman,' he murmured, focusing his eyes on a wisp of hair against her cheek. Without conscious thought or awareness that his actions were being noted by more than one pair of curious, speculative eyes, he tucked it behind her ear, feeling the velvet texture of her skin against his fingers. She stood perfectly still. 'I'm enjoying your being here and getting to know you better. I wish you didn't have to leave tomorrow. I shall make a point of bringing you back very soon.' He could sense she was trying to relax, trying not to show what she was feeling, but in the charged atmosphere between them it was impossible.

'In the short time we have known each other, you know more about me than any other man I know.' She glanced at him obliquely, a slow, tantalising smile curving her lips. 'You kissed me, Edmund. That is more than I have allowed any man. You will have to be satisfied with that for the present.'

His eyelids lowered seductively as he devoured her lips with his gaze. 'Not for too long, I hope. I long to know you better, Marietta. One thing I learned from that kiss is that that you like being kissed and would not object if I were to do so again.'

'Edmund, please!' Marietta said, aghast, her face heating as she glanced at the people observing them. 'We are not alone.'

'That doesn't worry me in the slightest. Let them look their fill. Would you like me to repeat the kiss?' he asked on a quiet, teasing note, enjoying her embarrassment.

'Yes, I would,' she confessed quietly. 'Now as I asked you before, will you please stop tormenting me about my slip from propriety.'

His eyes darkened. 'You know I enjoy tormenting you. I take great delight in seeing your face go pink with embarrassment. It suits you— getting all hot under the collar.'

'You may not have noticed, but I am not wearing a collar.'

His gaze dropped to her delectable decolletage, her firm breasts peeking over the low bodice. 'I have noticed.'

She smiled. 'I know you're teasing me, but please stop it. What do you want from me, Edmund?'

He studied her, bemused by the sheer perfection of her. She was graceful and as slender as a wand, and he wanted her. More importantly, he knew, as an experienced man of the world, that she wanted him, too. Suddenly he laughed and his eyes began to gleam with a wicked light. Taking her hand, he tucked it into the crook of his arm as dinner was announced.

'I want to talk about us, but not here—not now. Now come along. Despite your tumble, I hope the fresh air has given you an appetite.' As they were entering the dining room, he lowered his head to hers. 'If I don't have the opportunity to speak to you alone, Marietta, meet me in the library when everyone has settled down to their coffee and brandies. You are to leave in the morning and there is something I would like to ask you. We will speak in private.'

Marietta glanced up at him as he pulled out her chair at the beautifully decorated table, curious as to what could be so important that he wanted to ask her. 'Yes—yes, I will.'

Chapter Seven

Marietta waited for the dinner to end in a state of helpless anticipation. What did Edmund want to say to her, what did he want? Whenever she caught his eye her thoughts became so irrational and the feelings slipping through her body made her melt inside.

When dinner was over she waited until her mother was settled with her coffee and brandy before going to the library. Edmund was there already, two glasses of wine poured and waiting. Leather-bound volumes lined the walls of the room and it was dominated by a large mahogany desk and comfortable chairs and the piano she had enjoyed playing the previous day. Above a white marble fireplace was an ornate, gilt-framed mirror and English landscapes and

exquisite miniatures adorned the walls not occupied by bookshelves.

Uncertain of why she was there after closing the door, she waited before moving further inside. Edmund looked straight at her, his
firm mouth curling slightly at the corners, his
eyes suddenly alive with interest. He was one of
those men who always managed to move with
an air of assurance, looking as if he would fit
in anywhere. Seeing her hesitate, he crossed
the room and took her hand, drawing her further inside.

'Come and sit down—and don't look so worried. Here,' he said, handing her a glass of wine
and sitting across from her.

Marietta took a sip of wine and placed the
glass on a table beside her. 'I'm curious, Edmund. What is it you want to talk to me about?'

'Tell me. What do you think of Ashborne?'

'Think of it? Why—I told you—I think it's
quite splendid.'

'Could you live here?'

'Of course—but then, who could not.'

'Could you live here—with me?'

His face was calm, determined, Marietta
thought. The tension in his face did not make

it easy to read. Why was he asking her this? She had to know what was behind the words.

'Edmund, what are you saying?' She continued to watch his face closely. It did not flinch.

Getting to his feet, he went to her and, taking her hand, raised her to her feet once more. 'Earlier, when I told you that I love you, I meant every word. Never doubt that.'

Marietta's cheeks burned and her heart began to throb in deep, aching beats. The reminder of his kiss, his touch, the words he had said to her, were branded on her memory with a clarity that set her body aflame. She raised her eyes to his, seeing them darken and his expression gentle. 'Yes—I remember—but I had just suffered a bump to my head and I did wonder if you had said them in the heat of the moment.'

'Not a bit of it,' he said, slipping an arm about her waist, bringing her full against his hardened frame. 'And you, my love, are blushing.'

'Any female would blush when you say the things you do and look at them like that.'

With his lips close to her cheek his voice was husky and warm, his eyes devouring her with a ravenous hunger. 'I want you, Marietta. It is my dearest wish to make you mine. I am asking you to marry me. I want you to be my wife.'

Tilting her head, she stared at him in shocked amazement. 'Wife? You want to marry me?'

He nodded. 'Absolutely. I have never been so certain of anything in my life. I do love you.'

Marietta's heart soared. 'And I you, Edmund—as I have already told you,' she whispered, unable to believe this was happening.

She watched him as he smiled at her, surprised, trying to untangle her thoughts. She acknowledged that she wanted him—that if the strange new feelings and emotions he aroused in her were indeed love, then, yes, she did love him and she would be happy to be his wife. But she was reminded, as she found herself drawn into those introspective, secret eyes—eyes that could bewitch any woman—that there was still so much about him she did not know. She did not know the inner man, the core of him, to touch the passion in him. This was what she wanted.

'You must forgive me if I appear surprised,' she murmured. 'I—I did not expect this. It is all so sudden.'

'I have never felt like this about a woman before. You are a beautiful and very desirable, intelligent young woman, Marietta—a special kind of woman.'

'Special? There is nothing special about me. I am just an ordinary woman—just plain, ordinary Marietta Harrington.'

'There is nothing ordinary about you. You are special and I hold you in the highest regard. You, Marietta Harrington, are so much at variance and a complete contradiction in terms of appearance. Not only are you beautiful, but you also have a frail vulnerability—yet beneath it all there is a strong, wilful determination which belies your outward appearance. I admire you greatly. I admire your forthright character and strength of mind. If you had been born a man, without the restrictions imposed on your sex, I believe you would achieve anything you so desired.'

Marietta was filled with astonishment—he never failed to surprise her. She stared at him, her eyes wide in her flushed face, more than a little shocked by what he had said. 'You—you jest,' she murmured.

'I am not jesting. I never jest about serious matters. Whenever we meet, you always succeed in making our encounter unforgettable. No woman has ever done that. So what do you say? Will you be my wife?'

Marietta took a deep breath. Could she gamble on being able to reach into the inner core of this man? Was her will strong enough for her to continue loving him, to make him continue to love her so that he would never look back and have cause to regret this moment? He was offering her something she had been looking for all her life. She had to trust that it would.

'Yes,' she said softly. 'Yes, I'll marry you. I'll be very happy to marry you.'

'Thank you. We have an agreement.'

'Yes—if that is what you want to call it. But there is one thing I would like you to make clear.'

'And that is?'

'You and Lady Russell, Edmund? Have you been lovers?' A kind of coldness engulfed her and she was beginning to regret asking the question. She had a premonition that the knowledge she sought might turn out to be more than she wanted to know. Suddenly his expression changed. There was no mockery in his voice—the tone was softer. He peered into her face.

'I see you are not having an easy time of it where Francine is concerned. I'm glad you've asked as it's clearly troubling you.'

Marietta was reassured by the way he was looking at her. His expression betrayed a concern she had not expected, and she was glad he wasn't about to shrug it off. He answered seriously.

'The answer to your question is no, Marietta. No, we are not and never have been lovers—although I am not unaware that Francine would have it otherwise.'

Marietta smiled thinly. 'I imagine she would. She reminds me of a glacier sliding down a mountain.'

'She does? How?'

'Slow but implacable in her determination to have you. There's no stopping her.'

'She will have to. I first met her when she was just weeks away from marrying Andrew. She was beautiful then, lively and amusing... No, wait, Marietta,' he said when she opened her mouth to make some remark. 'I am not saying this to hurt you, but to try to make you see how it was. Andrew and I spent a good deal of time together. Francine became a friend—and then when Andrew died she came to rely on me—and Aunt Dorothy to some extent. She became a frequent visitor to Ashborne. Her husband was my friend—my closest friend. That was what Andrew was to me—my only friend. I was devastated by his death. It was sudden—

a fall from his horse—a bleed on the brain, the doctor said. One has acquaintances and such like, but true friends are hard to come by.'

'Yes, I can understand that.'

'As a child, I had a difficult time. My father was a difficult man—there were issues I would rather not go into now. What I will say is that when my uncle found me and brought me to Ashborne, I was in a dark place. Between them my uncle and Aunt Dorothy and Andrew brought me out of it and restored my faith in human nature. I owe them all a debt I could never repay—especially my uncle—not while he was alive. There wasn't time.'

Marietta listened, wondering what his childhood had been like. Where had he lived if not at Ashborne? What had happened to his father? She understood the depth of the despair that must have settled on him when his friend had been killed. Edmund would have been less than human if he did not still grieve for his loss and the obligation he still felt toward his widow. Edmund seemed to know her thoughts. He nodded towards her as if affirming them.

'Andrew and I were of an age. We went to Cambridge together—we were never apart. The fact is that we were close. Now let us talk of something else. I did not ask you in here to talk about my neighbours.'

'Then what?'

Standing up, he reached out and took her hand, raising her to her feet and drawing her into his arms. He smiled crookedly, his eyes lingering on her lips, parted and moist and vulnerable. 'This,' he murmured. 'Now it is agreed that you will be my wife, I would like to seal the promise with a kiss.'

The first moment of their embrace felt to Marietta like a return from a long journey—and yet she had waited only since the previous night. She was amazed how familiar Edmund had become to her, how she was already totally absorbed with him. She did not know him well, only what her heart and her senses told her of him and they were never wrong. But so much remained unspoken between them. She abandoned herself to the feel and the touch and the excitement of him.

He kissed her then. She didn't resist. Everything else about her receded, leaving her open only to the present moment. Hot and cold waves swept over her as she closed her eyes and swayed in his arms, feeling the hard strength of his body pressed to hers. Once again she felt that melting sensation low down inside her as his mouth made sensuous movements on hers. The fact that she was in danger of falling under his spell once more did occur to her, but she wasn't thinking rationally and she wanted more of what he had made her feel when he had kissed her in the garden yesterday.

His kiss was devastating, firm and demanding, stealing away any measure of resistance she had left. Her arms crept over his chest and of their own volition her fingers curved around his neck, sliding into the soft, thick hair at his nape, feeling a pleasure and an astonished joy that was almost past bearing. She pressed herself against him, answering his passion with the same wild, exquisitely provocative ardour that had haunted her dreams since she had first met him. The arms around her tightened, moulding her body to his. She clung to him as ivy clings to a tree and the strength in that hard, lean body gave her strength, gave promise of more pleasure.

Feeling his hands stealing up her back to the warmth at the back of her neck, his fingers firm, strong, yet caressing in a way that sent her senses reeling, Marietta trembled with a desire so great she thought she would die of it.

He filled her body with a liquid fire that melted the core of her heart, raising a hunger she had tried to deny for so long, and she yearned with a craving she had never known before for this strange and new feeling she believed was love.

When at last he withdrew from her lips, he raised his head and looked down at her face. Marietta lowered her head in confusion, a delicate pink flush on her cheeks. She felt so very vulnerable, completely at his mercy, as if she hovered on the brink of something quite extraordinary—and the excitement of the unknown, the expectancy of it, almost overwhelmed her.

As if Edmund divined her thought, with one arm still about her he placed the fingers of his other hand gently beneath her chin and turned her face up to his. His thoughtful gaze caressed her face, searching and probing the depths of her eyes.

'Never, in all my life, have I seen eyes such as these—as lovely as these—nor have there been lips as tempting since Eve's in the Garden of Eden. You want me as I want you. I can see confirmation in your eyes—I felt it in your response to my kiss. Your lips do not lie.'

They stood looking at each other, as if the

whole world had paused in its turning to contain this special moment. Edmund spoke with so much conviction that Marietta was unable to do anything other than stare at him in wondering awe, unable to believe what had just happened between them. But what he said was true.

Despite her determination always to remain her own person, to be in control of her emotions and feelings, Edmund's kiss had been her undoing. The way her body had quickly and wantonly responded to his lips, greedily craving more, told her that, where he was concerned, she did not have the power or the will to control them. What had just happened had flung open a door between them, allowing sunlight to flood in, revealing their true feelings for each other and covering Marietta in its luminous glow, so that Edmund was almost blinded by it.

'Thank you for agreeing to be my wife.'

She smiled. 'Thank you for asking me. But can we keep this to ourselves for the time being?'

'I agree. This is between us—of course I will have to seek your father's consent. Will there be any objections to my suit, do you think?'

'I cannot say. My father holds you in the highest regard—and in ordinary circumstances he would deem it a great honour to give his consent to a match between us—but he is determined that I shall marry a title—and that you don't have. I have told you that he considers me some kind of property to be bartered at will. He has always made decisions about my future without even pausing to consider my opinion. I have yet to discover if he has been successful in finding me a husband in the north.'

'I will go up to London and speak with your father within the next two weeks.'

'And if he has found someone else for me to marry?'

'He will have to cancel it. You are going to marry me, Marietta. No one else.'

They had just stepped out of the library when Marietta saw Lady Russell walking towards them. In a shimmering gown of saffron taffeta with a darker trim, her dark hair pinned and curled high on her head, she really was quite stunning. Like everyone else, Marietta had found it difficult to keep her eyes off her during dinner.

When Edmund saw her he stiffened. His face was blank, all emotion withheld by an iron control.

Pinning a brilliant smile on her face, Lady

Russell hurried towards them. 'Why, Edmund, I did not think I would have to come looking for you. You cannot have forgotten that you promised to partner me at whist. Our opponents are impatient to begin.'

'Francine! I apologise. No, I did not forget. I had a matter of considerable importance to take care of.'

Lady Russell gave Marietta no more than a brief glance—as if she were of no consequence—before settling her gaze once more on Edmund. 'Yes, so I see.' Immediately her attention was drawn back to Marietta. 'I am sure Miss Harrington won't mind if I steal you away.'

'Of course not,' Marietta said. 'I apologise for keeping Edmund for so long.'

'Really?' Lady Russell smiled as her insolent gaze passed over Marietta.

'Edmund and I were—'

'Stop it, Marietta,' Edmund was quick to retort. 'There is absolutely no need to explain to Francine.'

'Well, since I have just observed the two of you coming out of the library together, I can only assume that Edmund has been entertaining you there. I am sure it is none of my business, but had any of your other guests come upon you as I did then it would have given rise to gossip.'

As the three of them began to walk towards the terrace where most of the guests were gathered, Marietta took exception to Lady Marietta's tone, lightly contemptuous and at the same time more than a little suspicious, which made her hackles rise.

'You're right, Francine, it is none of your affair,' Edmund admonished. 'Now you have found me I will join you in a few minutes. Aunt Dorothy is beckoning me. I'll see what she has to say and then I'll be with you.'

He moved away to speak to his aunt, but it meant leaving Marietta alone with Francine.

'Well,' Lady Russell murmured, 'when I saw you coming out of the library I thought you looked like the cat that got the cream.'

Absently Marietta noted that rubies like droplets of blood dripped from Lady Russell's ears and neck. Marietta's flesh turned to ice when she met her stare. This woman was vain and supercilious, although, Marietta thought, anyone as beautiful as she was could afford to be. 'Edmund and I had a matter to discuss,' Marietta said coldly. 'Make of it what you will, Lady Russell, but it is not your concern. I apologise if I have kept him from you, but I think his game of whist with you must have slipped his mind. Now if you will excuse me, I will go and find my mother.' Unfortunately Lady Russell wasn't done with her just yet.

'Let me be understood, Miss Harrington. Whatever it is you aspire to where Edmund is concerned is presumptuous and can never happen. I thought I had made my position plain when you arrived here. I am resolved in my determination and will not be dissuaded from it.'

'Goodness!' Marietta exclaimed. 'If that is indeed the case, then you need have no worries, for if he does indeed belong to you, then he is hardly likely to make overtures to me.'

'Why did you come here?'

'I was invited,' Marietta reminded her.'

'Yes, but you suddenly walk in to what I've been building since Andrew died and try to take it from me. And I am supposed to disappear, I suppose.'

'You are mistaken, Lady Russell. I have not tried to take anything from you. How could I when the subject of the matter isn't yours to take.'

'You are very frank, Miss Harrington.'

'It is my nature to be so. And what was all

that about earlier today when you purposely over-rode me, causing me to part company with my horse? Were you deliberately trying to cause me injury by some chance? Or was it merely an impulse acted upon?' Marietta thought the very notion quite absurd, so she was surprised by Lady Russell's reply.

'Injure you?' The bitterness of Lady Russell's tone was a recognition of her feelings. 'I wouldn't be human if I hadn't thought of it. But the deed when it comes down to it is more difficult than the wish.'

'So you did. You admit it?'

Their tones were quiet and controlled as if what they spoke of was not outrageous in its content.

Lady Russell smiled coldly, her eyes hard. 'As for that, you'll never know, will you? So there you have it. Your father is to arrange another marriage for you, I believe—which is what your mother told me and others who cared to listen—although it will be hard to compete with the one you have already rejected or to silence the scandal mongers, who have done your reputation no good at all. It is indeed fortunate that your father is a man of great wealth— although rather shaming for you that you have a monetary value. It will cost him more than a shilling or two for the privilege of securing a title for his only offspring.'

'How dare you say that to me,' Marietta said, her eyes shining with tears of humiliation and wrath. The shock of Lady Russell's outburst remained and left an uneasy taste on her tongue. She could argue that Gabriel's actions on the day had left her with no choice but to abandon the wedding, but she felt the shame of it and, for the first time since that fateful day, she realised the extent of it.

'I dare because it's the truth.'

That was the moment Edmund returned to them. Overhearing Francine's callous, cruel words, slowly and with purposeful menace he allowed his hard eyes to fasten on Francine's maliciously smiling face. The coldness of that appraisal chilled Marietta.

'I think you have said quite enough, Francine.'

Lady Russell's eyes shot to his, a heated flush rising to her cheeks on being caught out. 'I—I only meant...'

'I know perfectly well what you meant. No one could blame Marietta for rejecting my cousin—a known reprobate and a gambler like his father. As for her reputation being sullied by it—that is nonsense. Yes, there were those who tried to blacken her name—rumours spread by poisonous tongues with nothing better to do— but I will not listen to it here in my home by anyone who has no compunction to using it as a weapon to sully her reputation further.'

Lady Russell opened her mouth as if to say something further, then it closed like a trap, sealing her words within, her face flushed with temper. Marietta smiled inwardly and her feelings for Edmund swelled that he should come to her defence so quickly, while Lady Russell looked as if she had been slapped and whatever it was she saw in Edmund's metallic eyes made her leave without further comment.

Marietta tossed in restless frustration as she tried to get to sleep. A cold breeze was blowing in through an open window, billowing the curtains, carrying the cool current of air to the bed. She considered getting up to close it, if she could stir herself from the comfortable bed. Stifling a yawn, she threw back the covers and tottered to the window, pulling it shut.

She was just about to scramble back into bed, hoping to settle her mind into the haven of sleep, when there was a light tapping on her door. Wrapping her robe about her, she went to open it, more than surprised to see Edmund standing there. He had removed his jacket and his white shirt accentuated the muscular trimness of his shoulders and tapering waist, leaving him looking extremely virile for this time of night.

'Edmund?'

'I hope I didn't wake you. I have something for you. Can I come in?'

'I—I...' She stared at him, lost for words, for what he asked was most inappropriate, but the lopsided way he was grinning at her was lethal and went some way to stripping away her resolve. If she had already been his wife, she would have opened the door wide for him to enter. She laughed a little nervously. 'You startled me.'

'Did I?' His white teeth flashed briefly in a wayward grin. 'That wasn't my intention,' he said, striding past her, not to be deterred.

Marietta peered out on to the landing to make sure no one had seen him enter her room, before shutting the door.

He tilted his head and contemplated her. 'You weren't asleep, were you, Marietta?'

She shook her head, unable to believe he was in her room, standing close to her. 'No. I couldn't sleep.' The hand she raised to draw her robe tighter about her trembled slightly—his presence never failed to evoke within her an inexplicable excitement to some degree. If she had any sense she would ask him to leave—this unexpected visit was telling her that Edmund Fitzroy wasn't the honourable gentleman he appeared on the surface. 'I hope no one saw you coming to my room.'

'Everyone has gone to bed. I have something I want to give you. Everyone will be leaving together in the morning and I may not have the opportunity to get you to myself.' Removing a small velvet box from his trouser pocket, he opened it and produced a diamond and sapphire ring. 'This was my mother's ring, Marietta. I would like you to have it. Call it a betrothal ring—a true statement of my love. You may hide it until after I have spoken to your father if you wish.'

Marietta gazed at it in his fingers, unable to believe he was doing this. She did not doubt his sincerity in the heated atmosphere of the bedroom. 'It—it's beautiful, Edmund. But I—I never expected—I never thought…'

He laughed. 'No, I don't believe you did. Would you like to wear it?'

She nodded without taking her eyes off the sparkling ring. Lifting her hand, he placed it on her ring finger, satisfied to see that it was a perfect fit.

'I hope you like it.'

'How could I not?' she breathed, holding her hand out in front of her to admire it all the more. 'But until you have spoken to my father I will keep it in its box. My mother has eyes like a hawk and would be sure to question me about it.'

'As you wish.'

Reluctant to remove it just then, Marietta clasped her fingers. 'But I think I will wear it for tonight.'

'Good. Now that's settled, I think a kiss is in order to seal the deal. Are you in agreement?'

'Yes, of course,' she replied.

Taking her hands and drawing her into his arms, he lowered his head to hers. His mouth was warm and firm against hers. He kissed her deftly, tenderly, gauging her response intuitively, before deepening the kiss, demanding more of a response. Marietta gasped, totally innocent of the sort of warmth, the passion he was skilfully arousing in her, that poured through her veins with a shattering explosion of delight.

It was a kiss like nothing she could have imagined, a kiss of exquisite restraint, and unable to think of anything but the exciting urgency of his mouth and the warmth of his breath, she felt herself falling slowly into a dizzying abyss of sensuality. His hands glided restlessly, possessively, up and down her spine and the nape of her neck, pressing her tightly to his hardened body.

Trailing her hands up the muscles of his chest and shoulders and sliding her fingers into the crisp hair at his nape, with a quiet moan of helpless surrender she clung to him, devastated by what he was doing to her, by the raw hunger of his passion. Inside her an emotion she had never experienced before began to sweetly unfold before vibrantly bursting with a fierceness that made her tremble.

Edmund's mouth left her lips and shifted across her cheek to her ear, his tongue flicking and exploring each sensitive crevice, then trailing back to her lips and claiming them once more. His kiss became more demanding, ardent, persuasive, a slow, erotic seduction, tender, wanting, his tongue sliding across her lips, urging them to part. Temporarily relinquishing her mouth, he raised his head slightly.

'Kiss me, Marietta,' he demanded thickly.

And Marietta, lost in a wild and beautiful madness and with blood beating in her throat and temples that wiped out all reason and will, did. When she moaned softly beneath the sensual onslaught and opened her mouth and kissed him deeply and as erotically as he was kissing her, he groaned with pleasure, the sweetness of her response causing desire to explode inside him.

Between his kisses he paused to murmur passionate endearments and Marietta closed her eyes and melted against him, allowing herself to be carried away on this overwhelming wave of passion, experiencing a joy which temporarily effaced everything.

Edmund caressed her, sliding his long, determined fingers, as light as thistledown, down her spine and over the gentle curve of her buttocks. They seemed to burn her flesh beneath the silken fabric of her robe, the sensation causing a spark to flicker and flare within her, racing through her veins like liquid fire, filling her with a craving for love like she had never experienced before or known could possibly exist.

When he finally relinquished his hold on her, she knew that kiss had been too urgent to be contained for long and she was shocked to find herself wanting to move on to the next stage. Her mind shied away from delving too deeply into the exact nature of why she would want this—she had little faith in trying to judge her own emotions.

She had always responded warmly to his closeness and she certainly wasn't indifferent to him. He desired her, this she knew, and he had said he loved her. No one had ever said that to her before. He cared enough about her to want to marry her and it seemed silly to pretend she hated the idea of marrying him, considering how she felt about him.

She looked at his lips and then into his eyes and any panic that was left smoothed away. They were smiling. With those eyes watching over her she would never feel afraid and insecure again, not until the very end and that was a long time away.

Forcing her senses back to some kind of normality, Marietta gazed up at him from beneath the thick fringe of her lashes. Edmund looked down into her dark, velvety eyes, large with love and desire, and she was offering no resistance, just a calm contentment of acceptance.

'So—I was right in my suspicions, Marietta.'

'Why—what do you mean?'

'Beneath the cool exterior you present to the world, you are like a smouldering volcano.' He smiled, his eyes warmly devouring her upturned face. 'I cannot wait to witness the eruption.'

'I'm afraid you'll have to,' she whispered, pulling back slightly within the intimate circle of his arms, seeing the tenderness filling his eyes. But unable to resist his closeness, she melted against him once more. The pleasure that took hold of her was too wonderful to be denied. Sliding her hand inside the opening in his shirt she ran her fingers over his flesh to trace his broad chest and the ridges of hard muscles. She revelled in the feel of him, and of the touch of his hand when his own fingers caressed her. She moulded herself into him and allowed no threatening thought to interfere. But then, on a return to sanity, she pulled back a little and gazed up at him.

'What is it?' he murmured, his lips caressing her cheek. 'Why stop now?'

'I don't understand any of this,' she murmured breathlessly. 'I don't know what is happening to me. I've never felt like this before.'

'It's quite simple really. I want you—and I believe you want me,' he said in a tone of tender finality. He took her chin between his thumb and forefinger and lifted it, forcing her to meet his steady gaze as he quietly added, 'You have no idea how much I want you—and you are going to marry me. I am determined. But you are right. This has to stop,' he said, holding her away from him. 'I have no wish to tempt you beyond your power to resist.'

With a final kiss on her lips he turned and walked towards the door. Marietta's eyes followed him, already feeling bereft of his presence. He couldn't go. She didn't want him to leave her, not now, not when she wanted him so. She wanted to feel and savour what she had felt just moments ago—and more. Tomorrow she would leave Ashborne and her life would go back to the way it had been before. She wanted so badly for tonight to be different. She wanted to taste life and love to the full.

Suddenly the full impact of what she was thinking hit her. Panic engulfed her, but she managed to cling to her composure with strength and fortitude as if it were a shield with which she could protect herself—as she had when she had been a child and her naked body had been an alien thing to her, when she had been made to cover herself, being told repeatedly that it was a sin to look on her own nakedness.

The young Marietta Harrington would have been shocked at what she was contemplating to do with Edmund. With her face flushed with embarrassment she would have lowered her eyes and turned away. The older Marietta Harrington did none of these things. She could not let what had been done to her then influence what happened to her now.

Could she reach out to Edmund—for him to show her how it could be? And could she live with the knowledge of what she had done afterwards? She stood and watched him walk to the door in an agony of uncertainty. She might feel the pain anyway, but she wanted to feel the passion first. She knew how she should behave, but she was so sick of being proper and subservient to her father, to obey his every wish whether she agreed with it or not.

'Edmund, wait.' He paused in his stride, but did not turn. 'Please—don't go. I—I don't want you to. There is something I want to ask you,' she said, trying to keep the nervousness out of her voice. When the words left her mouth she wondered where they came from. She had spoken without thinking. But she had no doubts. She wanted him more than she had ever wanted anything in her life. *Let him love me—just this once*, and she'd never ask for anything again.

'What is it?'

She took a deep breath. 'I—I've told you how it was for me when I was a child—and later—of how strict my parents were—still are—and how I don't measure up to the image of what they would like me to be—obedient and silent and subject to their every wish. I was always alone and there were few opportunities when I could laugh and behave like other children.'

He turned and looked at her. 'Marietta, why are you telling me this?'

Her heartbeat quickened to a frantic rhythm and she swallowed twice and gathered all her courage. 'I want a little of what I missed. I don't want you to go. Make love to me,' she whispered. 'Please.'

Edmund looked startled. Clearly he had not expected that. 'Marietta...' he started to say.

'Please, Edmund. It is what I want.'

Chapter Eight

'Do you realise what you're asking for?'

'Yes,' she whispered, meeting his intense gaze. He was looking at her, bathed in the light of the lamp. She stood motionless, her eyes dark and with a hint of wariness and with the innocence and vulnerability of a young deer—which was exactly what she was—innocent. 'Please, Edmund. Don't refuse me.'

'You are sure, Marietta?'

'I think I am perfectly capable of deciding what I want—and that's you. But—if you don't want to… If you don't want me…'

Those were the words, spoken with an aching caress, that were Edmund's undoing. 'Want you?' He immediately went to her and pulled her into his arms. 'Of course I want you. I want to refuse what you ask of me, but I want you more than anything in my life. My desire for you is eating away at me. But if I stay you may hate me in the morning.'

She smiled and tilted her head back to capture his eyes. 'No, I won't,' she murmured. 'I will love you all the more.'

Edmund looked down at her, his expression grave, thoughtful and with a depth of understanding for the enormous step she had chosen to take. The silver-grey eyes abruptly darkened with a new tangible hunger as his gaze ran a slow, thorough path over her slender body. His eyes flooded with desire and he seemed to shrug away his reasons for leaving her.

'So, you want to pre-empt our nuptials. And if so, what of your father?'

Swallowing hard, she nodded. She saw the purposeful gleam in those heavy-lidded eyes and drew a swift breath. She had said she would marry him, but had she given in too quickly? No, she told herself. This was what she wanted. 'Why should I concern myself with what my father would think or say? This is my decision, no one else's, and he need never know. Of course he would be incensed if he were to find out, but you have asked me to be your wife—you have also given me a ring, so where is the harm in it? And don't worry. I'm not so easily shocked. I won't scream and make a fuss.'

'Well then,' he said, his hands encircling her waist with practiced experience, 'what more is there to be said?'

Taking her face in his hands, he kissed her gently. Sliding his hands inside her robe, he smiled when the sweet shock of his touch made her gasp. Untying the belt, he slipped it from her shoulders, casting it on the floor. Her night-dress was quick to follow. Stepping out of it, she kicked it away. She felt a fleeting anxiety, embarrassed that he should see her without her clothes, but remembering that this was what she wanted, what she had asked for, she stood before him, unashamed of her nakedness, her hair tumbling about her shoulders, her shyness and embarrassment drifting away.

Edmund didn't touch her at once. 'You are exquisite—so beautiful I cannot believe what I am seeing,' he breathed.

Relief washed over Marietta. He wasn't disappointed as he looked at her, his eyes told her. His fingers lightly caressed her shoulder, trailing around her neck. A slow, aching warmth began spreading through her and she felt as if she was melting beneath that magic touch.

Bending his head, he pressed a kiss to her breast. She gave a startled cry at the quivering sensations that shivered through her. Raising his head, he drew her closer.

As he brushed his lips along her shoulder, down her arm, her throat, her breast, she arched against him as he teased her nipples with his tongue. He ran his hand slowly up the length of her back and pulled her hard against him, finding her lips. Something carnal stirred within her, something she had never felt before and could never have imagined. A flicker, a leaping, a reaching out. When he kissed her and tightened his hold on her, she relaxed against him with the familiarity of the most successful courtesan, little realising the devastating effect her naked body was having on him.

Releasing her, he went to the bed and drew the covers down to the bottom. Returning to her, he lifted her in his arms and placed her in the middle before sitting on the edge and removing his shoes, then stood up, his clothes soon following. Marietta watched him, unable to look away as his magnificent male body was revealed in all its splendour.

He moved to lie beside her, drawing her to him and relaxing against the soft pillows, the full length of their bodies touching in the most intimate of ways. He kissed her mouth, then proceeded to kiss his way down her body, slowly, deliberately, gently biting and caressing. She moaned and stretched and he laughed softly, nibbling her belly. He felt her twine her legs around his and shudder against him.

'Dear Lord! How I love you. I am in thrall to your beauty, Marietta. You are so achingly lovely in every way, flawless,' he murmured, maddened with desire as he caressed her tapered waist, the curve of her breasts and the generous flare of her hips, the softness of her thighs, losing himself in her then, in the sweet softness of her.

Marietta took his lips once more. He was irresistible. His body was a powerful magnet drawing her to him. His lips were warm and firm, his kiss long and deep. He was taking his time and savouring the moment. She was so starved of love that her lips yielded beneath his gladly. She shivered, but it was not from the cold. Suddenly she was warm—far too warm. Something was happening to her. It was as if a spark had been lit that could not be extinguished. A need was rising inside her—a need to be even closer to this man, to wallow in the desire that had suddenly taken hold of her, to saturate herself in this newfound passion.

Carried away by desire, she lay beside him. She reached for him, twining her legs around his. He was so different from her—earthy, vital and strong, all rippling sinews. His mouth, hard and demanding, tasting of brandy, was on hers, kissing her lips, her shoulder, her ears and her neck.

'You are wanton, Marietta,' he murmured, 'and how perfect you are. Thank you for not shutting me out.'

'You're welcome,' she whispered against his lips in the warmest tone. Her body was burning and she wanted more of him. He cupped her breast before his hand slid between her thighs. Never having been touched and fondled by a man like this before, shocked by the intimacy of it, she thought she ought to put his hand away, to tell him to stop, but she could not. The feel of his hands on her naked flesh almost melted her bones. He crushed her to him again and again and her mind reeled from the intoxication of his passionate kiss.

It was when her thigh brushed the scorching heat of his manhood that she was suddenly made aware of her innocence. Suddenly primeval fear mixed with the awesome pleasure and excitement of what was to happen to her. He covered her with his body, growing more purposeful, his hungering lips insistent. With his mouth against her flesh his tongue teased the soft peak of her breast while his spreading hand caressed the soft flesh of her inner thigh that began to tingle and to glow.

Her fear was gone. Incapable of reason, she felt her body respond as if she were another person. And though her mind told her this was wrong, her female body told her mind to go to the devil—for this was what she wanted. There was nothing she could do but let go of herself— but what was happening to her? What was he doing to her? Every fibre of her body came alive. A shuddering excitement swept through her and the strength ebbed from her limbs as his lips travelled down once more over her flat belly, hips and thighs. And then he was on top of her and she pulled his face down to hers.

She strained against him. They were entwined and a burning pain exploded in her loins, and as they had linked their fingers together in the garden, so their bodies were linked as one. Joined with him in the most intimate way imaginable, crushed beneath his strength, Marietta became aware of a sense of fullness as he plunged deep within her and she was moving with him. With lips and bodies merged in a fiery fusion, she gasped. His hungering mouth searched her lips and he kissed her with a slow thoroughness, savouring each moment of pleasure before beginning to move. And then she felt something new and incredible, and it all seemed so effortless as she began to respond to his inner heat.

Never would she have believed that she could feel such pleasure, nor that she could respond so brazenly as she yielded, giving all her desire and passion, as if an ancient, primitive force were controlling her, driving her on. Then his control shattered and as though he were seeking a much-needed release for his mind and body he claimed her fully, filling her with an urgent desire until he collapsed completely, his shuddering release over. Her arms went round him and she held his hard body, overwhelmed by lust and love and glistening with sweat, to her.

'I love you, Edmund,' she whispered against his ear. 'I love you so much.'

'No regrets?'

'No,' she breathed. 'No regrets, no shame,

just an overpowering joy and I want nothing more than to be with you for the rest of my life.'

She was aware of nothing but an immense, incredible joy beyond which nothing was comparable. Sated and deliciously exhausted, her body and lips tender from his caresses, she nestled against her lover's warm, hard body, closed her eyes and slept.

How long she had slept she didn't know. She opened her eyes to an enormous feeling of contentment, her body rosy and drugged with love. Her eyes were warm with the unfocused stare of a woman who has been utterly fulfilled, brought about when Edmund's body had entered hers. She felt so alive, as if for the first time in her life.

Edmund was dressed and leaning over her. Tenderly he placed a kiss on her cheek, taking her hand and sitting on the bed facing her. She was surprised to find that while she slept he had pulled the covers over her naked form and she suddenly felt shy and embarrassed.

Noting the soft flush that mantled her cheeks, he smiled, kissing her fingers. 'What is it, Marietta? You are blushing.'

'It's hardly surprising when I remember how I have so brazenly exposed myself.'

'You needn't. I intend to see a lot more of you in the future.'

'My mother would be scandalised if she knew. When I was a child I wasn't allowed to look at my own body and certainly not to show it to anyone else.'

Edmund stared at her in disbelief. 'Did you not object to this unusual practice imposed on you?'

'No. How could I? I was a child. I thought that was normal. I was told that to see one's body was a form of sin.'

'But were you not curious about your body?'

'Yes, of course I was, but the sin weighed heavy on my mind and I was frightened of looking. Apparently it was done to keep my mind pure.'

'You poor love,' he said, taking her hand from the top of the sheet and holding it firmly clasped between his own. 'How you must have suffered. Who did this to you? Your nurse—your mother?'

'Both—as I remember. But I didn't suffer—not knowingly.' She sighed, seeing the horror clouding his eyes. Gently she touched his cheek and smiled. 'Don't look so shocked, Edmund. It wasn't so terrible. I learned to control my emotions from an early age.'

'But you shouldn't have to.'

'It's behind me. I'm happy now—very happy. I have you and your love, which is all that I want and more than I ever thought I would have.'

'Nothing like that will happen to you again— I promise you that. You will be in my protection always.'

'So, it is settled then,' she said quietly, stifling a yawn and snuggling down into the bed to go to sleep. 'We really are to be married.'

'It is settled. The two of us are heading for the altar.'

And then he left her.

As Edmund made his way back to his own room, with the scent and the feel of Marietta filling his senses, she dominated his thoughts— sadness at what she had gone through as a child and anger directed towards her parents seething inside him. It was strange that Marietta, who had followed and tried to adhere to her parents' dictates all her life, should be like himself, affected by a hard past she'd had no control over. But he was sorry, sorry to the very core of him, for Marietta. How many more indignities had been heaped on her when she had been a child? Thinking of her parting words, he wondered how a woman as lovely as she could have thought for a second that a man's love was more than she could ever have.

She had told him of small part of her childhood with an open honesty that put him to shame. He wanted to be as honest with her, to tell her about himself, his past, but he couldn't, not yet. The memories were still too painful, too raw to speak openly about. His uncle had taken him from a life of deprivation and brought him into a loving world where he was robustly fed and nurtured. He'd had the companionship of other boys at school, but to this day he preferred his own solace.

Thinking of Marietta, he was unprepared for the rush of remorse that washed over him when he thought of what he had done. What in God's name had he been thinking? He should have waited. How could he have been so thoughtless, so stupid. But it was done now and there was no going back. The sooner he made her his wife the better.

However, he was well satisfied with the way she had responded to their lovemaking. He could only marvel at how much Marietta had lowered her defences toward him, like a wild pony gentled to his touch only and yet hungry for more. Her body was perfectly aligned with his and he sighed, savouring once more the unfamiliar pleasure of her naked body next to his.

He had slept briefly, no longer alone, where his nightmares were relegated to the dark corners of his mind, hidden and secret. He had been content to hold her in his arms, to feel the warmth of her breath on his chest. Even now he could feel her vulnerability and it made him tremble inside to think how much she trusted him when he wasn't even sure he could trust himself.

It was time to leave Ashborne House. Guests were saying their goodbyes and climbing into carriages that would take them to their respective homes or the station for the train to London. Marietta expressed her appreciation to Lady Fitzroy, thanking her for her hospitality.

'You are more than welcome, my dear. I am so glad you came. Have you said your farewells to Edmund—he is about somewhere,' she said, scanning the groups of guests and array of horses and carriages, her eyes coming to rest on her nephew speaking with Lady Russell, his head bowed low as he listened with interest to what she was saying. 'Ah—there he is, speaking to Francine.'

'Yes,' Marietta replied drily. 'I see he is occupied at present.'

Noting the coldness of Marietta's tone, Lady Fitzroy looked at her with understanding. 'Ah, Francine.' She smiled. 'Yes, I see. I really do see. Francine can be cruel in her possessiveness. Has she warned you off Edmund?'

'She implied that I should.'

'And does that bother you?'

'No, not at all,' Marietta replied, remembering the night and Edmund's loving. If Lady Russell figured in his life at all, it was not as a future bride.

'Oh, dear, I'm sorry if she upset you. Ever since Andrew died she's concentrated all her formidable energy on making Edmund notice her—for him to see her and no one else. He has shown no inclination to love anyone else—until now,' she said with a meaningful look at Marietta, which brought a flush to her face. 'Yes, I know how things are between the two of you—Edmund has always confided in me.'

'Does Lady Russell live alone at Stanford House?'

'Yes—the title died with her husband, I'm afraid. She inherited everything. She is a social person with friends galore and lives a life of pleasure. Our neighbour, Thomas Sheridan—you have met him, I know—a dear friend of ours—would dearly like her to pay him the same attention she pays Edmund. He lives in hope that one day she will.'

Looking away from where Edmund was still speaking to Lady Russell, Marietta fixed her gaze on Lady Fitzroy. 'I remember you telling that your husband was a military man, Lady Fitzroy—that he fought in the Crimea.'

'Yes—I was so proud of him. When he died I missed him terribly—we were close.'

'What happened to the title?'

Lady Fitzroy's smiled faded and she looked away. 'Ah—now that is a subject we will save for another day. For now, you have a train to catch. I look forward to seeing you back at Ashborne House very soon—although I shall be travelling to town very soon. I don't get up there as often as I once did, but I shall be there to witness the celebrations of Queen Victoria's

Golden Jubilee. I wouldn't miss that. It will be a truly grand occasion.'

When Marietta was walking to the carriage to join her mother, who was already comfortably ensconced, Edmund waylaid her and drew her aside. He was smiling seductively, the shared secret of his proposal and the night spent in each other's arms still vibrantly alive in both their minds. He wanted to draw her into his arms. With everyone looking on, saying their farewells with a proper degree of casualness was more difficult than he had expected when he remembered the night before.

'Goodbye, Marietta,' he said softly, realising how much he would miss her. Seeing her against the backdrop of Ashborne, it was the first time he had seen her so apparently carefree and casual and he thought how much it suited her. How lovely and vibrant she looked in her violet-coloured travelling clothes, with her skin aglow and the fetching feathered hat shading her eyes. At that moment he wanted nothing else in the world but to make love to her again. 'I will see you very soon, I promise. I shall be in London within two weeks when I shall call and see your father.' His gaze caressed her face. 'Will you miss me?'

'You know I will. Will you miss me?'

'Every minute of every day. Now away you go lest you miss your train.'

More hurried goodbyes were said as they climbed into the carriage taking them to the station. When they moved off Marietta looked back and saw Edmund watching them leave. Memories of her time at Ashborne House assailed her. She burned with the memory of the short time she had spent in the garden with him and again in the library when he had asked her to be his wife—the feel of his lips on hers. But the memory of the night they had spent together stood out the most, bringing a softening to her senses. Whenever she thought of his kisses, which had been ardently and expertly given, her face crimsoned with the wanton abandon with which she had yielded, sending a warm tide of pleasure flooding through her heart.

He had awakened her to all the pleasurable sensations she had only ever dreamed of, primitive, rapturous sensations she had always associated with being in love. She felt no shame in this, for she could not escape the fact that she adored him. When she closed her eyes, she could still see in every detail his darkly handsome face, and mentally traced its outline. She would live in hope that he would journey to London to speak to her father very soon.

Edmund stood and watched the retreating carriage carrying Marietta to the station. He hadn't wanted her to go. He'd wanted to tell everyone that they were to marry, but he had refrained. He had to be content to let things unfold as their knowledge of each other grew, for what they had was too precious, too important to hasten. She was like a flower opening and unfolding and stretching towards the light.

After he'd left her bed he'd returned to his own room, but he hadn't wanted to go to sleep. He wanted the night to remain in his memory, to remember the feel of her, the scent of her. He'd told her he loved her and he'd meant it. For the first time in his life he had found a woman he could say that to.

To make the time when he would see her again pass quickly, he had thrown himself into his work, but it was Marietta he saw in his mind, Marietta who stole his thoughts away from important matters at hand. When she'd been with him he'd had difficulty keeping his eyes off her and at times he'd been unable to keep his hands off her. What was she doing in London? Had her father found her another suitor for her to wed? He could hardly contain his jealousy at the thought of any other man touching her. After almost two weeks the need to see her became paramount to all else. Without more ado he set everything aside and prepared to leave Ashborne for London.

Unfortunately it was not to be. The morning of his departure brought a visitor to Ashborne. He had a letter from Switzerland that needed Edmund's immediate attention. Within the hour he had written two letters, one to Marietta and one to her father, leaving them with his steward to post them, before heading for Switzerland to be with his dying father.

He would have been outraged if he knew how his letters had fallen into the wrong hands. Lady Russell called on Lady Fitzroy and, seeing the correspondence on a tray in the hall ready for posting, her eyes narrowed when she recognised Edmund's neat, sloping handwriting and saw to whom the letters were addressed, Then offered to post them and saving the steward a journey into town. Happy to take her up on her offer so he could deal with other matters at Ashborne, the steward handed them to her. With a smug smile on her face, Lady Russell left the house with every intention of reading the contents when she was alone.

On Marietta's return to London her father lost no time in informing her that he had secured a union between her and the eldest son of the Earl of Rainford—Christopher Lovat. He was five years older than Marietta and very much looking forward to meeting her.

Marietta looked at her father with a mixture of horror and anger and humiliated to the depths of her being that he should have arranged another marriage for her so soon after the last one, if at all. 'How could you do this to me? How could you offer my hand in marriage to a man I have never met? Could you not wait, Father? Do you have to cast me off in so callous a manner, as if I mean nothing at all?'

'No time like the present,' he said coldly. 'You are my daughter and I've acted within my rights.'

'And if I object?'

Her father settled his eyes on her. Angry

emotion coated him from head to toe, a determination that he would be obeyed. 'You won't. There will be no repetition of the last time. You *will* go through with it and I will stand no nonsense. The two of you will meet when the family come to town shortly for the Queen's Golden Jubilee.'

Both Marietta and her father knew such an illustrious family would not have considered the suit had the family not been in dire straits.

Awaiting Edmund's arrival at any time, Marietta made little comment after that on her father's arrangements. When Edmund came, all would be resolved. While she waited, the self-perpetuating routine in her studio absorbed her totally and effortlessly. She put her visit to Ashborne House to the back of her mind as she mixed the paint on her palette and applied it to her latest creation, but that did not stop her thinking of Edmund.

The fact that she felt completely alive when she was with him made her realise the potency of the strange elixir he exuded and she found herself savouring those moments they had been together and she couldn't deny the way her senses seemed to soar to new heights when she remembered his mere touch. Her desire to see him again increased by the day—to tell him all that was in her heart—but the opportunity for doing so did not arise. Two weeks went by and he had not come, then another two weeks passed and still there was no word from him.

She waited and hoped and struggled against helpless tears. Her mother, so taken up with another betrothal and wedding to arrange, failed to notice. A doubt crept into Marietta's mind and a small grain of fear that took root until she could think of nothing else. Determined to behave as if everything was normal, the long-drawn-out days began to be a drain on her and all she wanted to do was hide herself away in her studio and lose herself in her art. As more time went by, she was determined not to give in to her fear, telling herself that she must be patient, that she must have faith in Edmund, that something must have happened to prevent him coming and that he would come soon.

After six weeks had passed and he had made no attempt to contact her or her father, every time someone came to the house, her heart would leap with anticipation. A strange kind of panic began to inhabit her mind with all the possible reasons why he had not come. What was the problem? Was it her? After that one wonderful night together had he fallen out of love with her, wishing he had never done as she had asked? He could not have known how deeply he had insinuated himself into her heart, how much he had come to mean to her, and whose absence had become a source of grief. But as her despair grew, so did her pride and she found herself drawn further and further into her old reserve.

Three days before the Lovats were to travel down from Derbyshire and she would meet Christopher for the first time, accompanied by Faith she did some last-minute shopping. They were returning home with their packages when Marietta saw the sleek black carriage drawn by four bay horses stationary outside the Pulteney Hotel in Piccadilly. Immediately she instructed the driver to pull up behind the equipage she recognised as belonging to Edmund. There could be no mistake.

Telling Faith to wait in the carriage, with her heart beating madly she climbed out and hurried inside the prestigious hotel that played host to dignitaries visiting London. She wanted to see him. She needed to know how he could have done this cruel thing to her. How could he tell her he loved her, made such wonderful love to her and then walked away?

It was early afternoon and the hotel was quiet. She glanced through the open doors into the luxuriously appointed dining room where the candelabras glowed, burnishing the gilding throughout the room and gleaming upon the fine silver and exquisite painted china. Her eyes did a scan of the vestibule, searching among the arrangement of palm fronds and huge white lilies and neatly arranged chairs, her heart beating with hope and uncertainty.

She saw Lady Russell coming down the stairs before she saw her. Marietta froze and stared at her, beginning to realise her mistake in coming here. An awful dread clutched at her heart. It was too late for her to leave. When Lady Russell raised her head and saw her, her initial reaction was one of shock. Her mouth tightened and an icy coldness hardened her eyes. Her eyes flickered over Marietta, noting every detail of her midnight-blue gown and matching jacket.

'Why, Miss Harrington. This is a surprise. What are you doing at Pulteney's?'

'I—I recognised Edmund's carriage. I—I thought he...'

Lady Russell smiled smugly. 'What? That he is here? Well, as you said—his carriage is parked outside. Are you here alone?'

'My maid is waiting for me in the carriage.'

Lady Russell laughed. 'That's one of the advantages of being a widow. I don't have to drag a maid around with me all the time. Still, I have no intention of being a widow for much longer.'

Marietta looked at her, not having noticed when she had first seen her how flushed her cheeks were—the flush of passion and the warm light of desire in her eyes. This was no grieving widow, but a woman in the full flush of desire. An icy shiver slithered down Marietta's spine. The thought that Edmund might at that moment be in Lady Russell's bedchamber, waiting for her, was too much. But, no. She could not believe that of him.

'Is Edmund here?' she asked, trying to make the question sound casual, yet unable to keep the hesitancy from her voice.

Lady Russell smiled and let her words fall like a dead weight upon Marietta. 'He might be,' she replied flippantly.

Lady Russell's mouth curved derisively, her eyes smoky with vindictiveness. She knows why I have come here, Marietta thought, and now she was exulting in it. She fought the conflict raging within her. Wanting to get out of the hotel, she stepped away. The last thing she wanted was to come face to face with Edmund, to watch him turn those extraordinary silvergrey eyes on her and to address her with the engaging charm that he exuded in abundance.

But then something happened. What was it? Was it a look she caught in Lady Russell's eyes? Was it her own knowledge of the trust that Edmund had imbued in her from the start and his declaration that Lady Russell meant nothing to him? Pulteney's was a well-established hotel where people came together not only to stay while in London, but to conduct their business affairs. Lady Russell's sanguine expression said otherwise, but Marietta didn't believe her. Lady Russell was lying. A calm settled on her, the complete severing of all emotions, a coldness that left her in control. She managed a smile.

'I must go. Faith will be wondering where I've got to.'

'Of course. I understand.

On the point of departure Marietta turned once more and faced Lady Russell. 'How remiss of me. I quite forgot to tell you my news.'

'Oh?'

'Yes.' She forced a smile to her lips. 'I am to be married.'

Lady Russell's eyebrows rose to a lofty level with surprise. 'Really? Do I know the gentleman?'

'I really have no idea. It is Christopher Lovat—the Earl of Rainford's son. Their estate is in Derbyshire.'

Lady Russell stared at her, as if for once in her life she was lost for words. 'Lovat?' she said at length. 'Goodness! Which one? The Earl has two sons, as I recall?'

'Christopher—the eldest.'

Lady Russell laughed. 'Good Lord! Now that is a surprise. The man is seriously immature and feeble and ruled by his father—a ruthless, greedy little man if my memory serves me well.' Her smile turned sour. 'So there you are. As the daughter of such a wealthy man you will always have a value. When is the wedding to be?'

Marietta ignored the jibe, but an icy finger ran slowly down her spine, a ghostly foretaste of what was to come. 'The date has yet to be decided. Goodbye, Lady Russell.' Pulling on her gloves Marietta turned and walked away without another word—too late to see Lady Fitzroy emerge from the ladies' rest room, keeping her appointment with Francine Russell to take tea with her.

As Marietta travelled back to Berkeley Square, the calmness left her and her face flushed with fury, but it was also wet with tears. She brushed them away angrily. Tears! Tears for Edmund Fitzroy! Whatever his reason for being at the hotel, why had he not sought her out? It was inexcusable. She felt sorrow and anger for what he had done to her and guilt for having let it happen.

She had been used, rejected and discarded and left alone without explanation or comfort. Recalling her treatment of Gabriel when she had left him standing at the altar, humiliated and angry—had he felt as she did now? But of course not, he had not been in love with her— then perhaps in the light of Edmund's abandonment, she was getting her just deserts. Looking back, she realised that the past weeks had made her grow up quickly. But no one would know of her misery.

Pale faced and tired she might be from lack of sleep, but her expression was set and a proud resolve hung about her as she awaited Christopher Lovat's arrival in London. They might not have met, but she had decided she would marry him come what may. If this was to be her fate then she would accept it with a bitter coldness. She was desolate, but pride and anger would carry her on.

Edmund's reasons for not calling on Marietta's father as promised were of a nature that Marietta could not have imagined. On reaching the clinic in Switzerland where his father had been a patient for the past eighteen years, he was just in time to see him before he died. Edmund looked down at the man who was a mere shell of his former self and for the first time in many years, he felt at peace with himself, not restless, not tossed about with memories and feeling as if he were bleeding inside from a wound that never healed. At last he could let his father go. He'd found love and happiness with a remarkable woman. His father belonged to the past.

With the funeral behind him, seated on the train taking him back to England, he reached for his drink and sipped it absently, his thoughts on home and Marietta. He stared at the passing scenery and listened to the noise of the train as it sped along on the rails. His thoughts turned to that magical weekend they had spent together at Ashborne, which was the beginning of a relationship that was important to them both.

She intrigued all his male sensibilities and his senses, her sharp mind stimulating his own, and she had captured his imagination with her gift for her art and her spirited opinions on everything from literature to the issues of the day, possessing a capacity to think for herself and to assess what went on around her. His hand reached again for the glass of whisky and, as he drank, he began to marshal his thoughts with the precision taught him by years of doing business with all manner of people.

He had told Marietta he loved her and he did. He could not deny that and he was certain that as time passed and they got to know each other better, the bond would strengthen. Her father was a wealthy man so he could believe that Marietta could love him, not for his money, not his power, not his flesh, but him. She was the only woman he knew he could ever imagine risking his heart for.

Suddenly he was impatient to get back to London, to Marietta. He wanted to speak to her father and hurry the marriage forward. He had finally found a woman he wanted, a woman who wanted only him. He would grasp marriage with both hands and rejoice in it.

On reaching his London house it was to find his Aunt Dorothy in residence. She lost no time in informing him of Marietta's imminent marriage to someone else. Paralysed by the revelation, he stood in the wreckage of his dream of marrying Marietta. He was seared with it, more deeply hurt than he had ever been in his life. He wanted her and he was unable to bear the intensity of the pain of losing her.

In the splendour of his home he poured himself a generous brandy and tossed the fiery liquid back, immediately pouring himself another, knowing he would get no sleep that night. With the woman he wanted more than any other, he intended getting well and truly foxed to stop himself thinking about her, to keep his mind from riveting upon the way she had looked when he had last seen her at Ashborne House.

He paced the carpet and with each footstep he swore violently under his breath. He found it incredible that, as a man who with cold logic could override his emotions whenever he wished, he should find himself in this intolerable situation.

* * *

At this time there was great excitement in London as everyone prepared to mark Queen Victoria's Golden Jubilee, the fiftieth anniversary of her accession. The Lovat family were no exception. Every hotel in London was full to bursting with people converging on the city to celebrate the event so it was fortunate that they possessed a fine mansion to the north of London.

The Countess of Rainford was tremendously excited about visiting the metropolis and the social gatherings they would attend. On arrival they came to the Harrington House in Berkeley Square to be introduced to Marietta and her mother. Thick set and with a balding pate, the Earl of Rainford did not make a favourable impression on Marietta. He was a loud irritating man and his wife, a small nervous woman, very much in his shadow. The Earl knew all about Marietta's previous failed wedding and it would have been better if it had not happened, but beggars couldn't be choosers.

'We are delighted you have agreed to marry Christopher,' the Countess said in a softly spoken voice. 'We will be delighted to welcome you into the family.'

Marietta smiled while all the time her heart was breaking. 'I aim to please.'

On meeting Christopher, she relaxed and returned his welcoming smile. He was not tall and his hair was brown and curly. His remarkably attractive face, his skin as soft as a girl's, was marred only by the hint of sulkiness about his soft, bow-shaped mouth.

'I was so happy when you agreed to meet me and that we will marry. We will be happy, Marietta, I know we will—and for the time we are in London I would like you to meet my friends. It's all so exciting.'

His father's eyes fell on him like a black cloud as he watched his son survey his fingernails in a lazy fashion and buff them against his jacket.

During the build up to the Jubilee there were many society events to attend. There was such an extraordinary outburst of enthusiasm as Marietta had never seen before and she became caught up in Christopher's excitement. Accompanied by their parents there was a succession of garden parties and receptions to attend and everyone was in no doubt that the celebrations would continue long after the day of the Jubilee.

The more Marietta and Christopher came together, a close camaraderie developed between them. Christopher was nothing but courtesy itself. More than that, he was charming and treated her with a thoughtfulness that almost undermined her control. He also made her laugh, but she sensed that something was not quite right, that he was unlike all the other young men she had met in the past. He had a tendency to babble when he became excited and an animated gleam would glitter in his eyes. He made no attempt to kiss her or take hold of her hand when backs were turned. He smiled affably enough, yet Marietta found herself mistrusting it—it was a smile that hid something and that something she felt instinctively would not be to her liking or advantage. Despite her willingness to marry him, she did not know how she felt about this unlooked-for complication. There was no one to give her advice or words of assurance—certainly not her mother.

The day of the Jubilee was warm and the sun shone. The streets were thronged with people positioned from dawn to get the best view of the Queen's open landau and all the pomp that accompanied it as it made its way from Buckingham Palace to Westminster Abbey.

On the evening of the Jubilee both families were invited to Lord and Lady Rycroft's ball at their mansion in Mayfair. It was to be Marietta's first big society event.

'The Rycroft ball, Marietta!' her mother stressed, as if trying to inspire enthusiasm in her daughter. 'Invitations to their events are as coveted as jewels. We have to go.'

Marietta presented a pleasing appearance in her tightly laced gown of deep blue taffeta, low necked at front and back and with capped sleeves. The front panel of the skirt was richly ornamented with elaborate embroidery. Faith had curled and braided her hair in an exquisite coiffure, with one fat ringlet draped over her shoulder. She looked exquisite and drew the eyes of many curious and admiring gentlemen. Even the Earl's eyes were seen to pass over his future daughter-in-law several times with a puffed-up pride.

As they arrived at Rycroft House dancing was already in progress, the dancers, both male and female, looking like brightly coloured peacocks. The house was richly decorated with gilded ceilings, polished parquet floors and crystal chandeliers. A hundred guests or more crammed into the rooms. Excited guests were all caught up in the excitement of the occasion, threading their way through the glittering crowd or lounging on couches and chairs in shadowed alcoves. A lavish buffet had been laid out in the supper room, the tables laden with every kind of delicacy imaginable. Above it all an orchestra played.

The Earl immediately excused himself and wove his way carefully through the dancers, intent on accosting one of the footmen bearing liquid refreshment. Marietta loved the bustle and brilliance, the colour, the music and the atmosphere, and the raw, pulsing energy that seemed to emanate from the dancers. With a sudden stirring of excitement and well-being she had not felt in a long time, feeling quite reckless, she smiled at Christopher and insisted he dance a lively country dance with her. It was a boisterous dance, considered bold, a dance much favoured by everyone. It was unusual in that they moved and turned in a close embrace, with Christopher's arm around her waist.

She caught a glimpse of Gabriel, standing on the side watching the dancing. This was the first time she had seen him since leaving him standing at the altar. Their eyes met across the distance that separated them, but he turned away, making no attempt to speak to her. Marietta made sure they did not come into contact with each other. What could they possibly have said to each other that wasn't full of denunciation and blame?

Taking a respite from the dancing and sipping a much-needed lemonade, her eyes were drawn to a man who had just arrived. She gazed at him with mild interest. And then she became numb, for the way he held his head and the thick dark hair brushed into obedience into his nape she recognised. It was Edmund. For a moment she doubted, but the moment was short lived. It was only a moment, a moment she spent in a daze of emotions—joy, bewilderment, hopelessness and despair.

She felt her heart leap at the sight of him. For one wild, hopeful second, she allowed herself to believe that he was there to see her, that he had sought her out at last. Then she silently scolded herself for her foolishness. He wanted nothing to do with her. Had he not made that perfectly clear by staying away from her?

Chapter Nine

Edmund stared round the room in an uncompromising fashion. He was grim faced, unsmiling as his eyes swept the occupants, lingering here and there when he saw a familiar face, moving over Marietta and then passing on. They snapped back, instantly arrested. He was not so immune to her presence and nothing had prepared him for his first sight of her after two months apart.

His heart wrenched when he looked on her unforgettable face—so poised, so provocatively lovely, so regal, glamorous and bewitching that he ached to hold her in his arms and send her present suitor packing. Shifting his gaze to her companion, cold anger stole over him as he acknowledged what he saw. Tonight he was seeing the truth of it. There was no way to avoid it and there was nothing that could douse the rage that was beginning to consume him.

Was she being forced into it by her father? Edmund despised Samuel Harrington. That man would give his daughter to a man for a title, the title not only his daughter's future security, but his own introduction into the elite society that had held him at arm's length because he wasn't one of them.

He had not expected to see Marietta here at Rycroft House. She was beautiful, even more beautiful than he remembered. She was innocence and purity, and worth far and above all the other ladies pressing around him. He inclined his head to her in deference to her beauty, but her rejection of him still burned in his heart. On hearing she was to wed Christopher Lovat he needed time to come to terms with this devastating news and to decide how he was to deal with it. He loved Marietta desperately. It was their brief time together at Ashborne House that had carried him through the past weeks. The memories paraded across his mind during every waking moment. He was not prepared to see her wed someone else.

Marietta continued to stare at Edmund. She felt as though she had been struck dead, unable to form any sort of coherent thought. She was deaf and blind to those around her, her one conscious thought being that Edmund was close. She could feel his presence with every fibre of her being and, despite the shock of seeing him again after so long, an increasing comforting warmth suffused her. A strange sensation of knowing he was close at hand pleased her.

They looked at one another from across the distance that separated them and once more, as though their minds were linked by some invisible thread, their eyes and hearts spoke to one another. Despite his rejection of her, the pain of which was immeasurable, Marietta's heart had not stopped yearning for him, hungering for him, no matter how fiercely she pushed the feelings away.

Her female body was not concerned with what went on in her mind, only the physical need to be close to this man. His face was as hard as a granite sculpture, his eyes filled with a kind of savage rage she would never have thought him capable of. She saw his entire body stiffen, saw his gaze snap to her face, his eyes turning an icy, paler grey.

Until then Marietta had thought she remembered exactly what he looked like, but she hadn't. In black and white formal attire, his waistcoat gleaming pristine white, his jacket clung to his shoulders that were broader and more muscular than she remembered. His face was one of arrogant handsomeness and she noticed the cynicism in those silver-grey eyes and the ruthless set of his jaw. Everything about him exuded power and an unshakeable confidence, and that in turn made her feel even more helpless as she searched his features for some sign of softness in this aloof, forbidding stranger.

Her heart had been filled with angry recriminations and rancour, for she had not fully understood why he had rejected her. But her flesh had not stopped wanting him, needing him, loving him. He was still every bit as handsome—the perfect gentleman. But she didn't want to feel anything for him—that part of her life was over.

She watched him cross the room to her, his face in shadow, moving with that long, easy stride she remembered so well. But her desire was not so strong that it blotted out everything else. She could sense his anger as it turned cold and the more deadly for it. She could feel it emanate from him. A muscle flexed along his jaw, the only sign of his temper.

There was a change in him, a strained look

about him, a gravity and a deepening of the lines about his mouth not created by laughter. What had happened to him in the weeks they had been apart to do that? When he stood before her, he inclined his head slightly, his indomitable male pride coming to the fore.

'Marietta. I did not expect to see you here. You look well.'

He spoke as if to a stranger. Marietta's throat constricted with pain. Shaking beneath the blast of his gaze, she tightened her hands in the folds of her skirts. She was dimly aware that this was worse, much worse than anything she had experienced in her life, but then she reminded herself that none of this was of her making. It was not her fault. He was the one who had abandoned her.

His mouth was set in a bitter line, his black brows drawn in a straight bar across his angry eyes, and she saw how resolute his expression was. The harsh light made him look judgemental. His iron-hard determination, his rigid resolution to treat her as no more than a passing acquaintance tore her to shreds, but he would not know that.

'As you see,' she replied, her expression tight. 'And you? You are well, Edmund?'

'Are you pleased to see me, Marietta? Or have you forgotten I exist? Unless that is what you want and that you forgot my existence by choice.'

Furious, Marietta shot her eyes to his. 'Choice? How could I do that? Despite what has happened in the time we have been apart, I have thought of you all the time.'

He smiled grimly. 'I will take some convincing to believe that.'

'Believe what you like. It is the truth.'

He nodded. 'You are here with Christopher Lovat, I see.'

'You know him?'

'I know his father. I have not been introduced to his son but I have seen him on occasion.'

'We are betrothed, Edmund.'

'So I've heard,' he said coldly. 'Have you forgotten so soon that you are supposed to be betrothed to me?'

'No, but things changed—when I didn't hear from you I thought perhaps you didn't care. Besides, you are aware that I am under age and you had not spoken to my father.'

'And you couldn't wait. For God's sake, Marietta, I asked you to be patient. I did not imagine you would do something so reckless as to tie yourself to someone else. I expect your father has forced you into it. Have you taken leave of your senses? I would like to be polite and say that your betrothal suits you, but your eyes tell me it does not.' His gaze slid to Christopher standing several paces away.

'And what is it to you?' Marietta retorted with calculated scorn.

'I am simply trying to understand. So you are going to do your father's bidding after all. Is he so desperate to acquire a title that he will marry you to a man who is a complete stranger to you, a man you know nothing about? And you have agreed to it after all.'

'After all what, Edmund?'

'After all that we shared at Ashborne. Do you forget so soon that night you spent in my arms? Everything we did that remains branded on my mind for all time?'

Marietta turned her face away, her cheeks burning at that shared, beautiful memory. 'I cannot do that—but it is best forgotten, Edmund. Do you think that what happened between us gives you the right to question me? It was just a short interlude in time. I was just someone you had invited to help occupy a dreary time for you and then I left.'

'If you believe that then you are a fool. And in no time at all became affianced to Christopher Lovat.'

Marietta followed his gaze, feeling suddenly cold. Christopher was conversing heatedly with a young man she had often seen in his company, who was lounging indolently against the wall. His name was Sir John Emery, a good-looking slim young man with pretty, effeminate looks. Aware of Marietta's attention, the young man shoved himself upright and, with all the swagger of his title and privilege, sketched a mocking bow.

Marietta frowned, for her feelings for this particular gentleman were not pleasant. She disliked him intensely. He gave Christopher an incriminating look that made her wonder at the nature of his feelings for her betrothed and, having seen how Christopher followed him around like a lovesick calf, she was beginning to realise just what Christopher's feelings were with regard to that young man. Hopefully it would all change when they married.

'Your betrothed exercises small regard for you, Marietta. He is friendly with young Emery, I see, a man who is devious and greedy, a man who lives only for pleasure.'

Marietta's cheeks turned poppy-red and she looked away, deeply embarrassed. "You are impertinent, Edmund. Please don't speak of Christopher in this way. It—it is not polite and it is none of your affair.'

'Damn it all, Marietta, I don't feel like being polite. How well you defend him.'

'Of course I do. We are to be married.'

Placing his finger beneath her chin, Edmund turned her face back to his. His expression was a mask of cynicism, one brow arched over flinty eyes. 'It is only a few weeks ago that you agreed to marry me.'

'Please don't remind me of that. It is in the past and I am going to marry Christopher.'

'A marriage in name only, I'll wager.' A smile of bitter satisfaction curved his lips when he saw her confusion about his words that she was too innocent to conceal in her eyes.

'I don't know what you're talking about.'

'No,' he said quietly. 'I don't believe you do. But you really should think twice about marrying him.'

Edmund studied her with the casual interest of a man who meets a woman for the first time, a woman he does not find particularly attractive, he would have her believe, but in his eyes was a darkness, a darkness that concealed his innermost thoughts and his emotions.

Marietta searched his eyes for something, to see something of the tenderness he had shown her at Ashborne. There must be something, there had to be, but those incredible silver-grey eyes only stared back at her, cold as a block of ice and without emotion and memories of tender kisses and passionate embraces they had shared. Determined not to make a fool of herself, with her heart breaking, she lowered her eyes.

'It has already been decided.'

As she raised her head her eyes were drawn across the ballroom to see Lady Russell standing in the doorway watching them. She was in the company of Thomas Sheridan. Marietta steeled herself against any display of surprise, any indication of agitation. Instead she forced herself to look nonchalantly away and stepped back.

'I see you have company, Edmund. I won't keep you. I will arrange for the ring you gave me to be returned to you. Please excuse me.'

Marietta turned and walked away, clinging on to her pride like a drowning man clings on to a floating piece of wood.

* * *

Edmund watched her go. In the frozen silence that followed that announcement, white-hot fury, the like of which he had never experienced before, consumed him. Hatred and jealousy directed against young Lovat were sinking their poisonous fangs into his heart and were almost destroying him. Passing before his eyes were visions of a bewitching, tantalising young woman strolling through the gardens at Ashborne House with him, Marietta in his arms, kissing him, laughing with him, naked in his arms in bed. Why had she done this? Why had she not waited for him to return from Switzerland? Why had she rejected him when she had agreed to be his wife?

Unable to tolerate the dancing, the heat and the packed bodies mingling with the scents of hothouse flowers and wine welling in the air, feeling that she'd had enough of the frivolities and that she must have some fresh air, Marietta slipped out on to the terrace. Taking in some gulps of much need air, she walked further along the terrace where it was quiet. She turned her face up to the breeze, welcoming its coolness. Suddenly a hand shot out of the gloom and drew her in.

'And about time,' a voice growled. 'I was beginning to think you would never leave the revelries.'

Her cheeks aflame with indignation, Marietta spun round to see Edmund, his face darkened by shadows. 'Edmund!' She stared at him in bewilderment. 'What are you doing here?' He had clearly been waiting for an opportunity to confront her, but what could he have to say to her that wasn't unfavourable? 'If you have anything further to say about Christopher, then you might as well tell me and have done with it. It is clear that you are angry about something—'

'Angry?' he snapped, flinging his arms wide and restlessly beginning to pace the terrace. 'God above, Marietta, anger doesn't begin to describe what I am feeling. Why did you do it?'

Marietta paled, glancing about to make sure they weren't being overheard. 'Have a care what you say, Edmund.'

'Have a care, you say. I will have my say, Marietta, and you will listen. Had I a glass I would raise a toast to you. Your beguiling beauty and vulnerability had me fooled and quite undone for a time. When you left my home I truly thought you would be waiting for me in London when I came.'

'Waiting for you! Why, you conceited beast. Did you really not stop to ask yourself why I chose not to wait for you?'

'Tell me. I would like to know.'

'Because I loathed myself for being so weak and stupid that I succumbed to your seduction. I know we had only known each other a short time, but I thought that we had a profound depth of understanding of each other.'

'I thought so, too. I did not expect you to agree to wed someone else as soon as my back was turned.'

'You knew my father was in the north arranging a marriage for me, so it should not have come as such a surprise.'

'Damn it, Marietta,' he growled, 'it was. I never thought you would do something so reckless as to agree to wed a man who—who—'

Marietta drew back in the face of what she expected to be a harsh attack on Christopher. 'Say no more,' she snapped. 'I—I know Christopher prefers the company of men to that of women—as many other gentlemen do—but he is kind and generous to me and I know things will change when we marry.'

'Change? Never. Generous, you say.' Suddenly he pulled her to him. His arms were around her and she could only lean helplessly against his familiar body. 'Does his generosity lead to kissing you, Marietta—kissing you as you deserve to be kissed?'

'Let me go, Edmund,' she flared, pulling herself from his arms. 'How dare you?'

'I do dare, because, unlike you, I did not renege on our arrangement.'

'Renege? What are you talking about? I did no such thing. Why did you not come to see my father? If you no longer had feelings for me I could understand, but the permanent uncertainty was cruel.'

His eyes held hers. 'You little fool. I love you as much if not more than I have ever done.'

'No, you don't,' she fumed, 'otherwise you would not have left me for so long. You are a tyrant, Edmund.'

'So you have actually decided you do not like me.'

'Definitely.' Her voice sounded sharp and angry, though she could not meet his eyes.'

He moved closer. 'And you are certain of that, are you?' he pressed.

'Yes—yes, I am.'

He chuckled. 'That certainly deflates my ego. And here was I, a man who is notorious for the effect I have on women, hoping you, too, had fallen under my spell.'

'Me? Never.' Marietta's cheeks flamed. 'You should know by now that I have a mind of my own.'

'I do know, but it is difficult to believe when you follow your father's dictates without objection. Does he know the kind of man he is committing you to? If I did not love you so much, I would walk away and leave you to it.'

Marietta was not to know that the harshness of his voice was to conceal his own feeling of rejection and frustration. She could only feel the humiliation and pain of his criticism, as cold and cruel as to bring her to her senses like a slap in the face.

'Why do you speak to me with such anger, Edmund? I am the injured party, not you. And please don't make it any worse by trying to excuse yourself.'

'What are you talking about?' he asked, frowning. His voice was taut, his brows drawn together in a frown.

'You told me you would speak to my father. You asked me to be your wife before I left

Ashborne.' She did nothing to stop the words, even though he was looking at her as if she had taken leave of her senses. 'What happened? You didn't come. I trusted you, but you did nothing to give me hope. Lady Russell tried to make me believe she was entertaining you at the Pulteney Hotel when I saw your carriage outside and I went in, hoping to see you. I didn't believe her, of course—but what was I to think when you made no attempt to come and see me?'

A group of revellers chose that moment to come on to the terrace and continued laughing and talking with raised voices close to them. Edmund threw them an irate glance and did his best to ignore them, but with difficulty.

'Enough, Marietta. You talk in riddles. I was never at the hotel so there had to be some mistake—but now is not the time to discuss such an important matter with all this noise. Just think about this. If you wed Lovat, you will live a lifetime of regret—it will be a lonely existence with little comfort.'

'Regret? Lonely?' She stared at him in disbelief. 'I cannot believe you said that.'

'Were your husband to be so inclined to take you to his bed on your wedding night, he will know you are too innocent and inexperienced to simulate a virgin's first night,' Edmund said, stepping close to her. 'How would you explain that?'

Marietta's small chin squared up to him and her clear shade of transparent amber eyes warned him to keep away from her. 'Unfamiliar with the kind of world you inhabit, I really have no idea. It is thanks to you that I am no longer pure, but used goods. To his credit, Christopher has tried to be open with me. To my shame I could not bring myself to be honest with him.'

He caught her by the shoulders. She tried to twist away, but he held her fast, and in spite of everything she was all too aware of his closeness, the slight, angry flare of his nostrils, the tension line around his mouth. 'I am disappointed in you, Marietta. Have you forgotten everything that I said to you before you left Ashborne? What we did and then that dreadful moment when I was told you were to marry Lovat, that I might be too late—I lived a lifetime in those seconds. When I asked you to be my wife I meant every word of it. I told you I love you—that has not changed, so I can't understand what all this is about.'

'You can't—no,' she said. 'Maybe not.'

Shrugging his hands from her shoulders, she

stepped away from him, knowing that if she stayed with him any longer, that if he touched her again, she would be lost. They stood in shadow, but the light from an occasional lantern suspended from the nearby branch of a tree made his eyes shine silver like the eyes of an animal in the dark.

'Excuse me, Edmund, I must get back to Christopher.'

'Not yet. Not until I prove something to both of us.'

Marietta opened her mouth to object, but then he looked at her in such a way she couldn't resist and the words died into a whimper in her throat as his mouth covered hers. So strong were his arms that it was useless to struggle and break free, and just as useless, she discovered a moment later, to fight against her own treacherous response of her own senses. She rediscovered the feeling of being carried beyond herself to some place far away, where nothing mattered but the two of them and their desire.

She felt the heat inside him and the heat in herself and suddenly she wanted him, desperately, as she had never wanted anything before. She would have gone on kissing him if Edmund himself had not shattered the spell and thrust her from him so suddenly that she almost lost her footing. It was only pride and anger that came from rejection that made her reach out for the balustrade that kept her on her feet.

Reaching out, he steadied her, and she could read no expression on his face. She had to moisten her lips with her tongue before she could speak.

'Edmund—I... Please stop it. Do you make a habit of seducing women in dark places?'

'No, only you,' he murmured, a glint of humour in his eyes, 'and since you've already been seduced by me, you don't count. Now,' he murmured and his voice held a more tender note, 'are you going to tell me what this is all about?'

On a sigh she looked up at his face. 'I—I thought you had abandoned me.'

'You little fool. I didn't. Why would I not come back to the woman I love? Who I believed loved me? You should have trusted me, Marietta. Did you think I would turn away from you?'

'In truth, I didn't know what to think. Since our parting I've been living in a state of betwixt and between, unsure of everything. The longer we were apart the chasm grew ever wider. The estrangement hurt me beyond bearing.'

'It did me, too.'

'Then why did you not come? Why will you not tell me what it is that has kept you from me?' And what did you mean when you said I hadn't done as you asked?'

'I wrote everything in the letter I wrote to you—and one to your father, explaining my absence.'

Marietta stared at him in bewilderment. 'A letter? What letter? I received no letter—and as far as I am aware, neither did my father.'

Edmund frowned, puzzled by this. 'I had to leave Ashborne urgently. I wrote to both you and your father, leaving the letters to be posted by my steward. I can't think what happened, Marietta. At last I understand why you behaved as you did.'

'What happened, Edmund? What was so urgent that you were unable to come to me in London?'

'When you left I received a letter from Switzerland informing me of my father's imminent death. I had to go.'

She stared at him in amazement. 'Oh—I am so sorry. Of course you had to go—how awful and upsetting for you. I wish I'd known. Were—were you in time?'

He nodded. 'He lingered a few weeks before he died at the clinic where he had been a patient for eighteen years.'

'But—I thought your father was dead. You implied it.'

'Did I? I apologise if I misled you.'

'It doesn't matter now. It has been a difficult time for you, I can understand that. So that is what happened to the title. I did wonder why it wasn't passed to you when your uncle died. Silly me. I should have guessed.'

'Anything to do with my father I find difficult to talk about. We will speak of it, but now is not the time.'

'No—of course it isn't.' She glanced along the terrace where more boisterous revellers were noisily enjoying themselves. 'I—I should go inside. I must speak to Christopher.'

'Yes, talk to him, Marietta. You owe it to yourself. It is as well you know the nature of the man you are about to marry. That his father favoured his younger son, William, five years Christopher's junior, is no secret. He has known for years that Christopher is not like other men and he doubted he would ever take a woman. People will always take advantage of him. The Earl would rather pass the estate to his younger son. He has sought a marriage for Christopher for some time. Although he doubted the marriage would prove fruitful, he lives in hope that Christopher will surprise him and prove him wrong. If you don't like what I'm saying, then ask him.'

'I will, Edmund. You can depend on that.'

'If you decide to go ahead and wed Christopher Lovat, then consider this. You will be everything he needs in a woman—as mother, sister, friend—but you'll never be a lover or a wife. If you decided not to marry him, then with two failed betrothals behind you—both instigated by you—you will be ruined. A man might be capable of shrugging off a broken engagement, but a woman cannot.'

'If Christopher is as you say, then I am willing to trade my reputation to tell him I will not marry him.'

Edmund's eyes darkened with hunger as his gaze did a slow sweep of her slender body and lovely face. 'Do not forget that you promised yourself to me, Marietta.'

It was her response to that glance that had Marietta stepping away. 'No, Edmund, I never did forget that. I need time to extricate myself from marriage to Christopher.'

'Do that. The love that we declared for each other must not be allowed to become nothing more than a wonderful illusion under the weight of misunderstanding and distrust.'

Without another word Marietta turned from him and walked away. She had much to consider as she went back inside, not the least of which was the thought that she would not be marrying Christopher Lovat.

Edmund let her go. Everything that had happened to her on leaving Ashborne—her miseries, her father's motives in forcing this marriage to Christopher Lovat on her—were written clear as black ink on white paper. Not having received the letters he had written, she believed he had rejected her. Vulnerable and misguided, she'd had no choice but to fall in with her father's wishes. What she believed to be his rejection of her as she saw it had drawn the bitterness from her. He saw it all now. The whole sorry mess began to unfold.

Making his way back inside, he stood on the side lines and watched her as she sought Christopher Lovat. He pondered the scene, watching her. She was changed. She had changed since that day he had first seen her riding in the park. He had watched her in the way he was doing now.

Her hair had come loose beneath her hat and tumbled about her shoulders and then again in the touching and slightly pathetic recklessness and vulnerability of her youthfulness when she had run from Gabriel at the altar. He had seen how young she was as she struggled into adulthood. She had run from him as she had run from Gabriel and he suspected she was about to do the same to Christopher Lovat, but he sensed that this time she didn't fully understand why she ran.

Seeing her tonight had been unexpected and a shock. He was torn between anger, torment and tenderness. After speaking to her and listening to what she had to say, he felt his anger and pain diminishing and he could finally think more rationally. Remembering his anger when he had been told she was to marry Christopher Lovat, he had been seized by a terrible rage, but not for one moment had he been able to purge her from his heart and mind. It mattered to him what happened to this beautiful, intelligent young woman.

One thing puzzled him. What had become of

the letters he had written to her and her father? He was determined to get to the bottom of it.

Having seen Marietta exchange words with Mr Fitzroy, Christopher left his friend and his comfortable vantage point at the refreshment table, where he was able to supply himself with a never-ending amount of wine, and came to her. 'You are acquainted with Mr Fitzroy, Marietta?'

'Yes, I am,' she replied. 'My mother and I stayed at his house in Kent some weeks ago.'

'I see. Then would it not be polite to introduce me?'

'I think not, Christopher. Mr Fitzroy is just leaving.'

'Then come and dance with me.'

'Not just now, Christopher. I—I would like to speak to you first.' Taking his arm, she guided him to the door and into the passage beyond. Fortunately everyone was in the ballroom or the supper room. Drawing him to a window embrasure, she faced him.

'Tell me about Sir John Emery, Christopher. He is a close friend, is he not?' His eyes were on her face, his expression one of nervousness as he studied her.

'Why—yes. We have known each other since school days. Why do you ask?'

'I think you know, Christopher. This is difficult for me, but I have to ask. Will—will we have a proper marriage? Will you share my bed?'

He swallowed and glanced away. 'I—I'm sorry, Marietta. You must forgive me...'

With a sinking heart Marietta sighed. 'I see. You don't find me attractive enough? Is that the reason?'

'No. Please don't think that. You are the most beautiful woman I have ever seen, but—but I...'

'I know,' she said softly. 'Please don't feel you have to explain. But—you must realise that I cannot marry you now, Christopher. It would be a mistake.'

He nodded. 'Yes, I can see that—although I fear my father will take it badly.'

'Then why did you agree to it?'

'To placate my father.'

'And what about me?'

He looked at her pleadingly. 'Please try to understand. All my life I've tried to be what my father wanted me to be—to be the son he wanted—and the harder I tried the more difficult it became. I—I'm not like other men, Marietta. It used to upset me—until I met others like me at university. That was when I recognised who I was and accepted it. I sincerely hope that you can, too.'

'Your father is aware of how you are?'

Christopher blanched. 'He is not ignorant of any matters concerning me.'

The blood burned hotly in Marietta's cheeks. Angrily she glared at Christopher's pretty face. 'Little wonder your father was so eager to accept a marriage between us—and as for my own—so desperate is he to buy me a title that he would accept this without consideration. Not only does your father acquire a very generous dowry, but also a wife for his son who can never be a husband to me in the true sense.'

'I could not go against my father's demands on me. I should have done so. I realise that now.'

'Yes, Christopher, you should. I am thankful I have found out in time, before we marry.'

'I—I know what I am about to say is most unfair, but—but if you agree to go ahead with the marriage—you can take a lover, if you like. I would not object—providing you are discreet.'

'How very noble of you,' she retorted, unable to conceal her disappointment and the bitterness that was eating away inside her. 'It amazes me that you should even suggest such a thing.'

'I can see you are angry—'

'Angry is not the half of it—but I am less angry with you than I am with our fathers. How dare you? How dare all of you do this to me? I should have been told from the start. I would have respected you more had you been honest. You should have told me that I would be a bride in name only,' Suddenly she couldn't bear to look at him a moment longer. 'Will you please go and find my mother and tell her I am not feeling well and would like to go home? I will wait for the carriage outside.'

'Yes—of course.' He made to turn away then he looked back at her. 'I'm so sorry, Marietta…'

'What are you sorry for, Christopher? Agreeing to marry a woman who can never mean anything to you but as a companion and friend? At least I hope that's what you're apologising for. But do not apologise for the way you are. Never that.'

He smiled sadly and, taking her hand, he placed a gentle kiss on the backs of her fingers. 'Thank you for saying that, Marietta. Unfortunately the world is not a very friendly place to people like me.'

It wasn't until he had gone that Marietta realised he had been on the verge of tears. She regretted her harsh words and was tempted to call him back, but it was too late.

At home in her bed she lay back with her eyes open. When she could no longer hear movements in the house she relaxed and closed her eyes. She was amazed how surprisingly calm she felt and enormously relieved, when she should be feeling sick with humiliation, hurt pride and failure. No, she thought, snuggling into the soft warmth, she would not miss Christopher Lovat from her bed.

The morning after the ball Marietta prepared to tell her parents she would not be marrying Christopher Lovat after all. Before going down to confront them over breakfast, she checked her appearance in the mirror and straightened her skirts, having dreaded this moment and knowing exactly how her father would react, but it had to be faced.

On entering the breakfast room, she was glad they were both there. Her father had eaten and was about to leave. He cast his eyes over her with little interest and, placing his napkin on the table and gathering up a newspaper, he shoved his chair back and rose, ready to be about his business.

'You're late this morning, Marietta,' her mother said, buttering a piece of toast. 'Did you sleep well?'

'Yes, thank you, Mother.' She glanced at her father, her legs trembling with apprehension. 'Before you go, Father, there is something I must speak to you about—and you, Mother.'

'Oh,' her mother said without interest as she bit into her toast.

'What is it, Marietta?' her father said, eyeing her with suspicion. 'Has something happened?'

'Yes—it has.' Drawing a long, deep breath, she said, 'I'm sorry to have to put you through this again, Father, but I cannot—I will not marry Christopher.

For a moment an ominous silence fell on the room as her parents digested the enormity of her words.

'Indeed,' her mother said frostily at last, shoving the plate away from her, her daughter having gained her attention at last. 'And why not, pray?'

'I—I believe you know why.'

'No,' her father thundered, shaking with suppressed rage, a repetition of the last wedding she had walked away from striking him with painful force and knowing he would have to clean up the mess once more if she didn't go through with it. 'We do not know why. You will go through with this marriage if I have to drag you all the way to the altar.'

'No, I won't,' she said, looking at her father with pain-filled eyes. She had only once defied him before. 'It's no use intimidating me, Father. Nothing you can say will make me marry him. I have told Christopher and he understands.'

'Damn you,' her father roared, his fist crashing down on to the table, the crockery jumping and rattling with the force. 'You will do this.'

Recoiling as much from the anger in his voice as the words he said, she looked to her mother for support. 'Christopher—he is not like other men,' she said, the words almost choking her. 'I didn't know until last night. If I marry him, it will not be a normal marriage. It would not be fair to either of us to put ourselves through that.'

Her father strode to the door. 'I will not listen to this,' he retorted, his voice raised. 'It is arranged. You will do as you are told.'

'Does it not concern you that there will be no children—no grandchildren in the future?

Do you not care that my life will be one long misery?'

'Only if you let it,' he snapped. 'Things will change when you are married.'

'But they will not, will they?'

Scalding tears sprang to Marietta's eyes and, with a feeling of desolation weighing her down she looked to her mother for support. She had made up her mind long ago that her mother was frigid in matters of a sexual nature, which was why Marietta was an only child, but she hoped she would see her problem and understand her concern. 'Mother—please tell me you understand. Please tell me you will not try to force me into this.'

Her mother got up slowly and looked at her husband, unable to believe what she was hearing. 'Samuel, what is Marietta talking about? If it is what I think, then of course she cannot marry him. It wouldn't be right—not for either of them. Did you know?'

'I had a good idea, but like his father I thought he would change with marriage.'

'And you were willing to risk our daughter's happiness on the off chance that he would—to turn a blind eye? And if he didn't? What then?'

'She would have to learn to live with it.'

Fuming inwardly, he strode to the door. 'I will speak to the Earl about this. Be prepared for another scandal. Word about this will go around the city like a fire in a dry cornfield. If you will not go through with this marriage, then I demand that you leave London immediately—for Italy, I think. A time spent with your sister will give the gossip time to die down and for you to drum some sense into our daughter.' Opening the door, he spun round and looked at Marietta. 'You do realise this will ruin you socially.'

'Yes. I am sorry, Father.'

He glared at her and started to say more, then stopped, as if he could no longer trust himself to speak. Without another word he went out.

Preparations for them to leave for Italy were put into motion immediately Marietta's mother took care of everything with an energy that left Marietta breathless. Marietta actually believed she was relieved to be going away.

Since arriving home the previous night from the ball, she hadn't had time to give much thought to what had passed between her and Edmund, but she had to see him before she went away. Her feelings for him remained unchanged—she loved him deeply and always would, but after two failed betrothals, both terminated by her, it would not be fair to expect him to ignore this.

Misunderstandings had driven them apart and she would leave it up to him to decide the best course to take. Besides, her father was right. After calling off her betrothal to Christopher a terrible scandal would ensue. It would not be fair if Edmund were to become caught up in it. She could not ask that of him.

He had told her he'd sent a letter to her and one to her father before leaving for Switzerland, explaining his absence. She was curious as to what could have happened to those letters and how different things might have been had they received them. She desperately wanted to see him one more time. Not knowing how long she would be in Siena, she put the ring he had given her in her reticule. To her mother's exasperation she said she had just one thing to do before they left London.

Taking the carriage to Edmund's town house she was disappointed to find he was not at home and was not expected back soon. Marietta could have wept with frustration. Utterly dejected she had no choice but to go, leaving the ring with Henry to give to him.

She could never love anyone as she loved Edmund. Edmund was her heart and soul and he always would be. The pain of that knowledge would torture her night and day, so she would leave London broken-hearted and despairing.

Chapter Ten

They took the boat train from Victoria Station for the Continent the next day. From Paris they travelled to Italy.

Although singularly uneventful, it was a long journey and, unlike the other times when Marietta had made this journey, the distance that separated her from the man she loved and to whom she wanted nothing more than to devote her life to, a man who not so long ago had vowed that he loved her above all else, tore at her heart and overshadowed any joy and excitement she would normally have felt when going to visit her aunt and her cousins.

The train puffed its way through villages and towns and beautiful farmland threaded with rivers. It was midsummer and the weather was pleasantly warm for travelling. The Alps were an awesome, splendid sight and had a strange and solemn beauty. They were highly picturesque, with effervescing springs rushing down the mountainsides into the valleys below, the lofty peaks reaching up into a cloudless clear blue sky. The hotels along the way were respectable, the perfect places to enjoy the taste of luxury as they journeyed south.

Desperately she tried to thrust Edmund into the shadows of her mind and not to let the memories encroach as she settled into her life in Siena, but it was impossible. She felt a sense of loss and bewilderment about everything that had happened and heavy clouds of apprehension hung over her. She had never felt so wretched in her life. There were things that had been left unsaid between her and Edmund, their separation was cloaked in confusion which she wished she'd had a chance to put right.

Her spirits had lifted on seeing Siena and Aunt Margaret. As a girl she had always been happy here in a household full of her cousins' laughter and teasing. And now here she was again. The sun, the warmth—here she could relax, be herself. Even her mother seemed more relaxed now she was away from her husband's domination.

'I thank you for receiving me,' Edmund said when he was admitted to the study in the Harrington House. Samuel Harrington rose to meet him.

'You are welcome, Mr Fitzroy.' He seated himself behind his desk, offering Edmund the seat opposite. 'What can I do for you?'

'My circumstances have changed. On the death of my father recently I have acquired the title of Lord Fitzroy of Ashborne House.'

'I see. Well—I commiserate on your loss, Lord Fitzroy.'

'Thank you.'

They spoke of business matters for several minutes before Edmund turned the conversation to the real purpose of his visit.

'I have not come here to talk about business matters, Mr Harrington. I am here to talk to you about your daughter.'

Mr Harrington glanced at him sharply. 'Marietta? What about Marietta?'

Edmund nodded. 'I—know she is betrothed to Christopher Lovat…'

Mr Harrington shifted irritably in his chair.

'Not any longer. She's cried off—refuses to marry him. I don't know what gets into the girl. This is the second time she's done this.'

'Perhaps she wouldn't *cry off*, as you put it, if you allowed her to have a say in her choice of husband. After all, she's the one who has to spend a lifetime living with him.'

Mr Harrington's face became flushed with anger. 'You are impertinent, sir. My daughter is my concern and I know what's best for her.' He looked at Edmund narrowly. 'I'm curious. What is Marietta to you?'

'She has become important to me. In short, I want her to be my wife.'

'Your wife? You must excuse me if I appear shocked by your announcement, but I appear to be missing something, Baron Fitzroy. Just how well do you know Marietta?'

'I got to know her quite well when she stayed at Ashborne House.'

'Does Marietta know you are here by any chance?'

'No, she doesn't. I saw her at the Rycroft ball the other night. She seemed far from happy. She had begun to realise what marriage to Lovat would mean so it comes as no surprise to know she refuses to marry him.'

'So—you want to marry her yourself.'

'I made up my mind before she left Kent. I love your daughter, Mr Harrington, very much, and I know she feels the same about me. When she left I arranged to come to London and speak to you, to ask your permission to marry her. Unfortunately, before I could do that a letter arrived at Ashborne informing me that my father was close to death. He was in a clinic in Switzerland—had been for the past eighteen years. I wrote you a letter, explaining everything. Unfortunately something happened to prevent you receiving it.'

Mr Harrington frowned, shaking his head, weighing his words carefully before he spoke. 'I received no such letter. Had I done so and had the letter warranted a reply, I assure you, Baron Fitzroy, I would have done so.'

'I am sure you would. I also wrote to Marietta, informing her of my urgency for me to leave for Switzerland. It didn't reach her either. I left the letters for my steward to post. I cannot imagine what went wrong. I will look into it.'

'Yes—do that. In the meantime, be so good as to tell me how well you know Marietta. Do you still want to marry her?'

'Yes, I do.'

'You do realise she has a reputation for rejecting her bridegrooms? The first—your own cousin—she left standing at the altar and you assisted her in her escape.'

Edmund grinned. 'I do. But there is something in the proverb of third time lucky, Mr Harrington. I believe that the third time something is attempted is more likely to succeed than the previous two attempts. I am now Baron Fitzroy, which is not quite as illustrious as a viscount or an earl, but I know I could make her happy.'

'Then I wish you luck. I have yet to inform the Earl of Rainford that the wedding is off and brace myself for the scandal that will ensue.'

'Where is she? Can I see her?'

'She isn't here. I sent her away when she told me she would not marry young Lovat. My wife is with her. They left for the Continent this morning. They are to travel to Siena to stay with my wife's sister indefinitely—leaving me to deal with the fallout from this latest debacle.'

Edmund was rendered speechless. He had not expected this. 'Good Lord!' he uttered at length. 'I didn't expect that. I would have come to see you sooner, but I thought I'd give her time to sort things out with Lovat first. Do I have your permission to go after her?'

'To Italy?'

'Yes.'

Mr Harrington sighed and nodded. 'Very well. If you can talk some sense into her, then you have my full permission. But you may have your work cut out persuading her to be your wife. I no longer have the power to compel her to do anything any more. I know my daughter. If she should prove stubborn—whatever argument she puts to you, don't lose her, or you will end up being the kind of fool your cousin was— and Christopher Lovat.

His aunt, who was staying in their London house for the duration of the Jubilee celebrations, had been happy to see him arrive back from Switzerland. She never ceased to stress her concern for him. He was either working too hard or worrying about his father in the clinic in Switzerland. At this present time she made no secret of her concern over his state of mind. Since he had returned from Switzerland his manner was like that of a man being stretched beyond endurance by an internal struggle. When he had returned to the house from a business meeting, Henry had told him Marietta had called to see him and left a small package. On opening it and finding the ring he had given her, in reply to his aunt's questioning he had told her how, after seeing and speaking to her at the ball, there was much that had been left undecided.

His aunt was shocked and deeply disappointed when Edmund told her of his visit to Mr Harrington. 'So, Marietta is betrothed to the Earl of Rainford's son?'

'Not any more. It's all been a terrible misunderstanding. I left some letters with the steward to be posted when I dashed off to Switzerland. Have you any idea what happened to them—if he didn't post them?'

'Well—I remember you mentioning them before you left. It was such a worrying time—knowing how ill your father was and if you would reach the clinic in time to see him before… Well, you know what I mean. As for the letters, perhaps Francine can shed some light on where they are. I believe she offered to post them to save the steward the trouble.'

Edmund became quiet, his face like hard granite, his mouth so tightly clamped he could barely speak. 'Francine took them?'

'Yes. Why do you ask, Edmund?'

'They were intended for Marietta and her father. They didn't receive them.'

His aunt stared at him, her mouth half open. 'Oh, dear! Are you saying she never posted them?'

'It would appear not.'

'Deliberately?'

'Yes. Another thing has been puzzling me. Marietta did mention that she saw Francine when she was in London—that she had seen the carriage outside the hotel and believed I was inside.'

'When was this?'

'Three or four weeks ago.'

'Then it could have been me. I called at the hotel to have tea with Francine one day. I know Thomas was in London and that he called to see her at some point. That must have been when Marietta saw the carriage.'

'Francine implied that she was entertaining me in her room.'

'Then that was very wrong of her, very wrong indeed. I am disappointed in her that she could do this.'

Edmund was unable to control the anger gathering pace inside him. 'Thank God Marietta had enough sense not to believe her.' The suspicion that Francine had purposefully kept the letters from reaching their destination was farfetched, yet the moment it presented itself he couldn't rest until he had proved or disproved it. And to exacerbate the situation by implying he was visiting her at the hotel was outrageous. The rage he felt at the mere suspicion that, out of spite, Francine might have tried to keep him apart from Marietta was so powerful, so great, he could feel it thicken in his throat.

'I think I can understand why Francine would do this,' his aunt said.

'So can I,' he said, his voice strained. 'She would do anything to keep me and Marietta apart. When Andrew died, I really should have kept her at arm's length.'

'Francine is not the kind of woman who would be satisfied with that. She wants nothing more than to be your wife.'

'And I cannot be held responsible for the way she or other people think. If destroying letters I intended for Marietta and her father and knocking Marietta from her horse are the lengths she will go to to get her own way, then her malevolence knows no bounds. Her interest in me is more mercenary than affection.'

'Perhaps you're right. Where is Marietta now?'

'She has gone to Italy—to Siena. Apparently her mother's sister, who married an Italian, lives there. They will be gone indefinitely—until the scandal of her ending her betrothal to Christopher Lovat dies down.'

'I see. What will you do, Edmund?'

He cast his aunt a determined look. 'Go after her, of course.' He grinned suddenly, looking more like his old self. 'Siena is supposed to be the most romantic city in Tuscany. The magic of the town will be the perfect place to court her—before making her my wife.'

His aunt returned his smile. 'That would be wonderful. And you are sure you can persuade her?'

His grin widened. 'I have no doubts—when I have confronted Francine. I have a few choice words to say to that particular lady.' He looked at his aunt as a thought occurred to him. 'Why don't you come with me to Italy? You'll enjoy it—and you wouldn't want to miss the wedding.'

She brightened. 'You wouldn't mind?'

'No. I'd like you to come. I have things to do before we can leave—instructions for my secretary and where I can be reached.'

'I'd love to come with you. In fact,' she said, getting up from the sofa and heading for the door, 'I shall begin preparations at once.'

Edmund found Francine at the Pulteney Hotel where she was staying to enjoy the Jubilee celebrations. He was cool and calm when she let him into her room, and he wasn't smiling.

Poised and beautiful, Francine sat gracefully on the sofa with her hands folded in front of her. Edmund looked at her hard. Until Marietta had appeared in his life he had enjoyed her company on occasion, but, she lacked Marietta's goodness and her fresh and lively wit, and she didn't look at him with two adorable amber eyes and smile that wonderful warm smile.

'Well, this is indeed a pleasant surprise, Edmund. I didn't expect to see you today. I'm so glad you've come up from Kent for the celebrations. I have no doubt it is business that has brought you, but you must leave time to enjoy yourself. The celebrations promise to go on for weeks.'

With his hands clasped behind his back, Edmund looked down at her, finding it virtually impossible to restrain his anger. 'Neither business nor celebrations have brought me to

London at this time, Francine. I am here to see Marietta—as well you know,' he said without preamble, watching her closely. 'I have come to see you on a matter which has been giving me one hell of a headache and which I am told you can clear up. Where are they—the letters you offered to post for my steward? It would appear they have not reached the people for whom they were intended. What have you done with them?'

Francine stared at him, her face as white as the petals of the huge daisies which filled the porcelain vase on the dresser. Unable to lie her way out of a predicament she had not foreseen, she said, 'The letters? Why, yes, I…'

'Failed to post them. Where are they, Francine?'

Edmund watched her face as several emotions struggled for supremacy in her. He could read her like a book. He knew that she was trying to think her way out of it, but he stood there, fixing her with a penetrating, relentless silver gaze, all feeling ruthlessly extracted from his face. He had no intention of making it easy for her.

'I simply forgot to post them. It's as simple as that. I'm so sorry. I didn't realise they were so important.'

'Don't insult my intelligence. How could you know whether they were important or not—unless you opened them and read them,' he said harshly, looking down into her eyes with a hard, murderous gleam, his lips curled over his teeth. 'I've known some dirty fighters in my time, but never have I known a woman who would stoop as low as you. Why did you do it?'

'Because I loved you and I couldn't bear to think I might lose you,' she said, trying to put the softness back into her voice and school her features into a tender look, but it didn't work on Edmund.

'If that is what you think, then you deceive yourself,' he told her scathingly. 'You and I have been friends, Francine—you were the wife of my closest friend. Not once have I given you reason to believe you are anything more than that and I never will. I will make Marietta my wife and we will live at Ashborne. By withholding those letters you have done harm to more people that you will ever realise—not least to Marietta herself. You will accept my marriage to Marietta and if you can't, then stay away from Ashborne.'

Francine sprang to her feet, anger she could no longer contain flaring in her eyes. 'Marry her if that's what you want. It will be interesting to see how it will work out. No matter what she tries to aspire to, she will always remain what she is. A nobody. The daughter of a social climbing parvenu.'

The callous bluntness of her statement jarred every one of Edmund's nerves. He moved close, looming over her. 'And you have a warped definition of how a well-bred young woman should behave. Marietta could give you lessons in the art of being a lady. One thing you should know about me, Francine, is that I'm a very determined man. If any harm comes to Marietta by your hand again, I'll destroy you. Believe me when I say that you don't want me for an enemy.'

He turned from her and strode to the door. Opening it, he looked back. 'Marry Thomas, Francine. He's besotted with you—has been for years. You've kept him dangling long enough. For God's sake put him out of his misery.'

Through half-closed eyes Marietta looked up into the cerulean blue sky. The afternoon was peaceful, the air heavy with the perfume of blossoms and the drone of bees. The sun's warmth had an invisible, embalming quality and she sighed languidly, apathy and inertia calling the tune. Little wonder, she thought, that the Italians retired to shaded rooms when the heat was at its fiercest. She was content to forget the passage of time as Dario, clad in the green and black livery of the Sansone household, flitted in and out of the house to wait on Marietta and her mother, lounging beneath large parasols in the garden.

Margaret Sansone, her mother's sister, was a widow. She had married Flavio Sansone and come to live in Siena thirty years ago. Their three offspring were married and scattered about Italy. The Sansones were an old wealthy family of merchant stock and lived in a beautiful ancient house on the outskirts of Siena.

After a while she stirred herself. Picking up her sketch pad, she looked across at her mother. 'I won't be long. I'm just going to do some drawing now it's beginning to cool down.'

'Don't forget to wear your sun hat, Marietta. You don't want to get your face burnt.'

Securing the wide-brimmed hat on her head, her hair tumbling over her shoulders, she set off to her favourite spot outside the grounds of the Sansone house which overlooked the city.

Siena was steeped in history and she loved the richness of the different buildings and styles.

The hills offered wonderful vistas of the countryside—of vine and pasture and cypress groves, lofty castles and Romanesque churches. In fact, it was an artist's paradise and Marietta loved it. Siena was a city full of candlelit palaces and churches, shuttered and secretive, magnificent and ancient, its towers and crenelated buildings soaring at random.

Settling herself on a hillock shaded by trees, she opened her sketch pad and began sketching the city spread out before her, the rooftops and the distinctive bell tower of the Palazzo Pubblico in the centre. When she had first come to Siena as a child, she had been overawed by its elegance and patina of charm. And now, with her sketch pad on her knee, she felt privileged to be following in the footsteps of writers, poets and artists who had been drawn into its mesmeric aura through the ages.

'Well, isn't this just the perfect place,' a male voice said softly behind her.

Marietta hadn't heard him approach. Looking up, she saw the tall figure of a man looking down at her. She had to shade her eyes against the sun's glare, blinking hard to see him better, telling herself that she was losing her mind, that it was her imagination playing tricks on her—it couldn't possibly be Edmund. But she sensed it was him. It was as if some tangible, powerful force told her so. She even recognised the elusive, tangy smell of his cologne, borne to her on the warm breeze. He was smiling, as though it were the most natural thing in the world that he should be there.

'Edmund!' she gasped. At the sound of his voice she experienced a rush of feeling, a bittersweet joy.

Edmund's gaze was long and sure and Marietta found herself unable to move as she feasted her eyes on his handsome face, her heart pounding as she looked with loving eyes at his tall form. He was still smiling, his teeth a white slash in his tanned face, and his eyes glinted as the sunshine shone directly in them. His smile closed like a fist round her heart and a warm rush of pleasure washed over her.

She thought how casual he looked dressed in a loose white shirt tucked into cream-coloured trousers. Ever since she had last seen him at the ball, when they had exchanged harsh words, he had occupied all her waking moments and she had longed to see him again and despaired of not doing so.

Swallowing uneasily, she was disturbed by his sudden presence and the scorching heat of his perusal in the quiet setting. He was lithe and powerful, all hard sinew and rippling muscle, his shining black hair falling in an unruly casual sweep across his forehead. The atmosphere was sultry, the tiny insects spiralling in the shaft of light through the trees.

'What are you doing here?' she asked, placing her sketch pad on the grass and getting to her feet.

'Your mother told me I might find you here,' he murmured. 'It wasn't difficult to locate you.'

'Yes—I like to come here to sketch the city. But what are you doing here—in Siena? And how did you know where I was staying?'

'Your father told me.'

'My father? Oh—I see.'

'I'm here with my aunt—along with her maid and my valet. We have accommodation in a hotel in the city.'

'But—but *why* are you here, Edmund? For what reason?'

'To see you. What else?'

'What else indeed.'

* * *

All the way to Siena Edmund had been rehearsing in his mind what he would say to Marietta, and now he was with her he couldn't remember a thing. He looked out at the landscape that so enchanted her, but somehow he didn't see it. Ever since she had left him at Ashborne House he had thought of no one else, his male body remembering her warmth, her sweetness and melting in his arms when he had made love to her, the surprise of her complicit compliance. She had lived in his heart, in the pure agony of his mind and in his soul since their first meeting, and, no matter how hard he tried, he had been unable to wrench her out of it. She had settled there and there she would remain for the rest of his days.

The Marietta he now saw was still the same. Her face was slightly tanned by the Italian sun and she was still as beautiful. Her eyes had lost none of their challenging intensity—the same restless, questing soul that lived in him. When she lifted her eyes to his and he saw the quiet yielding in their clear depths, it nearly sent him to his knees. He wanted to lose himself in her eyes, to pull her into his arms and unburden his heart. Taking a neutral course, he looked at her sketch pad.

'You are busy, I see, Marietta.'

Marietta met his gaze and swallowed nervously, smiling with shy uncertainty. 'I'm always busy drawing something. Siena is an inspiring city. There's always something of interest for me to draw.'

The sound of her voice was so soft and sweet, Edmund almost dragged her to him. Instead he looked long and hard at the city spread out before him. When he looked again at Marietta his face was inscrutable.

'You're surprised to see me?'

'Yes, of course I'm surprised. I never expected to see you here in Siena. Why are you here?' she persisted, unable to bear another moment of this awful suspense.

Edmund's brows drew together and he continued to study her. 'What brought me here at this time has nothing whatsoever to do with the restorative values of Siena.'

'No, I don't suppose it has,' she murmured. 'How are you?'

'All things considered I am remarkably well,' he assured her drily, fixing her with a level stare, 'for a man who has made love to a woman, asked her to be his wife, who then walked away and became betrothed to another. It did nothing for my male ego, my self-esteem or my pride—and a man is most sensitive about his pride. The woman I made love to that night at Ashborne was passionate, warm and responsive, with an ardour to match my own. What happened to her?'

'She's still here, Edmund. She hasn't gone anywhere.'

'I'm relieved to hear it. You returned the ring I gave you. Why, Marietta? Why did you do that?'

'I—I thought it would be for the best. I can imagine the scandal that has erupted following my cancelled betrothal to Christopher. It wouldn't be fair to you for you to become caught up in it.'

'Fair? You should have let me be the judge of that before running off to Siena.'

'I didn't run off, Edmund. My father insisted I left London at once. Everything happened so fast. I was so awful to you on the night of the ball—and I said some terrible things. Will you ever forgive me?'

'It is forgotten. I said some pretty offensive things myself. Thank God you gave Christopher his marching orders. Every time I thought of you marrying him, I was tormented with images of you. You see, my desire for you was unquenchable. It nearly drove me insane. You have put me through hell. You, my darling, are the most exasperating woman alive.' His voice sounded harsh, as if forged from his chest.

'I'm sorry. I didn't mean to.'

Reaching out he framed her face with his hands, gazing down at her lovely features, knowing perfectly well that their parting had been as difficult for her as it had been for him. Unable to resist her a moment longer, he wanted to taste the sweetness of her lips, to feel her closeness, the fullness of her breasts pressed against his chest, and his mouth locked on to hers hungrily, his kiss searing her lips, and she returned his kiss with a smothered moan of joy.

He rejoiced in her. To have her in his arms again, to feel her close to him, which was where she should have been all along, it was nothing short of a joy he had not felt since that night at Ashborne when he had made love to her. Twining her arms around his neck, she pressed herself close as he deepened his kiss, his arms sliding up and down her back as he moulded her closer to him.

'Dear Lord, I have missed you,' he murmured when he finally tore his mouth from hers, unable to relinquish his hold on her as he feasted his gaze on her long-lashed, amber eyes, turned languid and solemn with emotion. 'Do you know what you have done to me? Do you know what you have made me suffer? Do you know what I have been through these past weeks? I thought I should go mad. Never do that to me again, Marietta. We have much to talk about. There have been misunderstandings—I have a lot of explaining to do to put things right. Circumstances, I'm afraid, played a heavy hand upon my actions when you left Ashborne.'

'Then we will talk about them.'

'I have been most anxious to touch and kiss you again.'

'You did much more than touch,' she whispered shyly.

'I know—and I intend doing so again,' he told her fiercely. 'I intend taking you to bed and making love to you as thoroughly and leisurely as I can. I accept that the loss of your virtue was largely my fault and I find the responsibility a heavy burden to bear. If I could turn back the clock and put everything right, I would, believe me, but it's too late for that. Ever since I went to London and found you were to marry young Lovat, I have been dying inside.'

Marietta gave him a heartbreaking smile. 'It's been a difficult time for me, too.'

Unable to look at her a moment longer and not hold her, Edmund pulled her against him once more with stunning force, his mouth opening over hers in a kiss that demanded she return it with equal passion. She slid her hands up his chest and around his neck and arched herself against his rigid thighs. Edmund shuddered with pleasure, his hands caressing her back, and then pulling her hips tighter to him. He groaned aloud with rampaging desire and with the pleasure of having her in his arms and feeling the sweet softness of her mouth.

Tearing his lips from hers, he placed scorching kisses on her cheek, her temples. 'Say you still love me, Marietta. Say it.'

'I do love you,' she whispered, her lips against his. 'I never stopped. Do you still love me?'

'I wouldn't be here if I didn't. Do you remember when we were in your studio and you told me you had never known love in your life?'

'Yes, I remember.'

'I wanted to tell you then—my soul cried

out to tell you that I could love you, that I could give you the kind of love you could never have imagined.'

'Then why didn't you?' she whispered.

'It was too soon.'

'What about the letters you wrote before you went to Switzerland? Did you solve the mystery as to what happened to them?'

Edmund took her hand, his face grim with the knowledge that he had been unable to stop this estrangement. 'I told you I wrote two letters, one to you and another to your father. I left them with my steward to post. Francine offered to do it for him and she kept the letters. I cannot forgive her for that.'

'I see. Well—that explains a lot. She must love you very much, Edmund.'

'I don't think Francine knows how to love.'

'Love sometimes makes people ruthless in a way that hatred doesn't. When it comes to love, some people find it easy to stab someone in the back when they're not looking. In Francine's case, in her way she must love you very much and I stood in her path.'

'Francine is clever and devious in ways that would surprise you.'

'Perhaps not so clever—otherwise you would not be with me. It has proved one thing.'

He smiled. 'It has? What?'

'If our love can overcome Francine's machinations, then it can withstand anything. Thank goodness the missing letters have been explained.'

'Yes,' he said, looking down at her once more. 'But I can neither forget nor forgive the trouble it has caused—to the Lovats as well as the useless suffering it caused you. There is something else. Do you remember telling me you had seen and spoken to Francine at the hotel?'

Marietta's expression became grave at the memory. 'Yes, I do. I recognised your carriage outside. I thought you must be inside.'

'I was never at the hotel. It wasn't me in her room—it was Thomas Sheridan. He's been trying to get close to Francine ever since Andrew died. It would appear they are beginning to see more of each other.'

'I never thought for a moment that it was you. I knew that was what she wanted me to think, but I trusted you, Edmund, even though I had heard nothing from you.'

'Bless you for that,' he murmured, cupping

her cheek with his palm. 'Aunt Dorothy was in London at the time and had arranged to take tea with Francine at the hotel. She uses the same carriage as myself when I'm in town.'

'I see. So that explains it.'

'Where I am concerned, I think my money was the draw to Francine. I've made money, lots of money through my many enterprises, but money breeds distrust. The right kind of people you would like for friends shy away from you. The wrong kind are easily come by. Francine was one of those. I hope Thomas makes an honest woman of her—although she'll lead him a merry dance.'

'You said my father told you that I had come to Siena. Have you approached him with your offer to marry me?'

'Yes. Was that wrong of me?'

'No. I'm glad he knows.' She laughed, a teasing light dancing in her eyes. 'At least he gets his title—although a duke or an earl would have suited him better.'

'Minx,' Edmund said, kissing the laughter from her lips.

All the love that filled her heart was in her eyes for Edmund to see, a love so intense he was humbled by it. And when she opened her mouth to tell him again he silenced her words with his lips, his kiss becoming hungry, searching, primitive and potent. Breathing deeply, Edmund broke the kiss and looked down into her glowing eyes and soft mouth and had an impulse to bend his head and kiss them again, but a loud burst of laughter from a jolly party of youths coming along the path snapped them both back to the present. Irritated by the lack of privacy available to them, he shot the group an irate, disapproving scowl.

'Come, I will walk back to the house with you. We will talk later.'

Picking up her sketch pad and charcoal, they fell into step along the path. 'How long are you here for?'

'As long as it takes for me to marry you before you marry someone else. Aunt Dorothy has had her first taste of Italy and has fallen in love with Siena. She won't want to leave it in a hurry.'

'I'm glad she's come with you. As far as I am concerned nothing has changed. You pledged yourself to me at Ashborne. It still stands. Have you met my Aunt Margaret?'

'No, I have not had that pleasure.'

'I look forward to introducing you. Everyone loves her.'

'There is just one thing before we go,' he said, reaching into his pocket and producing the box containing the ring she had returned to him. Taking it out, he placed it on her engagement finger. 'There. It should never have been taken off—and it never will again.'

Never had he felt happier in his life as when he placed the ring on her finger. It seemed to seal the bond and to proclaim to the world that she was to marry him.

A softness entered his eyes. Idly he brushed a tumbled curl from her shoulder, becoming preoccupied with the way the breeze caught her hair, lifting the tresses. He admired the way it sparkled in the sunlight. Here in this open, relaxed setting, with the sky as blue as sapphire, and the beautiful city of Siena before them, she was a very beautiful young woman. Her face was flushed with the sun and her eyes warm and sultry.

Marietta walked beside him, unable to believe what was happening. Edmund was here and suddenly her fears about the future seemed to vanish. Acutely aware of her dishevelled appearance, removing her hat, she ran an ineffectual hand through her hair, which hung down her back in a shining, tangled cascade, thinking what a sight she must look. But from the admiration she saw in his eyes as she replaced her hat and the inexplicable, lazy smile that swept over his face as he surveyed her—from her head to her small and slender feet—she had the staggering impression that he actually liked what he saw, that the girl walking beside him was far more appealing to him than the woman he had seen in London at the ball. She had thought never to see him again. Now he was here she wanted to weep with joy.

They reached the house from the back. It was a charming house, with wrought-iron balconies and blue shutters at the windows. Marietta always thought it looked like a miniature French chateau, with its grey stone walls and pepper-pot towers. They approached through the lovely garden, with flowering creepers climbing walls and trellising and an abundance of flowers and sweet-smelling shrubs.

'See,' Marietta said, 'there is Aunt Margaret. One can't help but like her.'

Aunt Margaret came to meet them. She was a small, delicately built woman with a gentle smile. When her husband had died she had continued to live in the house and had no desire to return to England. Despite all the small tragedies in her past she maintained a cheerful, calm disposition. Her skin was bronzed by the sun and her white hair was held up with silver combs. Immediately she ordered refreshments to be brought into the garden, where Marietta's mother was resting, and they all sat around talking and drinking tea.

'So?' Aunt Margaret asked, looking at Marietta and Edmund in anticipation, unable to contain her curiosity any longer about why this gentleman had come all the way from England to see her niece. 'Do you have anything to tell us?'

Marietta laughed, reaching out and taking Edmund's hand. 'Yes, Aunt Margaret. We do. Edmund and I are to be married. There, does that satisfy your curiosity?'

'Oh—that's most splendid—don't you agree, Beatrice?'

'Yes—of course I do—although we have been here before,' Marietta's mother remarked drily. 'Several times, in fact.'

'This time I am serious, Mother,' Marietta said, wishing with all her heart that her mother would show some enthusiasm on hearing this happy news.

'Don't look so surprised, Beatrice,' Margaret rebuked her sister. 'You must have known what was afoot when Baron Fitzroy appeared, having come all this way to find her. I, for one, am so delighted that they are to be married that I could dance with joy.'

Edmund laughed. 'Then don't let us stop you.'

Aunt Margaret joined in his laughter. 'I would if I were able, but I'm afraid that with my arthritis, my dancing days are behind me.'

'You will be relieved to have me off your hands at long last, Mother, and Father will be ecstatic.'

'Well, he will be relieved, I know that. Of course we must go back to England so I can consult with your father.'

'We want to be married here in Siena, Mother—before returning to England.'

'But this is all so sudden—and your father...'

'Worry not, Mrs Harrington,' Edmund said. 'I have written permission from your husband to go ahead with the wedding if Marietta will have me.'

'You're not going to raise any objections, are

you, Beatrice?' Aunt Margaret said. 'You can see how it is with the two of them.'

'Yes—of course.' Her mother forced a smile. 'Well, then—what can I say other than the wedding can go ahead? It will be a relief, I can tell you. Although I will not feel easy until I know Marietta is suitably wed. I only hope she doesn't renege on the day. I don't think I could stand another walk out.'

'We will be married soon—here in Siena,' Edmund said. 'Marietta knows by now that I never take refusals. It's as well she understands the man she is going to marry,' he said with mock severity, a teasing light dancing in his eyes when he looked at Marietta.

Her mother relented and went along with the preparations, but she was still the handsome, somewhat imperious figure she had always been to Marietta.

Aunt Margaret had taken a fancy to Edmund and thought it was wonderful that Marietta was to marry such a handsome, rich man. 'We will get on with the wedding plans—informal, yes, because the time is short, but we'll still make it a grand occasion.'

'Thank you, Aunt Margaret. It will be a simple wedding. It is what we both want. We will honeymoon in Venice for a couple of weeks and then return to Siena before returning to England.'

Completely fascinated by Edmund, Aunt Margaret was blissfully happy for them both. She was in a state of feverish excitement to have it all going on beneath her roof.

Everything was golden about those days leading up to the wedding. Marietta would never forget them. Edmund and his aunt dined with them most evenings, the ambience contented and relaxed. Marietta was wonderfully happy and everything was different having Edmund around. The days were joyous and carefree and a kaleidoscope of shifting emotions and finding things new about Edmund and his different moods. Hand in hand they strolled through the streets of Siena, utterly devoted to each other.

She learned a great deal about him. He was knowledgeable about almost everything. He was something of a connoisseur in most things, especially about art and music, yet he could be critical about some issues which made discussion interesting.

There was a serious side to him that was not

given over entirely to pleasure and she could feel a sadness in him that he kept locked inside himself, something in his past he found difficult to talk about. She had tried drawing him out on occasion, but he was not forthcoming, until one day, knowing she had to every right to know everything about his past, he surprised her by opening up his heart to her.

They sat on the grass on the exact spot where he had come to her on his arrival to Siena. They talked of inconsequential things and covered the preparations for the wedding, before Marietta broached the issue uppermost in her mind—that of Edmund's past.

'I know you are reluctant to talk about it, but if you are to be my husband I would like to know all about you—especially that part of your life you have locked away inside yourself.'

He looked at her, his brow furrowed. 'I've given it considerable thought, Marietta, and you are right. The time has come for me to bare all. I have put it off for too long.'

Marietta sighed, shaking her head sadly. 'I know you find it difficult—and I don't mean to press you.'

'You're not. You deserve to be told. I want no secrets between us when you become my wife—and then we can put it behind us. I'm going to tell you things about me that will shock you.'

'And I am ready to listen. Were you not brought up at Ashborne?'

'Sadly, no. I was taken to live there as a youth.' He drew a long breath. 'The trouble began when my grandfather died. There was an inheritance issue—David, my uncle, as the eldest, inherited the estate. Charles, my father, who had a gambling addiction—he also drank way too much—was left very little. Grandfather had no faith in him—and with good reason since he had bailed him out many times when he had fallen into debt—so he cut his inheritance right down, leaving it up to David to finance him as he thought fit. You can imagine the effect this had on a proud, stubborn man—which my father was.'

'Was your father married at the time?'

'Yes—to the Earl of Waverley's sister, which you already know through your engagement to Gabriel. Until their father's death, my father lived at Ashborne with my mother and me when I was born. Sadly my mother wasn't a well woman—she died when I was four years old. My father made up his mind to go to Liverpool and take ship to America—to begin a new life. My aunt and uncle wanted him to leave me at Ashborne to be raised by them, but he wouldn't hear of it. I think it was more to spite my uncle than my well-being. So, we went north to Liverpool, but he couldn't afford the fare to America.'

'So he stayed in Liverpool.'

He nodded. 'He found cheap lodgings for us in a run-down area of Liverpool where the sun never shone, close to the docks. He managed to see I received some schooling and to find work for himself on the docks—it didn't last. I was neglected—as a boy I had to grow up quick and learned to live by my wits. The rooms were always cold and dank. We had to eat, to pay the rent and buy coal for heating. I saw and endured every kind of degradation. The smell of poverty never leaves you—the smell of the river and the salt of the sea.'

'Did your aunt and uncle not know what you were having to endure?'

'No—how could they? Had they known the conditions we were living in then they would have gone to Liverpool and forced my father to let them take me back to Ashborne, but they genuinely believed we had gone to America.'

'Did your father not write to them?'

He shook his. 'He was too proud to do that.'

Marietta had a painful vision of a dark-haired little boy with no one to care for him but a father who was careless of his needs and it nearly broke her heart. 'That is so terrible, Edmund. What an awful time that must have been for you.'

'My father's gambling became worse—along with his health. When I was no more than a child I took work on the docks—doing anything to keep us from starving and to keep my father out of debtors' prison. One night he didn't come home. I found out he'd been involved in a fight—he suffered a terrible head injury. I found him in the hospital. He was in a bad way. I wrote to my aunt and uncle at Ashborne—I also wrote to my uncle, the Earl of Waverly, but he would have nothing to do with me.'

'I only met the Earl on one occasion and he did not endear himself to me.'

'He is a hard man, inconsiderate of another's needs. Later, when he landed on hard times and I had become successful, I refused to help him financially. I would not give him one penny piece that would end up on the gaming tables. My aunt and uncle took me and my father back to Ashborne. We expected him to die many times. Convulsions were a frequent occurrence and he was often hysterical. At such times he had to be suppressed. He didn't speak. He didn't know who we were.

'When he could be moved, on the doctor's advice he was taken to a clinic in Switzerland, which dealt with head injuries and the like. But there was no improvement over the years. I went frequently to Switzerland to see him—they were difficult times for me, but I felt duty bound to go. It was after the weekend you came to Ashborne that word came that he was deteriorating. I went right away. He was skeletally thin, his eyes open, but they had a dead and empty look in them. I always talked to him, but all my efforts were in vain. There was never any response, no sign of recognition. There was nothing there—just an empty shell.

'I still feel the pain of memory, of that time as a boy and the awful experience of my father's drinking and gambling culminating in that fight that rendered him bedridden for eighteen years. He lingered a while when I got there before he… It was a blessing—he had suffered for years—and never did speak—not since the day of the fight.'

'I am so sorry, Edmund. His death must have affected you deeply.'

He was silent for a moment, considering her words. 'It was a relief and also a blessing.'

It was with a heavy, aching heart that Marietta looked at him. A lump of despair was in her throat when she thought of all he had told her of how awful his childhood had been. She was glad she was wearing her hat with a large brim because it shielded her eyes and the gathering tears. But Edmund was not fooled. The quietness of her mood drew his attention. Reaching across the table, he tilted her face up to his.

'What's this?' he said, touching the wetness around her eyes. 'You're upset.'

Through a blur of tears Marietta nodded, swallowing down the lump that had risen in her throat. 'Yes,' she whispered. 'I'm so sorry, Edmund. I—I had no idea.'

'How could you?' Standing up when a jolly group of young people came walking along the path, taking her hand he drew her to her feet. 'Come, let's walk. We'll find somewhere quieter.'

They remained silent until they reached the empty paths which would lead them back to Aunt Margaret's house. Edmund's expression remained grave, tortured even, but then he shook his head resignedly. 'You know all about me now—and no doubt knowing I was brought up in squalor has shattered any illusions you might have had of me.'

'No, it doesn't. It doesn't change a thing. I loved you before, Edmund, and now, knowing what you went through—a small boy who was so brave and strong—now I could not love you more. Now I know all about you—the best and worst of it. It makes no difference—truly it doesn't. I only wish you had told me before, but thank you for telling me. I'm glad you did. It helps me to understand you better.'

And it did, more than she could have imagined. She knew Edmund's scars went deep and her feelings for him went deeper than compassion. Now, knowing about his tortuous life as a child, if she hadn't already lost her heart to him she would now. She understood his private anguish and his suffering aroused her more protective instincts and she wanted all the very best for him.

'I have every faith in you that you will understand like no one else, Marietta.'

She nodded, wiping her eyes with the backs of her hands. She looked at him, really looked.

His mouth was compressed. She could still see the pain in his silver-grey eyes, a great deal of pain that shocked her. She looked at his proud, lean face with its firm jaw and stern mouth, but all she could see was a dark-haired little boy— alone, frightened, trying to do the best for his father and determined to succeed. He had been hurt almost beyond bearing, so badly that he'd kept his pain hidden, allowing no one other than his aunt and uncle to come close enough to uncover it. That he was doing so now to her told her he very much wanted her in his life.

'Did you love your father, Edmund?'

He considered her question. 'As a boy I did— he was all I had. I have an image of a man whose features were gaunt, with black hair like my own. When he had the time he would take me on to the river's edge and tell me about the river and the ships that sailed on her. He knew all their names. I believe in another life he would have made the sea his life. He loved being close to it. I would listen to him, full of wonder. They were the moments of happiness I remember.'

'I can't imagine how you survived what you did,' she whispered achingly, feeling a lump of poignant tenderness swell in her throat. Unthinkingly, she took his hand and raised it to her lips. 'I'm so sorry, Edmund.'

'What for? You have nothing to be sorry for.'

'Yes, I have—for doubting you. I should have realised when you didn't come to me in London that you wouldn't have deliberately kept yourself from me, that there must have been good reason.'

'You had your father to contend with. He is a difficult man to stand against, Marietta. I realised that when I went to see him.'

'We neither of us have had an easy time of it with our fathers.'

'It would appear not. My father loved pleasure whereas my uncle was of the more serious type. Apparently, my grandfather was of a stern disposition. Ashborne was important to him. He saw that my uncle was the one who cared for Ashborne as much as he did. My father he dismissed as an idler, a drunk, a gambler and a philanderer. I tell myself that he couldn't have been all that bad, for why did my mother fall hopelessly in love with him?'

'You love Ashborne, don't you, Edmund?'

He gave a nod. 'In some of his more lucid moments my father would talk about what it had been like for him growing up there. When he took me away when I was a boy, the thought of Ashborne gave me reason to carry on when I was struggling though the darkest of days. I will never forget what I owe my aunt and uncle. Ashborne was something to live for—and now,' he said, looking at Marietta with so much love in his eyes, 'I have even more to live for.'

'We both have and we have much to be thankful for. I am so sorry for what you have suffered, but despite everything that has happened to you, since then you have succeeded in everything you have done. You should be proud of yourself, Edmund. I don't care who your father was. It's who you are that counts. Whatever your past, we cannot allow it to affect how we feel about each other.'

'Bless you for saying that, Marietta. There is a gentle strength, an understanding and compassion about you that I saw from the start. You will be good for me and I love you deeply. It may surprise you when I tell you that when I invited you to Ashborne, before you arrived I told my aunt I was going to marry you. She was surprised when I told her I was coming to Siena to find you, saying that she could think of no other woman I would travel all this way to wed.'

'I'm so happy that you did.'

'And you still want to marry me?'

'Of course I do. Do you still want to marry me?'

Edmund stopped walking and, taking hold of her, he drew her into his arms. 'You know I do and not out of duty or obligation.'

'Then tell me why.' Her body became still in his arms, her cheek resting against his chest as she waited, not breathing, anticipating his next words.

Tightening his arms around her, Edmund placed his lips on the top of her head. 'It's because I love you,' he said fiercely. 'I cannot remember when I came to love you, but I can't deny that since the moment I set eyes on you riding your horse in Hyde Park that day, I love you very much indeed. I knew straight away that you were different to any other woman I have known. I didn't recognise what I was feeling. But suddenly you became the light of my life and my body and my soul craves for you.'

Marietta turned her face up to his, her eyes shining with all the love that was in her heart. 'I can't bear to think that through my foolishness I could have lost you.'

'Even though I had already asked you to marry me and you had accepted?'

'I know. I'm a very complicated woman.'

His lips curved in a leisurely smile. 'I'm beginning to realise that.'

'Do you mind?'

'Not in the least. It will add excitement to our marriage, I suppose.'

On reaching the house where Aunt Margaret was entertaining her sister and Lady Fitzroy beneath the branches of a spreading blossom tree, chairs were pulled out to accommodate the engaged couple. When it was time for Edmund and Lady Fitzroy to leave, Lady Fitzroy took Marietta aside, a worried look in her eyes.

'Edmund was quiet over tea, Marietta. He's told you, hasn't he—about his childhood?'

'Yes, he has. All of it.'

'And about time, too. I can imagine how it shocked you—but you are a sensible girl and you will deal with it, I know.'

'Yes, I will. We both will.' Marietta was grateful and relieved that Edmund had chosen to share the knowledge of his past with her. He had humbled himself in his need for her to know, to understand, handing it to her to share.

'Edmund is a generous man, Marietta,' Lady Fitzroy said, linking her arm through Marietta's as they strolled across the garden to the house. 'He cannot forget that time as a child he spent in the slums of Liverpool and he always gives generously to the charities that are trying to help the poor and destitute, charities that work on behalf of many—to make their lives better in any way he can. Because his father was badly injured, he was able to escape that life of destitution and hopelessness, but he could not forget the ones still there, the ones he left behind— still cold, still hungry. The donations he makes goes to the schools, for he believes only education can raise them out of their deprivations.'

Marietta smiled. 'That's just like him. I admire him for doing that.'

'Now, tell me how you will like living at Ashborne,' Lady Fitzroy asked, waving when she saw Edmund looking for her.

'I can't think of anywhere I would rather live.'

'Well, it's a relief for me, I can tell you. Now Edmund is to be married—and a new family. I will be quite content to move out to the dower house.'

'Oh, but I couldn't possibly—'

'Of course you can. This is what I've wanted for a long time. I couldn't be happier with the way things have turned out. I have thought for a long time that Edmund needs a good woman to love—and children. You have no idea how I have yearned to hear the sound of little ones at Ashborne—but it was not to be—not for me. For you and Edmund it will be different—and I will not be far away.'

'I sincerely hope you will be there to help me acclimatise to Ashborne.'

Lady Fitzroy smiled. 'You can count on it. Edmund tells me you are an artist, Marietta— and how talented you are. There are plenty of rooms at Ashborne you can choose for a studio.'

'Painting has been a big part of my life. I could not imagine being without it.'

'I look forward to seeing your work.'

'Thank you, I will enjoy showing you. Few people have seen what I do—only Edmund.' She sighed, glancing to where Edmund stood talking to her mother, thinking how wonderful it was that they had found each other once more, when for a while she believed she had lost him for ever.

'You have a faraway look in your eyes, my dear,' Lady Fitzroy observed softly. 'What are you thinking?'

Marietta hesitated, not quite knowing how to

phrase her thought. 'I was thinking,' she said quietly, 'what a wonderful place Siena is for our wedding—a place that has always been close to my heart. I was also thinking how lucky I am to have Edmund by my side—for always.'

'That's true. But remember that those days you were apart when you left Ashborne, the days you lost to misunderstandings, may add to the joy of others still to come. If my own experience with my dear husband is anything to go by, then they will by unrivalled.'

Whereupon, they sauntered back to where the others awaited them.

Epilogue

Unbelievable as it seemed to Marietta, they were married in a small Anglican church in Siena one mid-morning, before the intense heat of the afternoon. She wore a soft gauzy chiffon dress with short puffed sleeves and a square neck. A band of matching material emphasised her small waist. Her hair she wore drawn back from her face, a white camellia secured just above her ear, its pure white waxen petals in stark contrast to the rich auburn colour of her hair.

Her mother, looking oddly subdued, drew her aside as they were about to leave for the church. 'You look lovely, Marietta. I know there must have been times when you have resented me, but I only want what is best for you.'

Marietta hesitated, surprised by the sincerity

in her tone. 'Yes, Mother, I know. I am sorry for all the trouble I've caused, but please be happy for me now. This is what I want. I love Edmund and he loves me.'

'Then what can I say except that I wish you every happiness.'

Edmund was at the church, waiting for her. He came to her and put his arms around her. 'Sorry, Marietta. It isn't what I hoped for you. You deserve a grand affair with bells ringing and a choir singing.'

'Don't say that, Edmund. This is just perfect. I would not have it any other way.'

'I'm glad. That's what I wanted to hear,' he murmured, taking her hand. 'Now come. Let us go inside and get married.'

Marietta went through the ceremony in a daze and she hardly heard the final pronouncement. It was only when Edmund turned to her that she realised it was over. She was Edmund's wife, a Baroness, and he intended to kiss her to seal the vows. His eyes were warm and a little smile tugged his lips, then they found hers willing and softly yielding.

Afterwards there was a small reception at the house. Two of Aunt Margaret's offspring and their families had travelled from their homes in the south to attend and on the whole it was a lovely affair. Glasses were raised again and again. Time passed quickly and in no time at all they were on the train heading for Venice.

The hotel where they were staying overlooked the Grand Canal. Marietta fell in love with Venice as soon as she saw it. She stood on the balcony and gazed at the colourful craft on the water below. Edmund came up behind her, threading his arms about her waist.

'This is where it begins, Marietta.' Bending his head and placing a kiss on her cheek, he frowned when his lips met wetness. 'Why are you crying?'

'I can't help it. I'm so very happy. It will always be like this, won't it, Edmund?'

He kissed her lips. 'It's going to be wonderful.'

Leaning back in his arms, she looked up at him, loving him, revelling in the simple joy of being in his arms.

Over the days that followed, they wandered at leisure, meandering through an enchanting maze of alleyways, squares and bridges and whiled away the time beneath the tall tower of the Campanile in St Mark's Square, drinking coffee at Florian's.

Their love was still alive, even if it had been cooled for a while by the unforgiving wind of misunderstanding. Marietta and Edmund grew in the physical experience of their love. They came to know each other's bodies with every growing intimacy and their response to each other seemed endless as they honeymooned in Venice. She was loved by him, deeply, tenderly—more than she could have believed possible. With her whole life ahead of her with Edmund beside her, she wanted to live life to the full—with the joy of loving and being loved.

Sometimes when she stole a glance at him and realised she bore his name, a sharp thrill would shoot through her. He never ceased to amaze her. He was sophisticated, so elegant and full of charm, but he was forceful, too—a power held in restraint, a man with many diverse and complex shades to his character.

He was also a man who was meant to dominate and it amused Marietta that he often found it irritating that the gentle, naive young woman who had often been ignored as a child and had been reared in a sheltered, austere environment had a mind and will as strong as his own and had not been born to be dominated. The way it looked it was evident the two of them were not likely to lead a docile life.

But whatever their differences—which they always overcame in the nicest possible way—their love was undisputed. They knew they were meant to be together and the joy and happiness they found in each other was complete.

* * * * *

COMING SOON!

We really hope you enjoyed reading this book.
If you're looking for more romance, be sure to
head to the shops when new books are
available on

Thursday 20th
January

To see which titles are coming soon, please visit

millsandboon.co.uk/nextmonth

MILLS & BOON

THE HEART OF ROMANCE

A ROMANCE FOR EVERY READER

MODERN

Prepare to be swept off your feet by sophisticated, sexy and seductive heroes, in some of the world's most glamourous and roma locations, where power and passion collide.

HISTORICAL

Escape with historical heroes from time gone by. Whether your passi for wicked Regency Rakes, muscled Vikings or rugged Highlanders, the romance of the past.

MEDICAL

Set your pulse racing with dedicated, delectable doctors in the high-sure world of medicine, where emotions run high and passion, com love are the best medicine.

True Love

Celebrate true love with tender stories of heartfelt romance, from t rush of falling in love to the joy a new baby can bring, and a focus emotional heart of a relationship.

Desire

Indulge in secrets and scandal, intense drama and plenty of sizzling action with powerful and passionate heroes who have it all: wealth, good looks…everything but the right woman.

HEROES

Experience all the excitement of a gripping thriller, with an intense mance at its heart. Resourceful, true-to-life women and strong, fear face danger and desire - a killer combination!

To see which titles are coming soon, please visit

millsandboon.co.uk/nextmonth

MILLS & BOON

Coming next month

THE HIGHLANDER'S SUBSTITUTE WIFE
Terri Brisbin

'Bring her now. The MacMillan will greet his bride as he should.' Duty. Duty to his clan must come first. Too much depended on this agreement.

'You will accept her?' Dougal asked as he went to the open doorway. 'But she is…'

'I heard you the first time. The wrong bride. A disfigured bride. A bride from the nunnery. An insult to me and our clan. Anything else you need to tell me, Dougal? Och, aye, she is already married to me by proxy with no way out of that.'

Ross rolled his shoulders to relieve the growing tension. The urge to respond to this insult with one of his own grew within him. Yet, as the chieftain, he did not have the luxury of letting loose his fury. Too many depended on this arrangement. Too much danger surrounded them as they prepared for another attack, one that could be disastrous without the supplies, the support and, damn it, the gold that his bride brought to him.

After watching her approach through the gate, Ross could see…nothing of her. She was covered from head to foot in a long cloak that nearly overwhelmed her. A hood was in place and veils flowed over her face.

'Lady Ilysa, welcome to Castle Sween.'

'My lord, I thank you for your welcome.' Her voice was melodic and had a pleasing lilt to it.

'Father Liam,' he called out. 'If you would give us your blessing?' Ross moved down next to his bride and waited as the priest made their wedding publicly official.

When everyone watched Ross expectantly, he understood what they wanted. He turned to face the lady, his wife, and nodded at her. 'My lady?'

A simple kiss. That was all he must do in view of his people to seal this bargain. A kiss. Without knowing the full extent of her appearance, he could only wait for her to reveal herself.

As she reached up and lifted the hood from her head, everyone avidly looked on. For them, it was to see their chieftain's bride. For him, it was to see if the rumours were true. The hood slipped down as she pushed it back to her shoulders and she lifted the veils away from her face.

His indrawn breath was not the only one.

Ilysa MacDonnell was a beautiful young woman.

Continue reading
THE HIGHLANDER'S SUBSTITUTE WIFE
Terri Brisbin

Available next month
www.millsandboon.co.uk

LET'S TALK
Romance

For exclusive extracts, competitions and special offers, find us online:

- facebook.com/millsandboon
- @MillsandBoon
- @MillsandBoonUK

Get in touch on 01413 063232

For all the latest titles coming soon, visit
millsandboon.co.uk/nextmonth